THE DRAGON STONE

TALES OF TYRRATH 2

Lauren H Salisbury

SEAMOUNT PUBLISHING

Edited by Cathy McCrumb | www.cathymccrumb.com
Cover Design by Moonpress | www.moonpress.co
Map and internal artwork by Andrés Aguirre | www.aaguirreart.com

ISBN (e-book): 978-1-915438-06-5
ISBN (paperback): 978-1-915438-07-2

To all those who don’t feel like they belong anywhere:
You are exactly who you were meant to be!

THE KINGDOMS OF
EGREA
CRAEICK
LOCHANACK
BALEWICK MOUNTAINS
GOLDENOAK FOREST
STONETOOTH MOUNTAINS
ABBEY
TYRRATH
LAKE ARROL
FAERSTOLMERE
MOCHYNDEN FOREST
SUMMER PALACE
NORFELD
THE WHITE CITY
SWALLOWDALE
BRUNLAND
FARLING FOREST
DYNNFORD
JADHE
DEKARAT

DRAGONSPINE
ISKARIA
KASRKAN
VAAN'S RETREAT
ARALAN
ILDERDELL
CARELLION
ARDEN FOREST
RAVELAN
EINDAL
AKKIA
FIRSTPORT
WHISTLING COVE
FREE ISLES

Chapter 1
Joss

Princess Jocelyn Dalbot wiped her face with the back of her hand and sat back on her heels. She inspected the rabbit she had just gutted—not as messy as her first—and grinned up at Parker, her long-suffering guard and confidant.

"I think I'm getting better at this."

Parker raised a questioning brow. Then she leaned over, drew a finger down Joss's forehead, and showed her the blood smeared across the tip. "Mm-hm."

Joss blinked at it and looked down at her blood-splattered hands. "Oh."

She rubbed both palms through a nearby tuft of grass, found a cleanish spot on her wrist, and scrubbed it over the areas of her face she had touched earlier, but Parker's grimace suggested she had only made it worse.

Giving up, she tied her latest kill alongside two other rabbits and a pheasant at the end of a pole fashioned from a hazel branch. Then she pushed herself to her feet and tossed her thick, brown braid over her shoulder.

“Time for one more?” she asked, donning a pleading look.

Parker glanced at the dimming light filtering through the canopy, and her brows bunched. “We should’ve been back an hour ago.”

“But there’s still enough daylight left to—”

“Your Highness, you agreed—”

“Fine. Fine.” Joss waved her arms in front of her to ward off the rest of Parker’s admonishment. “Just don’t call me that outside the palace. You know I hate it.”

The reminder of her royal status, and the strictures that went with it, sent a chill through Joss’s body, and in the corners of her eyes, the surrounding trees appeared to close in around her a fraction. She snatched up her bow, quiver, and the pole laden with her brace of game and trudged along the forest trail in the direction of home.

Only shackles waited for her there—duty, propriety, a thousand unbending rules that must be obeyed. Invisible weights dragged at her feet despite the birdsong around her, the fresh scent of the outdoors, the sun’s fingers reaching through the branches to caress her nape.

“I’m not deliberately avoiding everything,” she called over her shoulder, though in her heart, she knew it most certainly was. “It’s just that I need to hone my skills, and it gives the servants time to prepare for Maddie’s return without me underfoot.”

The only response from behind was a low hum and the soft thumps of Parker’s boots on the narrow, packed-dirt path.

Joss scrunched her lips to the side and searched the trees ahead for the stream they needed to cross. She heard it first, gurgling through the forest on its way to join the Arrol river south of the capital, then glimpsed the light-flecked ripples between two ancient trunks.

When she reached the bank, she adjusted the quiver on her shoulder and focused on navigating the crossing without dropping her load. Though summer flowers dotted the margins, a healthy flow still sloshed along the pebbly bed and over the half-submerged stepping stones, turning them into a slippery test of balance that she always enjoyed.

She had just transferred her weight to the second stone when Parker cleared her throat. "Might want to stop and wash your hands, Your— Milady."

A grin tugged at Joss's lips. She would have been happy for Parker to use her given name when they were alone, but the serious guard always insisted on maintaining 'proper boundaries'. Though she had begrudgingly agreed to the compromise of Milady, this was the first time she had voluntarily used it.

Joss turned around, nearly losing her footing, and hopped back to the bank. She shoved the pole at Parker, who immediately leaned it against the nearest tree trunk and resumed her ready stance while Joss lowered her bow and quiver to the grass and crouched to dip her hands into the water.

Cool and cleansing, it soon washed away the traces of her attempts at gutting the rabbits, and she splashed a few handfuls over her face for good measure, gasping at the cold shock to her skin. She let the residue drip from her clean tanned fingers into the stream and watched the droplets turn to amber in the last of the dying sun's rays. A last moment of peace before she returned to reality.

"I still think you should leave the prep work to the kitchen staff, Milady." Parker stood a single pace away, one hand gripping her sword hilt and her eyes roving the treeline as if she expected bandits to jump out at any moment.

"No. If I'm ever stranded out in the wild, I need to know how to fend for myself."

The chances of that happening were as likely as Brunland giving away all their messenger dragons, or Iskaria embracing magic, but she longed for that kind of freedom with every fibre of her being.

She stood and patted her face dry with the arm of her sleeve, then eyed the water downstream. Sweat clung to her back, making her skin itch, and she considered detouring to her favourite secluded pool. Mochynden was the royal family's private forest, and the rangers were likely busy with their suppers, so she would not be disturbed.

But Parker cleared her throat, dashing any hopes of a woodland bathe. With a last glance in the direction of the pool, Joss retrieved her weapons and prizes, crossed the stream, and continued towards their original destination.

A quarter of an hour later, the outer wall of the palace rose above the trees ahead—a smudge of red stone underlining the orange and purple hues of sunset. Joss shifted the pole on her shoulder and dug in her waist pouch for the gate key as she approached the dense clump of shrubs hiding the private entrance to Redcairn Palace.

Parker rummaged through the undergrowth and, after a few moments' search, straightened with Joss's bundled dress in her hands.

Swallowing a groan, Joss swapped it for her load and shook the dratted thing out. As she tugged the split skirt over her hunting leathers, she glanced up at the mullioned windows of the palace, to the room on the second floor where her father lay trapped in a sleeping sickness no healer had been able to cure.

How different things would be if he were awake. He would be ruling the kingdom, mediating the conflict between Garellion and Iskaria as only an old friend of both rulers could, and she would be free to leave the palace and its constraints far behind her.

But he was not.

And she had responsibilities—to help her elder sister, Madeline, rule in his place and protect their younger sister, Olivia, from the pressures of court. Bad enough Joss was forced to endure the endless demands and constant scrutiny while Maddie visited Craeick. Timid as Olivia was, she would find it impossible, and Joss would never put her in that position. Better that she remained in the mage guildhall, learning how to control her magic.

"Ready, Milady?"

Parker's voice broke into her musings, and Joss forced her mind back to the present.

"As I'll ever be."

She slid the key into the lock, turned it until the bolt clicked home, and eased the door open a crack. After a cautious peek, she looked back at Parker, then pushed it wider and stepped through the gap. If she could get to the library without being spotted, she might just be able to relax for the evening.

A short path between two outbuildings led to the rear courtyard, which, as good fortune would have it, was empty. She eyed the pole Parker still carried and jutted her chin in the direction of the kitchen.

The guard huffed out a quiet breath but said nothing. She merely offered a respectful bow before strolling across the cobbled square, the rabbits and pheasant swinging in time with her near-silent steps.

Joss waited a few moments longer, then skirted the forge, hugging shadows lengthened by night's onset, and headed towards one of the palace's secret entrances. Once inside, she climbed to the main floor, followed the dusty passage around to her family's private wing, and emerged halfway along the deserted hallway.

Only it was not deserted for long. Half a dozen strides from her target, she bumped into a young maid rounding the corner from the servants' staircase.

"A-apologies, Your Highness." The girl dipped into a curtsey, nearly dropping her basket of cleaning supplies in her haste.

Steadying her, Joss lifted a finger to her own lips and let out a quiet "Shhh."

The maid responded with a shy smile and a single nod of her head before continuing on her way, and Joss hurried in the opposite direction.

She grinned to herself. Tabitha would never have let her get away with that. The old woman would have whisked her upstairs for a bath and stuffed her into an evening gown for dinner before Joss could say a word to stop her.

Fortunately, Tabitha was still in Craeick with Maddie and her husband, King Lucas Sinclair, for the couple's spring visit to his kingdom. Joss calculated the dates as she reached the library and slipped inside—maybe on the return journey already, but either way, blessedly absent.

No sooner had she closed the door and slumped against it when a squeal startled her upright, and her younger sister, Olivia, ran at her from one of the loungers by the fireplace.

"Joss!"

"Mouse?"

They hugged for a long moment, swaying from side to side, until Olivia stepped back. "What are you doing here?"

"Shouldn't that be my question? I thought you needed the head mage's permission to leave the guildhall."

Olivia gave a little shrug. "I've learned to control my power enough that Mistress Nessa agreed." Over a month earlier than anticipated—trust Mouse to overachieve. "But I meant why are you here in the library. This is the last place I'd imagine—" Her eyes widened, and she lifted an accusing finger at Joss. "You're hiding."

Joss wrinkled her nose. "You don't have to make it sound so childish. And you'd hide too if Ethan Ealley was here every time you turned around."

"Is he still trying to court you? Poor Lord Ealley."

"Poor Lord Ealley?" She pointed at her own chest. "What about poor me?"

Olivia winced, but her shoulders lifted in a placating shrug. "He does love you, Joss."

He had sworn as much for years, and since he had declared his intentions during Olivia's birthday feast the previous year, everyone in the capital knew it, much to Joss's frustration.

"Only because he doesn't know me." She huffed. His latest attempt to persuade her had included gifts of a jewelled choker and a corseted gown that he claimed was the latest style from Brunland's top dressmaker. Though clearly expensive and lavish enough to impress any other woman in Tyrrath, all Joss had seen was a suffocating trap.

She waved her hands to dispel the memory. "Anyway, enough of that. Let me get a good look at you." She held Olivia at arm's length and studied her from head to toe, taking in her pinned-up hair, gentle smile, and loosely clasped hands.

Her younger sister looked more like their mother with every passing year—the same amber eyes and snub nose in the same oval face—though she would never know it. Olivia had been a mere tot when their mother passed during labour along with their brother, leaving her with no memories of warm hugs and adventure-filled bedtime stories to fill the void their mother's death had left.

Joss released Olivia and stepped back, fingering the ends of her braid. The only things she had inherited from her mother were her lighter brown, wavy hair and her willowy figure. And maybe her unruly personality. The rest of Joss's features matched their father and older sister—dark brown eyes, sharp nose, and an angular jaw.

She looked back at Olivia and grinned. It was so good to see her, but Joss could not resist a little teasing. "Have you grown again, little Mouse?"

"I'm eighteen now. That doesn't work on me anymore. And I was already taller than you."

Linking her arm through her sister's, Joss tugged her over to the seats and loosed an exaggerated sigh. "I suppose not. So, tell me what you've been learning recently."

Olivia glanced at a sheaf of papers sitting on the side table and bit her lip. She reached for them, hesitating for a moment before picking them up. "I've been translating the books you found in Oslengil last year, and—"

The clatter of hooves and cry of voices outside drew them both to the windows. They looked down at the courtyard, where a dozen riders drew to a halt. In the dim torchlight, their identical cloaks rendered them indistinguishable from each other. The royal carriage rolled through the palace gates behind them, followed by another contingent of the same size, and one of the lead riders dismounted from his horse and rushed over to help the occupant down.

“At last. I thought they’d never get here.” Olivia rose on her tiptoes and peered at the couple talking beside the carriage.

A grin stretched Joss’s cheeks. Hodges would be spitting feathers. But the hawkish steward should have known by now that Luc loved to test their households’ readiness by arriving early. She was about to open the window and call out to them when Olivia’s statement finally sank in, making her pause.

“Wait. You knew they were coming?”

“Surprise.” Olivia spread her hands with a half grin half wince, then stepped closer and gripped Joss’s hand. “Maddie and I spent weeks planning so we could arrive on the same day, but they’re so late, they nearly ruined it.”

“You—!” Joss pulled her into a hug. “I love you.”

As soon as she let go, she opened the window, leaned out as far as she could, and waved at the others. “Maddie! Luc! Welcome home.”

Her sister looked up and grinned, then gestured for her to get back inside, saying something Joss could not hear over the general hubbub but could well guess. Maddie watched until she complied, then ascended the palace steps and out of view.

Joss crossed the room, flung the door open, and dashed towards the main entrance, Olivia close on her heels. They arrived in the hall as Maddie reached the bottom of the central staircase, and Joss almost flew into her sister’s open arms.

“Oof, Joss,” Maddie said at the same time as Luc growled, “Be careful.”

He may as well have asked the forest not to grow as ask them to restrain themselves. Olivia squirmed in between their arms on Joss's left, and all three held onto each other tightly. They had not been together, all at the same time, since Olivia left for the guildhall shortly after her birthday the previous year. And Maddie had been in Craeick for the past four months.

Joss breathed in her sisters' scents—sandalwood and dust from the road, sweet peas and old books—and the tension melted from her body. They were the only ties that did not leave her feeling bound.

Eventually, Luc gently called Maddie's name, and she broke the hug.

"We should go upstairs so we can talk comfortably," she said.

She squeezed their hands, and when she turned to the stairs, Luc immediately offered his arm for support.

Joss opened her mouth to comment on it, but Olivia spoke first.

"Can we go to the library inst—?" She glanced at Maddie and bit her lip. "Never mind. You look tired. I'll meet you upstairs."

She scurried back the way they had come before anyone could respond, leaving Joss staring after her. What was so important that it could not wait until after they had caught up with each other? Joss chuckled. Most likely her latest favourite story or a new fact she had discovered in some obscure historical text.

Joss returned her attention to her other sister, who, on second glance, did appear a little weary. "Why didn't you ride instead of taking the carriage? A run with

Midnight would've been far better than being cooped up and rattled about for days on end."

"She needed to rest," Luc said, his tone brooking no argument.

Maddie did?

"Why? Did something happen?" Joss scanned her sister for signs of illness or injury but found nothing obviously amiss.

"I'm well, Joss. Just tired. It's been a long trip."

Maddie twisted her head towards Luc, and whatever look she gave him sealed his mouth in a tight line. She started up the staircase again, and he scrambled after her, holding one hand out behind her back and tucking the other under her nearest forearm.

Brows shooting towards her hairline, Joss stared after them for a few moments. Anyone would think Maddie was made of spun sugar the way he was acting. And that was too good an opportunity to miss.

She took the stairs two at a time to catch up and tutted loudly until Luc looked around. "I don't know how you call yourself the fearsome wolf king when you cluck about your wife like an old hen."

Maddie nudged her with an elbow. "Tch, Joss!"

Luc, meanwhile, glared at her over Maddie's shoulder, his mouth working as though he had swallowed a handful of bees.

She smirked back and linked her arm through her sister's as they reached the upper floor and walked along the hallway to the family's private solar. Luc held the door open for them and then directed Maddie to the chair nearest the fireplace.

He plumped the cushion behind her, propped her feet up on a stool, and poured her a glass of water, throughout which they held a murmured conversation that Joss had no desire to overhear. When Maddie was completely settled with everything she could possibly need at hand, he straightened and addressed them both.

"I need to see Aiden, so I'll leave you to talk. Send for me if you need anything, Maddie."

"Go." She shooed him away. "I'm fine."

He stroked her hair, cupping her cheek for a moment longer than Joss was comfortable witnessing, then strode to the door and left.

Joss flopped down next to Maddie and rolled her head to look at her. "Glad to be home?"

"It's wonderful," Maddie confirmed.

"It is. You can take back control of the kingdom now."

Maddie let out a soft chuckle. "Anything happen while I was away?"

"Nothing much here in Tyrrath, just report after report of friction between the southern kingdoms."

A deep vee pulled at Maddie's brows. "Yes, we heard about it in Craeick too."

"Then I'll let you deal with the ambassadors the day after tomorrow." When Maddie looked at her, Joss held up both hands in refusal. "I've done my best. They're your problem now."

"Thanks."

Maddie was still chuckling when Olivia walked through the door with a couple of books cradled in her arm. She sat in the chair opposite Maddie's and rested the books on her knees, staring down at them and twisting her fingers together.

"What is it, Mouse?" Maddie asked.

Olivia's hands stilled, and she met their gazes with a mixture of pain and resolve swimming in her eyes. "I've finished translating the journal you found last year."

"The one from Oslengil?" Had Joss known the book would cause her sister distress, she would have left it hidden in the wall of the abandoned castle.

"Yes. I finally figured out the odd dialect, and there were so many interesting things recorded in there…" She fingered the journal's leather binding. "But the most important is that I think I've found out what's wrong with Papa."

"You have?" Joss straightened, sensing Maddie still beside her.

Hesitantly, Olivia nodded. "I told Mistress Nessa about my theory, and given the fact that he's been asleep for so long and no traditional healers can cure him, she agreed it was possible. That's why she let me come home early to see if I could find out. I can't be completely sure, but I'm fairly certain, or as certain as I can be—"

"Mouse." Maddie leaned forwards and squeezed Olivia's hands. "Just tell us what it is."

Olivia sucked in a deep breath and said, "I don't think Papa has a sleeping sickness. I think he's been cursed."

"What?"

"What?" Joss blurted the question at the same time as Maddie, their voices ringing together in her ears as her world spun. Who would do such a thing? And how? When? "Are you sure?"

"What makes you think it's a curse?"

Maddie's voice took on the steady quality she used in difficult situations, which helped to calm the maelstrom in Joss's mind. She collected her scattered thoughts and focused on the pages Olivia spread out between them.

"See this section here? And again here?" Olivia pointed to several passages, and Joss read the scribbled notes while her sister explained. "Back then, a series of young girls were all cursed with the same thing. The way it started varied—one pricked a finger, another ate something, a third simply went to bed one night and didn't wake up—but the result was the same. They fell into a deep sleep, almost like death, and nothing could wake them until the curse was broken."

"But how do you know that's what happened to Papa? None of the mage healers found anything suspicious."

Olivia hesitated, then ducked her head and said, "You know my mage power boosts others' gifts?"

They both nodded, though she did not look up to see it.

"Mistress Nessa's been training me to sense magic around me so I can connect with it more easily." She clenched her fingers together in her lap. "I went straight to Papa's room when I arrived, and I felt something. It was faint, just a thin trace, so I doubt anyone without my specific power would have noticed it, but it was definitely coming from him."

Joss's mind swirled. Rather than falling ill as they had presumed, their father had been cursed all this time?

"But if it is a curse, who's behind it?" She could not fathom who would want to keep their father trapped in eternal sleep. Beloved by his subjects and respected by the other monarchs across Egrea, he had no enemies to her knowledge.

"I don't know." Olivia shrugged helplessly. "There's no way to tell."

Maddie fisted her left hand. "Could there be a dragon stone controlling it?"

A shudder ran through Joss's body. No one knew how the ancient mages had made those rare stones, but the black rocks allowed even non-mages to perform magic. That was how they had almost lost Maddie the previous year.

Olivia shook her head. "I don't think so. There's no mention of a stone being used in the journal, just a rogue mage casting a dark spell. But it would take a lot of power, so whoever did this to Papa has to be extremely strong."

The room fell silent while her statement sank in.

Until the last couple of years, mages descended from the dragon-bonded legends of old had barely been able to do a fraction of what their ancestors could. But magic had been returning across Egrea, like a giant waking after a long slumber. Existing mages were finding their abilities increasing, and new ones like Olivia were being discovered in every kingdom.

"So we're not looking for an ordinary mage," Maddie said.

"No." Olivia frowned. "I don't know anyone powerful enough to do this. Whoever it is won't be easy to find, and they'll probably be dangerous."

"Especially since we don't even know why they cast the curse on Papa." Joss absently drummed her fingers on the arm of her chair until Maddie touched her arm, drawing her attention to the action, and she stopped.

"Let's keep this to ourselves for now," Maddie said, looking between them. "Until we know who's behind it and why, the fewer people who know what we've discovered, the better."

"You'll tell Luc, though, and Tristan?" Olivia asked.

"Yes, but no one else."

Maddie was right. They could not trust anyone. They had no idea how the person responsible would react to them learning the truth.

The thought of their father being cursed brought a sting to Joss's eyes, and she curled her hands into tight fists. Regardless of who had cast it, they needed to free him.

"How do we break it?" she asked.

Olivia's face scrunched. "Without knowing who did it and how, I can't be sure."

"But you have an idea," Maddie said.

"It might be nothing, but it's the only thing I've found that might work. Look here." She pointed at a note in the margin of the journal. "It says 'Yarin finally succeeded in creating a dragon stone that undoes magic. Most powerful stone I've ever seen. Still, not sure it'll stop the war at this point. Must ask her how she did it when she gets back from Iskaria.'

"That's the only reference I've found to her or a stone with that ability, and there's no record of it being used anywhere, but they're nearly impossible to destroy, so if it's real, it must still be out there somewhere."

Joss jumped to her feet. "So, if we find the stone, we can save Papa?"

"In theory, yes."

"Good."

"But I've got no idea where it might be. It could be anywhere—buried under ancient ruins or in the middle of Iskaria's desert."

"Or it could be sitting in a forgotten chest in one of the guildhalls. Where would you start if you wanted to look for it?"

Olivia bit her lip and stared down at the translated papers. "Garellion," she said, straightening. "The guildhall in Aralan has more information about that period than anyone else on the continent. We could search for the mage by name or see if there's another reference to the stone itself."

That made sense. The mage guild had been based in Garellion since the end of the ancient mage wars, and every mage travelled to the Aralan guildhall to officially register.

Silence wrapped the room once more. Joss paced as she thought, a plan forming in her mind.

"Joss?"

She turned to Maddie, who fixed a wary look on her and asked, "What are you thinking?"

Joss squared her shoulders, determination thrumming in her veins. "That I'm going to find that stone."

Closing her eyes, Maddie sighed. “I thought it might be something like that.” She popped them open. “Are you serious? We don’t even know if it’s real.”

“Better than sitting here and watching Papa sleep forever. And I’m serious as a dragon attack.”

Chapter 2
Theo

Atheon Taskil bent down to examine the bindings around the huge stone block. They were using both ropes and a net due to its size and weight, but this was the trickiest, most dangerous part of the construction, so he needed to be particularly careful.

The lines were well-placed and padded along the stone's edges to avoid fraying, and the net joints had all been properly reinforced. Theo straightened and tugged at the knots attaching the stone to the pulley. They held tight. Good.

A breeze lifted sand into the air, and he held his forearm over his eyes to protect them from the fine grains. The afternoon heat made their work uncomfortable enough without adding gritty vision to the mix.

When the air cleared, he turned to his apprentice and inspected the youth's harness, twisting him around to see the back. "You have the bolt and screws?"

"Yes."

"And you know what to do?"

"Push the hook into the groove, slide the bolt through, and use the screws to fix it in place." Daevi replied in the sing-song tone of one who had recited the same a thousand times, and he had practiced it twice that amount. "I'm ready. I can do it."

It was his first time being entrusted with such an important task, but he was right. Theo had trained the youth in mechanical construction since he could hold a ruler, and he was ready.

"And you've got a hammer in case the bolt hole's tight?"

Daevi patted his hip, where the tool hung from his belt on a leather cord. "Right here, like you taught me. Can we start now?"

He bounced on his toes while Theo circled the slab again.

"Check twice, build once. Check thrice…"

"Build the best," the youngster finished.

Theo's mentor had drilled that into him when he was Daevi's age, and he had lived by it ever since. Which was why no accidents or mistakes marred his record—a feat of which he was most proud. Besides, the mechanism they were building was too important to risk anything going wrong.

Once the counterweight was connected, the new system to regulate water flow to the fields beyond the city's northern wall would be complete.

Theo looked across the worksite, seeing in his mind's eye the freshly-tilled ground ready for planting. Between this mechanism, the wall protecting the fields from desert storms, and the fertile soil the merchant guild had bought from Brunland, the crops grown outside Jadhe should finally be sustainable.

He hoped.

The magic that had destroyed Iskaria during the mage wars and turned it into a dry, barren wasteland had killed off all their previous attempts within a couple of years. But they had kept trying, and this time, he was certain they would succeed.

"So… Can we get started?" Daevi asked again, bringing Theo's mind back to the present.

"Yes. I suppose we should." He checked the youth's tool belt was fastened securely one last time and waved him over to the ladder. "Up you go, then."

Shielding his eyes from the sun, he watched Daevi scale the scaffolding like a monkey after fruit. When he reached the top, he straddled the wooden crossbeam and shuffled along it until he was in position, then held his hand out, signalling that he was ready.

Theo wiped the sweat from his face and neck and joined the rest of the team. He caught hold of the pulley's rope, bracing himself to pull.

"Ready?" he asked, feeling the tension on the rope increase as the men behind him also braced themselves. "One. Two. Three. Four…"

Together, muscles straining, they hoisted the hewn rock into the air, length by length until it dangled high above their heads.

"There," he said. "Hold it steady." He looked up at his apprentice. "Secure it in place. Quickly."

Quiet descended while Daevi worked overhead, until the man behind Theo, one of the most experienced but oldest on the team, let out a soft grunt.

"Getting tired back there?" Theo asked, masking his concern.

"Just clearing my throat."

"If you say so," one of the others called out.

Several snickers accompanied the huff of air that brushed Theo's neck. Though the rope never so much as twitched and he trusted every one of them with his life, now was not the time to lose concentration.

"Focus, men."

"Got it," Daevi called down from above. "You can let go now."

Slowly, Theo and the others eased the tension on the rope, seasoned into caution by years of constructing the city's mechanisms. The counterweight held steady, so he loosened his grip and stood back to inspect their work.

His eyes traced from one end of the mechanism to the other, searching for any loose bindings or ill-fitted joints and finding none.

In the past, it had taken teams of twenty men working constant shifts to water Jadhe's crops. Now, a single man could do the same with the switch of a lever, and thanks to the counterweight system Theo had designed, they could set the required flow and leave it to work on its own until the levels needed adjusting.

Making such a contribution made Theo's chest swell. This was why he loved to design and build mechanisms—to make a lasting, practical difference to people's lives. But there was one final thing he needed to do before he could declare it complete.

"Come down now, Daevi."

The youth met his gaze and nodded, then retraced his path to the ground even faster than he had ascended.

Theo frowned. "Safety first," he said when Daevi bounded over to him.

Daevi ducked his chin. "Yes sir."

To avoid reaching out and ruffling the youth's hair, Theo wiped his hands down his trousers before walking over to the controls. Then, with a quick check to make sure everyone stood well clear, he flipped the main lever along with one other and looked up.

The brake released, and slowly, the gate dropped into the aqueduct. Water gushed along the new channel, diverting into the conduit for the field he had selected.

He threw another lever, and a second gate lowered with a dull thud. The flow of water shifted, sloshing down a different pipe.

It worked.

Pumping his fist, he let out a great whoop, which was soon joined by others from the rest of the team. They clapped each other on their backs, and one or two threw their neck cloths into the air. Seven months of hard labour had finally come to fruition.

Theo beckoned his foreman over. "Give them an hour to rest, then clear the site. And make sure the top men wear their safety ropes when you dismantle the scaffolding."

"Yes sir."

"I'll stop at the overseer's on my way out and tell him they can start using it as soon as you're done."

"You'll be missed while you're away." The foreman held out his hand and they clasped forearms in farewell, holding on long enough for Theo to feel the older man's respect.

Giving him a firm nod in return, Theo let go and walked over to where he had left his pack, tucked out of the way beside the compound's entrance. The slap of running feet behind him made him turn, and he raised one brow at his apprentice.

"Please take me with you," Daevi said.

Theo pushed out a long breath. "We've been over this. You need to stay here."

"But—"

"Master Hass is the best mechanical inventor in Iskaria—he taught me everything I know—so this is a good opportunity for you. Do as he says, work hard, and I'll see how much you've learned when I get back."

Daevi lowered his head and mumbled something that Theo decided to take as 'yes sir'. He started to leave, but the youth launched himself forwards and threw his arms around Theo's shoulders, nearly knocking him back a step.

Theo's stance softened. Daevi had been with him since his parents died when he was six. He patted the boy's back and said, "I'll miss you too. Now go on and help stow the ropes. I need to get to the gate before it shuts."

"Yes sir."

When Daevi stepped away, his eyes shimmered with moisture, but he straightened and blinked it away. He dipped into a respectful bow, then ran back to the others without looking back.

Theo watched him work for a few moments before shifting his pack on his shoulder and slipping out into the street. He would do his best to return as soon as possible, but if the worst happened, at least he had left Daevi in the safest hands he knew.

After reporting the project's completion to the merchant guild's overseer, Theo made his way through the city towards the northern gate.

The main thoroughfare was bustling with crowds by the time he turned onto it, the city's populace having emerged after the worst of the midday heat. They filled the street in both directions, bartering over goods or chatting as they strolled, the general hubbub underscored by the rumbling of the giant waterwheel in the distance.

The scents drifting from a perfume vendor tickled Theo's nostrils, and he sneezed. He put his head down and wove through the masses, passing between a generous mix of stalls, inns and teahouses, and private homes.

When a large shadow blocked the sun, he looked up. The aqueduct peeked out above the roofs and coloured awnings to his left. He was close to the edge of the city.

A few turns later, the gate tower rose ahead, looming over the nearby buildings with thick walls stretching into the distance on both sides. He kept walking and was within sight of the checkpoint when a familiar voice called his name.

"Theo, wait."

He spun towards the sound of his name, spotting his cousin emerging from a teahouse he had just passed. A grin slid across his face as he pushed back through the crowd, which scattered around his cousin like beetles before a sandstorm.

"Rai? What are you doing here?"

"Thought I'd learn the art of tea making." They clasped forearms, and Rai slapped him on the shoulder. "What do you think? I'm here for you, of course."

Theo pointed to the city gate. "Just in time to see me off."

A deep vee furrowed Rai's brow. "Are you sure you want to do this?" He leaned closer and whispered, "You'll be stranded if they catch you."

The mention of the feared punishment sent icy fingers down Theo's spine, despite the heat of the afternoon. He sucked in a calming breath and forced a smile.

"I know, but it's a risk I'm willing to take." He gripped Rai's arm and lowered his voice even more. "Magic didn't destroy Iskaria back then. Power-hungry mages did. But now magic's surging everywhere, and our hunters are getting too bold. Crossing borders to capture anyone showing new gifts? There's even a rumour they'll target the guild headquarters directly. We're so close to war with Garellion over it… If this remedy can restore life to our land, it'll make all our lives easier, and it might stop us from attacking the Garellis too. That's got to be worth trying."

His cousin opened his mouth and closed it again. They had been over it so many times already, he must have known it was not worth arguing anymore.

"I really can't talk you out of it." Defeat bled through Rai's voice.

"No."

He let out a deep sigh and looked off to the side in the way he usually did when Theo had won. "Then I'll keep it to myself. Just make sure you're careful out there."

"Mm." With what he hoped was a reassuring nod, Theo resumed walking towards the checkpoint beside the gate, and Rai jogged to catch up.

When they arrived, the few people in the queue ahead of them moved aside to let them pass, and the power of their status made Theo's skin itch. He scratched his neck, not at all sorry to leave that behind. Thankfully, he was such a minor member of his family that those around them would barely have noticed had he been alone.

"Leaving the city, Aadi?" the guard asked.

Aadi. Young Master in the common tongue, a title he enjoyed for having earned it. His lips curved into a genuine smile as he held out his papers. "Research trip," he said. Close enough to the truth.

"No need for those." The guard saluted Rai with a fist to his chest, clan tattoo showing, and stepped aside, allowing them to stroll through the gate and out into the blistering heat of the desert.

Rai stopped walking just beyond the towering city wall, where the paved road met dry, packed sand. "It won't change anything, you know, even if you do find the cursed thing."

"You're wrong, Rai." Theo shook his head and met his cousin's eyes. "If it works, it'll change everything."

Clapping his hand to Rai's shoulder, he gave it one final squeeze, then swung his pack up onto his back and set out for the border crossing to Tyrrath. He would find the ancient mage's cure for Iskaria or die trying.

Chapter 3

Joss

Joss hurried along the pitch-black passage, trailing her fingers against the uneven wall in lieu of carrying a lantern. She knew the twists and turns of this tunnel by heart, and she could not risk alerting anyone to her movements. If one of the palace guards found her, she would be marched straight back to Maddie—and possibly locked in her room until she promised not to attempt to leave again.

If only her sister had agreed to let her search for the stone, she would not have to sneak out like this. But Maddie had been adamant, claiming it was too dangerous and they did not have enough information to act, which was ridiculous because Olivia had said the best place to start would be the mage guildhall in Garellion's capital, Aralan, far from the troubled border.

So here Joss was, setting out without even being able to bid them farewell but finally doing something of use.

She hitched her pack higher up her shoulder and, at the hundredth step, turned to the right, where the faintest sliver of light pierced the gloom ahead. The dull slap of her boots on the rough stone floor echoed along the tunnel and kept her mind from straying to other dark places. Places where fear rather than purpose kept her company. Still, she knew every inch of these tunnels, had explored them before learning the taste of fear, and could navigate them well enough in the dark.

When she reached the door at the end of the tunnel, she rested her ear against the wooden panel and listened for any signs of life outside. Nothing. She eased back the bar, wincing at the scraping sound amplified by the darkness, and pushed on the handle.

The door swung slowly open, a thin layer of stones and mortar moving with it. Joss slipped through the gap and paused again, letting her eyes adjust to the moonlight. Two empty cottages owned by her family hid the secret tunnel entrance at the base of Faerstolmere's hill. Beyond them, a path followed the shoreline of Lake Arrol away from the capital.

No movement, torch, or voice warned of company in the immediate area. She eased the door closed, and the stone façade blended in with a retaining wall built into the side of the hill.

With a brush of her hands, she turned and set off down the path only to come to an abrupt halt after a mere four strides.

Parker stepped out from behind the cottage on Joss's left, arms folded, head tilted at the angle that said she was in no mood to negotiate. "Can we go home now? Milady."

A curse fell from Joss's lips. "How did you know I'd be here?"

"I've been with you long enough to tell when you're planning something."

"But this entrance—"

"Captain Karr made me find and memorise every inch of the palace's secret tunnels when he assigned me to guard you. Now." She held her arm out in the direction of the palace. "Shall we?"

Joss spun on her heel and marched up the slope without a word, but objections churned inside her, ready to be thrown at the next person to cross her path.

By the time they reached the palace, she had an entire speech prepared for her sister, but it died in her throat at the sight of Hodges fidgeting in the main entrance. The moment he saw them, his arms fluttered in their direction as if caught between waving them over and maintaining decorum.

"Please hurry, Your Highness," he said. "We've been looking for you everywhere."

Joss glanced at Parker, but the guard's tightened expression and grip on her sword said she knew no more than Joss. They hastened up the steps, and Hodges performed the most perfunctory bow Joss had ever seen from him before ushering them inside. "You're needed upstairs, Princess Jocelyn. The king…"

"Papa?" Joss heard nothing else. She dropped her pack without a second thought and raced up the stairs to the family's private wing, blood pounding in her ears.

When she reached the upper landing, her feet slowed of their own accord, her stomach hollowing as she approached the room at the far end. The doors to her father's bedchamber stood open, one servant rushing out as another couple scurried in with a bowl of steaming water and a stack of towels. The low hum of voices drifted from within, alongside the pungent scent of medicinal herbs.

A mixture of fear and guilt gripped Joss's body and pinned her in place. Her father was in trouble, and she had been too busy running away to be there for him.

Only when Olivia emerged from his room, tears staining her cheeks, did the hold on Joss ease. She ran to her sister. "What's happened? Is Papa all right?"

"Joss." Olivia's fingers trembled in her hand. "Where've you been?"

"I'm sorry I wasn't here." Joss held her sister tight and stroked the back of head, peering over her shoulder into their father's room. Whatever was happening inside must have been serious.

When Olivia's breathing evened out, Joss eased back, then gently clasped her upper arms and met her eyes.

"What happened, Mouse?"

"He had a fever."

The need to see him prickled beneath Joss's skin. "Will you be all right if I…?"

"Go. I'm well."

She gave her sister's hand one last squeeze and stepped through the doorway.

Additional candelabras brightened the interior, revealing her father's bed surrounded by people. The maids who had just entered stood at the far side, wiping his limbs with damp cloths. The palace healer stood at the foot, and Maddie sat on the near edge, her hands folded around one of their father's.

Another healer—a mage, by the guild medallion he wore around his neck—slumped in one of the chairs by the fireside opposite the bed, and Tristan Kaar, Captain of the Royal Guard, stood just inside the doorway.

Joss walked farther inside, treading on a creaky floorboard as she did.

Maddie looked up. Though her lips pressed into a thin line, relief swam in her tear-filled eyes. "You're here."

"I'm sorry—"

"Never mind that now. I'm just glad you're here."

Joss glanced around the room again. "Where's Luc?"

"Looking for you."

Guilt lanced Joss's chest, and a wince creased her face. "I'm sorry." Ducking her head, she joined Maddie by their father's bedside. Clumps of damp hair stuck to his face, which appeared paler and more sunken than the last time Joss had visited him the morning before. "How is he?"

The healer answered, "His Majesty's out of danger now."

"But it took much longer than normal to ease his fever," Maddie added.

That explained the condition of the second healer. The magical healing must have taken considerable effort, even assuming Olivia had used her gift to boost the man's power.

"Be at ease, Your Highness. We'll stay with him overnight in case it returns. Normally, I would advise plenty of rest, but..."

That would not be an issue where her father was concerned. The sleeping sickness—curse—confined him perpetually to bed.

Maddie looked from their father to the hallway outside and up to Joss. "Can you see to Mouse? She's exhausted. I'll join you as soon as Papa's settled with fresh linens."

Reluctant as Joss was to leave, she agreed without complaint. Bending down to plant a kiss on her father's cheek, she whispered, "Be well, Papa."

Then she straightened, donned a serene mask, and walked from the room. Olivia leaned against a tapestry of a hunting scene along the inner wall and barely twitched when Joss placed a hand under her elbow.

"Come on, Mouse. Let's get you to bed."

She half-carried her sister along the hallway to her chamber and had barely pulled the bedcovers back before Olivia sank onto the mattress. Joss lifted her feet up and reached for the blanket, intending to leave her to sleep, but Olivia grabbed her hand, eyes wide and alert.

"Did I figure it out too late?" she asked, her voice hitching.

Joss sat beside her. "Not at all. We'd never have known he was cursed without you. At least we have a chance to fight it now."

"His hand was so hot, and he was shaking all over. It was horrible."

"I'm sorry." It was all Joss could think of to say with the evening's events still pummelling her mind. Nudging Olivia over, she climbed onto the bed and wrapped her arms around her, paltry comfort after sneaking out while her sister faced one of their worst fears.

An hour or so later, the door opened, and Maddie slipped inside.

Olivia bolted upright. "How's Papa?"

"Better." Maddie moved a pile of books off the nearest chair and sat as if she carried an entire mountain on her back. "The healer's prescribed a tincture for him. They think it was caused by an infection in his chest, passed from someone with a cold, or from lying still for so long."

Joss tensed. "But he's been fine so far. Why now?"

Maddie spread her hands in a helpless gesture. "It's been two years. Maybe the curse has become unstable or the magic is wearing off. Or it could be that the long-term effects of it are only now starting to show. We can only feed him liquids and purees while he's asleep."

She rubbed her forehead, then straightened a little. "Either way, the healers can treat the fever and keep him stable."

Joss studied Maddie's face, trying to read whatever it was she was not saying, but her sister was an expert at hiding her thoughts. "But…?"

"He's not in any danger, and we have plenty of time, but his body won't last in this state forever."

The news pierced Joss's stomach so painfully she barely registered her younger sister's fingernails digging into her arm.

"So he'll die if we can't wake him up," Olivia whispered.

Maddie hesitated before answering, "Eventually, yes."

Joss swallowed. "Did this happen with others, Mouse?"

"I don't know." Her sister chewed her lip for a moment, as she did when recalling information. "Most were saved fairly quickly. I think one of them lasted quite a while, but they all woke up when the curse was broken."

Resolve hardened the wounds Maddie's revelation had made inside Joss. "Then we must do everything we can to save Papa, no matter how dangerous or how slim the chances." Before Maddie could argue, Joss scrambled from the bed and knelt at her side, gripping her hand. "I'm no use here, but I can look for the dragon stone. Please, let me try."

Moisture gathered in Maddie's eyes, but the line of her mouth remained firm. "Even if it's real, it could be anywhere. I can't risk losing you too."

"You won't. I can find it. I know I can."

Maddie opened her mouth to respond, but Joss spoke faster. "I'll start at the guildhall in Aralan, like Mouse said, and follow whatever leads I find from there. I can travel as a commoner to avoid attention, and you can tell everyone I'm visiting Aitha so whoever's behind the curse won't know what I'm doing.

"But it has to be me. We don't know who we can trust, so we can't send anyone else without risking word getting out. Besides, if necessary, I can use my status to get access to whatever I'll need without questions."

"She has a point there," Luc said from the doorway, causing both Maddie and Joss to start. "We can't keep her here forever, and she's well-suited for the task."

He walked forwards, and Joss stood back while he rested a hand on Maddie's shoulder and met her gaze. They looked at each other for a few silent moments, something passing between them that Joss could not decipher. Then he turned to her and Olivia, including them in the conversation once more.

"I spoke to the healer, and I agree with Joss. At this point, we should try everything, and if it's out there, she's got the skills and determination to find it. Besides, if she goes, we won't need to involve outsiders."

Joss bounced on her toes. He understood her need for action.

Then, he continued, "But only if you take Parker with you."

She opened her mouth to argue.

"Or we can put you under guard in your room to make sure you don't run away again."

"I'll take Parker."

Maddie grumbled under her breath, and Luc squeezed her shoulder, giving her a small nod when she glanced up at him. She huffed, looked over at Joss, and closed her eyes for a long moment. When she finally opened them, she said, "Very well. I agree. But promise me you'll be careful and follow Parker's lead if you find yourself in any danger."

Joss fisted both hands in front of her. “Yes. I promise.”

“And you’ll come straight home if you don’t find anything,” Maddie added.

“I will.” Joss grinned at Luc. “You’re my favourite brother, you know.”

Except for a tiny twitch at the corner of his mouth, his expression remained flat. “I’m your only brother.”

She shook her head. “Uh-uh. There’s Flynn too.” Luc’s young half-brother counted, even if they did only see him once a year.

He narrowed his eyes at her, the silver orbs slitting to sharp knives. “You called me a clucking hen last week.”

A laugh bubbled up her throat, but she forced it down and managed to keep her expression serious. “Never again. I promise that too.”

She escaped the room before they could change their minds, already creating a mental list of what else she could pack now she had formal permission to leave. She would not return without that dragon stone, and then she would wake her father and restore everything to its rightful place.

Chapter 4

Joss

Two days later, Joss stood in the palace courtyard, drumming her fingers against her thigh while Maddie inspected her provisions for the hundredth time.

"I do know how to pack my own clothes, you know?" Joss said.

"Just give me one more minute."

She had wanted to set out before dawn, but her sister had insisted on bidding her farewell, which in reality meant worrying over every little detail despite them having gone over everything several times the previous evening. And now the sun's sleepy head rose above the parapet along the eastern wall, though a chill still clung to the air in defiance of the heat that would soon banish it for the day.

"I've got it, Your Highness." Maddie's personal maid, Tabitha, bustled around the corner from the kitchen entrance, holding up what appeared to be a round of cheese.

Joss groaned. By the time they were finished, she would be carrying enough food to last an entire year. She turned from the elderly maid's attempts to squeeze it into her pack only for Maddie to grip her arm.

"Do you have enough chew sticks and soap?"

"I was actually hoping my stench would keep any bandits away," Joss said before she could think better of it.

Her sister pinned her with a narrow-eyed look.

"I'll be fine, Maddie. Between us, we've got everything we need."

Maddie waved a dismissive hand that almost struck Joss's nose, but the tightness in her shoulders and eyes finally eased. She searched her belt for something and looked up at the palace windows. "Oh, I must've left it upstairs. Tabitha?"

The maid paused halfway through tying the strings on Joss's pack and lifted her head. "Yes, Ma'am?"

"Could you go and fetch the package on my bedside table?"

"Yes, Ma'am."

She straightened and stretched her back, and Joss stepped in.

"No need, Tabitha. I'll go."

Whatever it was, it would be faster for her to get it herself. Her expression must have soured, for Maddie stopped her, her lips quirking. "Don't fret. You'll like this gift, I promise. But no peeking."

"I won't."

Joss ran inside and up to Maddie's room without stopping for anyone. She grabbed the package—a long, thin object that felt too solid to be clothing and too heavy to be a comb or chew sticks—shoved it in her belt, and ran back out, only to bump into a maid carrying a pile of freshly laundered bed sheets.

After ensuring the girl was not hurt and helping her pick up her load, Joss descended the main staircase at a more sedate pace. She was halfway across the entrance hall when a dreaded voice called out from behind her. Lord Ealley.

"Princess Jocelyn."

She eyed the open double doors ahead. Could she pretend she had not heard him and escape?

He called her name again, loudly enough for a courtier at the other side of the hall to look up, and his footsteps clattered across the marble floor towards her.

She closed her eyes and bit back a curse as her feet drew to a reluctant halt. If she left now, he would only follow and make her farewell with Maddie awkward. Slowly, she turned to greet him, pasting as serene a smile as she could muster over her clenched teeth.

"Lord Ealley."

He stood a little taller than her, his light brown hair tied back in a neat queue and his face freshly shaved. A gold brooch in the shape of his family's stag crest held a short tan cloak about his shoulders, and his doublet was embroidered with matching patterns. Everything about him whispered of quiet wealth and courtly elegance.

"Your Highness." He eyed her attire—a tan cloak tied with a simple wooden toggle over a plain brown tunic and trousers—and twin creases formed between his brows. "Wherever are you going… dressed like that?"

If she told him she was merely heading out for a ride, he would likely try to accompany her. She curled her hands into fists. Maybe this was her chance to finally end his delusional pursuit of her.

"I'm going to Garellion."

He blinked. "Garellion? So far… But why?"

A frisson of irritation scuttled across Joss's skin. She drew herself to her full height and said, "That is a private matter, Lord Ealley. Good day, then."

With a curt nod, she went to step around him, but he shifted into her path again.

"Forgive me, Your Highness, but I don't understand. If you're travelling to Garellion, why are you…? I mean, you'll be in a carriage. There's no need for… um, these."

He pointed in the general direction of her legs, and the tips of his ears turned pink.

Joss clenched her fists tighter. While part of her wanted to laugh at his blush, the larger part longed to lash out at his expectations. The bite of her fingernails pressing into her palms helped to ease that desire. "I prefer to ride, and trousers are more practical for extended journeys."

"But it's not seemly for you—"

Her control slipped. "Why not?"

"Jocelyn." His tone softened as though appeasing an intimate. "You're a princess of Tyrrath. If you must travel, you deserve every comfort and luxury—a carriage with a royal escort. It's not appropriate for you to ride so far by horseback." He stepped closer. "What if someone sees you dressed like that?"

So many objections surged up within her that they clogged her throat and made it impossible to utter a single word. She closed her eyes and fisted her hands so tightly her knuckles strained from the tension.

Fortunately, a new voice interrupted her struggle, allowing her to loosen her grip. "Joss? I thought you were outside with Maddie?" A moment later, Luc appeared in her periphery and added, "Ah, Lord Ealley."

"Your Majesty." Lord Ealley performed a much deeper bow than he had bestowed on Joss but spoke again as soon as he had risen. "Sire, Princess Jocelyn just told me she's leaving for Garellion today and will be travelling by horseback. Is this true?"

Luc folded his arms across his chest and pinned the shorter man with a steely gaze. "What of it?"

Lord Ealley froze, and his eyes rounded. Then he lowered his head and shuffled backwards.

Joss let out a quiet snort. He must have lost his senses to question her brother-in-law in such a manner.

The fastidious lord cleared his throat and smoothed his pristine doublet. "Surely it's not appropriate—"

"I notice you haven't visited the training yard for some time, Lord Ealley." Luc dropped a hand on the courtier's shoulder and squeezed, eliciting a squeak that forced Joss to suppress a grin. "Would you like me to accompany you after I see Joss off?"

"Um, thank you, Sire, but, um, I'll go later. I have… things to do first." Lord Ealley flapped his hands in front of him, ducked out of Luc's hold, bowed again, and half walked half ran back to the audience chamber.

Luc ushered Joss outside without speaking, for which she was grateful. When they emerged into the crisp morning air, she breathed deeply and managed to smile for Maddie. She tugged the package from her waist and gave it a little wiggle, showing her sister that she had refrained from untying it.

"Oh, good. You got it," Maddie said.

She watched Joss with an expectant expression, but Joss could not bring herself to open the gift yet. Instead, she walked over to her horse, where Parker now also waited with her own mount.

The guard looked different out of her leather armour. She pushed a stray lock of blonde hair back from her face, and her worn, grey cloak parted to reveal a light green tunic and darker trousers made of homespun cloth. Her usual sword peeked out at her hip, the only familiar part of the ensemble.

Joss tucked the package into her blanket roll. "I'll open it later, if you won't mind."

Maddie made a sound that cut off before any words formed, and when Joss turned to face her, Luc had his arm firmly around his wife's shoulders and was kissing her cheek.

He straightened and flicked his gaze between Joss and Parker. "There's been another incident between Garellion and Iskaria. Cross the border at Dynnford and take the western road through Farling Forest to Aralan. That way, you'll stay far away from any trouble."

Parker stood to attention. "Yes, Sire."

Joss wanted to complain—that route was much longer than crossing farther south along the River Siven—but she stayed quiet lest he change his mind and forbid her from going at all. With a dutiful dip of her head, she focussed on Maddie, who stepped forwards with her arms wide for a hug.

Joss walked into them and closed her eyes. The realisation that this would be the last time they embraced for some time made her tighten her hold, and she swung her sister from side to side, eliciting a soft swat on her arm before Maddie pulled away.

Sensing movement beside them, Joss glanced over her shoulder and spotted Luc pulling Parker aside.

He angled himself away from Joss and Maddie and spoke to the guard in hushed tones too low to hear. Then he passed her something that she studied for a moment before nodding once and tucking it inside her tunic.

Curiosity itched beneath Joss's skin, but she had no opportunity to discover more, for Maddie tugged on her arm.

"Joss, are you listening?"

"Hmm?"

Joss returned her attention to her sister, who pursed her lips, her forehead wrinkling. It cleared with a wave of her hand. "Never mind. Just make sure you write regularly."

"I promised I would, didn't I?" Besides, Joss was certain Parker had been instructed to ensure she put pen to paper at least once a week.

"And I'll send word via the mage guildhall if anything happens here."

Maddie stepped back at the same time as Luc returned to her side.

"Ready for this?" he asked Joss.

"Yes."

He bent to look her in the eye, his silver gaze piercing. "Parker's in command the moment things look dangerous, even if it means bringing you home."

"I know." After all, her acceptance of this condition was the only reason she had been allowed to leave.

Maddie clutched Joss's hand. "Just be safe, please?"

"I will, I promise."

An unexpected thread of reluctance to leave wound through Joss's body. She had never travelled beyond Tyrrath's borders and had never faced the probability of being apart from her sisters for so long. She held Maddie tightly once more, memorising her sandalwood scent and comforting embrace.

It took Luc patting her shoulder for her to let go. "Is Mouse not coming to send you off?"

"We said goodbye earlier." Olivia hated farewells. She had all but locked herself in the library for the last two days, scouring the records for another mention of Yarin or the sleeping curse.

"Ahh."

Joss swung up into the saddle and turned to Parker, who had already mounted. She sat quietly stroking her horse's neck as though they were about to go for a morning ride rather than set out to find an ancient stone that might not even exist any longer. Her stoic presence settled any qualms Joss may have had, and she cast the guard a grin as she turned Shadow's head towards the private forest gate and set off.

The ride through the forest felt like any other until they emerged into rolling countryside, pungent pig farms interspersed with fields of crops, smaller woods, and occasional villages. Joss paused at the top of a rise, soaking in the sights, sounds, and scents of the landscape ahead before turning to Parker.

"What did Luc give you back there?" she asked.

"Instructions in case of an emergency."

Nothing else was forthcoming, so Joss gave up and focused on the path ahead. They were on their own, heading outside not only the palace but the entire kingdom. A mixture of excitement and nervous energy filled her at the thought, making her heart pound and her skin prickle. What adventures awaited, and where would their search take them?

There was only one way to find out. She dug her heels into Shadow's flanks and lifted her head to the sun, eager to reach their first destination.

Chapter 5

Joss

They arrived in Dynnford several days later, Joss a little sore, both dusty from their hard ride. The town was smaller than she had expected, given its position on Tyrrath's river border. Only seven or eight dozen buildings hugged the nearside shore. Then again, most people would probably take the more direct road between the capital cities.

Joss and Parker dismounted and walked the horses into town, as much for Joss's rear as to cool the animals down. Rows of cottages and a smattering of larger houses around the outskirts soon gave way to stores, a meeting hall, and a couple of inns. The low hum of conversation clarified into individual voices—a couple haggling over the price of potatoes, a baker shouting at a small boy who dodged past him and out into the street, some older men chatting over their pipes on a nearby bench.

A group of young girls giggled behind their hands outside the smithy as they stole peeks at the apprentice working the bellows. Parker followed the direction of their gazes and snorted, eliciting a few dirty looks from his admirers as she and Joss walked past them.

The river cut through the settlement just beyond the square, with what appeared to be a market area and more buildings at the far side of the few-hundred-yard-wide expanse. Joss shielded her eyes from the sun and studied the slow-moving water. What adventures she might find if she could float away like the leaves idling past.

The cool water tempting after baking under a cloudless sky for days on end, and her skin itched to go for a swim. But they were in the middle of a town, not the privacy of the royal forest. Parker would spit dragon scales if she stripped down to dive in. Besides, who knew what undercurrents hid beneath the lazy surface?

“How deep do you think it is?” she asked Parker.

The guard clicked her tongue. “Deep enough for ships to sail up to the White City.”

Joss gave her a flat look. “I know that much already.” Ignoring Parker’s smirk, she kicked at a pebble and muttered, “Aitha sails upriver to trade and deliver passengers.”

Metal rattled and groaned somewhere off to their left, and she spun her gaze towards the sound. A wooden pier jutted out from the nearside bank, and a static ferry chain was attached to a sturdy post at the end. Beside the pier, a pair of shire horses turned a huge wheel that wound a second chain in and pulled the ferry away from the opposite bank.

Turning to Parker, Joss tilted her head in the direction of the pier. “Come on.”

"It'll be a while yet," Parker replied, but she followed anyway.

They tied their horses to a rail, leaving enough give in the ropes for them to munch on the grassy verge, and sat on the riverbank to wait. Joss watched the ferry for a few minutes but soon grew bored of its slow progress. Parker was right; it would take some time to reach them.

She jumped up and fetched the knife Maddie had gifted her when they set off. The design was simple, but it had a keen edge and a leather grip that fitted her hand as if made specifically for her. And the note her sister had tucked in with it still brought a smile to her lips.

My dearest Joss,

I know you have your bow and arrows, but you cannot carry them with you everywhere. Keep this on you wherever you go for added protection. Luc purchased it, so you may trust the blade's quality.

Be safe, and listen to Parker.

May the creator guide you to the dragon stone and return you to us soon.

Your ever-loving sister,

Maddie

Joss tucked the sheath securely into her belt, then hefted the blade and focused on a clump of grass several yards away.

Without taking her attention from the town, despite the small number of passers-by, Parker noted, "That's not the type of knife you should be throwing."

"I know," Joss said as she aimed. She released, and it flew through the air towards its target only to land flat on the ground. Scrunching her nose, she walked over to retrieve it. "But my throwing knives are at the bottom of my pack."

A glance at Parker showed she had pressed her lips into a tight line, her brow furrowed.

"We're still in Tyrrath, and I'm better with a bow and arrow anyway."

Joss continued to throw her knife back and forth across the space in front of her guard, getting used to its weight. When she stopped to wipe her brow and take a drink from her waterskin, Parker looked over.

"Loosen your wrist more," she said, and Joss hid a grin.

By the time the ferry docked, Joss had struck the same clump of grass five or six times in a row. She wiped the blade on her trousers, beamed at Parker, and re-sheathed it.

A small stream of passengers walked off the pier into town, but curious as to who would be crossing with them, Joss paid more attention to the handful gathering to depart. Three men stood beside a large hand cart laden with barrels and rolls of leather, a young boy carried a tray of pies that made her mouth water, and a lone figure who wore a cotton cloak with the hood pulled low leaned against one of the wooden support posts.

Whether a man or woman, Joss could not be certain, until the ferryman called for everyone to board. The figure straightened, revealing a tall, broad outline and a brief glimpse of muscular, tanned forearm. Definitely a man, she decided.

The farmers took the lead, two pulling, one pushing their cart of goods along the pier, followed by the hooded man and the boy. Joss and Parker stayed at the rear, keeping a tight hold of their horses' reins and soothing them when they crossed the small gap from the pier onto the flat-bottomed ferry.

"Ye can tie yer horses there."

Joss looked over her shoulder. The ferryman strode aboard and pointed at a couple of water barrels sitting in the corner of the deck.

"Thank you." She led Shadow to the nearest and tied her to the railing beside it.

Within a couple of minutes, the chains clanked taut, the deck lurched slightly underfoot, and the boat eased out into the river. Joss peered over the side into the dark green depths and caught the gleam of a silver fish darting away from their passage. Farther out, a dragonfly danced across the rippled surface.

"Can you sit down and be still?" Parker asked.

Joss stilled her bouncing leg and dropped onto the bench beside her guard. "Sorry." Though, there were so few people on board, it surely did not matter if she drew their attention. She glanced around but saw nothing suspicious, unless she counted the hooded man.

A shadow fell across her view of him, and the boy with the pies held one out to her. "Two for a penny?"

The savoury scent invaded her nostrils, and her stomach grumbled in response.

"We'll take four," she said, piling them up in her hands before Parker could refuse.

Parker handed him a couple of coins and bit into the pie Joss held out to her without comment, so she must have been hungry too.

They sat and ate the meat-filled, crumbly goodness in silence while the boy moved on to the farmers, who took several each, severely depleting the contents of the tray. He then made his way over to the hooded man, who stood at the front of the ferry with his back to everyone else. He appeared to ignore the boy behind him.

After a few moments, the boy returned to the middle of the deck and sat on a coil of rope to eat his own pie, but Joss continued to watch the hooded man. Who might he be beneath the tan cotton?

"Why d'you think he's wearing a hood?" she asked Parker.

Parker spared him a single glance. "Probably wants to be left alone."

"That's boring."

"Very well. He's a criminal running away from the sheriff."

Joss nodded. "That's more interesting."

"Just stay away from him." Parker popped the last of her pie into her mouth, leaned back against the side railing, and closed her eyes. The sun highlighted a smattering of freckles across her nose and left touches of gold in her blonde hair.

Joss finished her own pie in silence. Her guard rarely had moments of such peace.

She licked a blob of gravy from her fingers. With nothing better to occupy her, she returned to inventing backgrounds for the hooded man. Could he be a secret envoy with orders to help Garellion in their dispute with Iskaria? Her sister had sent no such person, but maybe Brunland had, though they would surely travel by dragon.

Or someone with newly awoken mage powers on their way to the guildhall in Aralan? No. If that were the case, why would he need to hide?

Maybe he was badly scarred? She pictured a slash bisecting his face like the one down her brother-in-law's cheek, then a large burned area.

"Let's go."

Parker's voice interrupted her imaginings, and Joss looked up to find they had reached the Garellion side of the river.

Leaving the horses to the guard, she ran to the front for a better view. The ferry thudded into the dock as she reached the railing, the judder sending her stumbling backwards.

She landed against a solid chest, and hands caught her upper arms in a firm grip. Warmth enveloped her along with the spicy scent of jeira soap.

The hands disappeared the moment she was steady, taking some of the warmth with them, and before she could turn and address whomever had caught her, he brushed past her to disembark.

Her eyes widened. It was the hooded man. His voice rumbled something that could equally have been a greeting or dismissal, and then he was gone.

With a shake of her head, Joss hurried along the pier and all but leaped from the wooden planking onto the hard-packed soil of Garellion. It was the first time she had left Tyrrath. She had not even visited Craeick because she always had to take charge while Maddie travelled to the northern kingdom. Pausing beside the water, she examined their immediate surroundings, only to deflate a little.

She had expected it to be different, exotic somehow, but this half of Dynnford looked, sounded, and smelled exactly the same as the side they had left. It was like any other small town. Stores and inns lined the small green in front of them, an animal market stood to one side, and more buildings—likely private homes—surrounded the central area.

Above the thatched rooftops, distant woods climbed the lower slopes of the Dragonspine Mountains that lay along the horizon like sleeping giants. Joss and Parker's destination—the capital of Garellion—lay beyond the peaks. Maybe there, Joss would find wonders beyond her imagination.

She and Parker mounted their horses and set off towards the southern road to Aralan. On their way out of the square, Joss spotted the hooded man entering a supply store and absently wondered where he was heading, but the thought was quickly pushed aside by the anticipation of leaving the town behind and travelling deeper into the unknown kingdom.

Chapter 6
Joss

Late that evening, Joss sucked the last of the rabbit meat from a thigh bone and tossed it into the campfire, sending a handful of sparks skyward. She licked her fingers and looked up. Moonlight silhouetted the treetops, creating a dark patterned frame through which a scattering of stars shone. The trees whispered faintly, and the fire's warmth countered the cooling night air. If only her normal life could be this peaceful and free.

They had stopped to rest for the night in a small clearing that bore the remnants of previous camps. A ring of stones sat in the centre, blackened on the inner sides from numerous fires. A couple of logs lay around it for seats. And a flattened trail through the undergrowth between the trees led to a nearby stream.

"How many days to Aralan?" she asked Parker.

The guard lowered the meat she was about to put in her mouth. "Two. Three if we want to spare the horses."

Joss nodded slowly. She picked up a nearby stick and poked it into a clump of grass by her feet. How long would they need to spend in the capital? Would they be able to find the stone before her father—

"Gah!" She cut the thought off and threw the stick into the fire, then turned her attention to the bushes edging the clearing. Were none of the berries ripe enough to eat yet?

The bushes shook, and beside her, Parker stiffened.

"Don't look, but there's someone out there," the guard said in an undertone. "More than one." She eased her hand towards her sword, and Joss fought the urge to jump up and search the treeline for suspicious movements.

Instead, she bowed her head and tuned out the crackle of the fire, focusing on the sounds of the forest. An owl hooted off to their left, and a few moments later, twigs snapped ahead and something rustled the bushes to the right.

Joss swallowed. No party who closed in from several directions had good intentions. She looked back at Parker, who casually rolled her neck and closed her eyes, blocking out the firelight as she had taught Joss to do to improve night vision.

"As soon as they show themselves, put your back to the tree by the horses, and don't move till I tell you. Understood?" Parker murmured.

"Yes." Joss reached surreptitiously for the knife tucked into her belt. She did not draw it—it would be of little use in a fight, and she would rather use her bow—

but the solid weight of the handle in her palm made her feel less vulnerable.

Before she could prepare herself further, a handful of men emerged from the surrounding darkness of the forest, their shadows solidifying into looming figures. None of them spoke or even made a sound. They simply brandished their weapons, knives glinting blood red in the firelight.

The moment the first stepped into the clearing, Parker sprang to her feet, sword drawn, stance ready to fight.

"Go. Now," she ordered.

Joss scrambled over the log and across to the large oak where they had hobbled the horses. Her bow rested against the trunk, and she snatched it up. The familiar heft calmed her racing heartbeat. With her back to the tree and the horses protecting her right flank, she nocked an arrow and pulled the string taut as she swung the bow up.

Then hesitated.

Where should she aim? The men closed in around Parker on three sides, their knives and one axe swinging for her flesh. She danced between them with the fire at her back, and the constant slashes and thrusts of her sword kept them at bay. The clash of steel echoed through the night, sending a flock of birds skyward.

They distracted Joss for a moment, and when she looked back, one of the men was creeping around behind Parker while she fended off two in front of her. Joss sighted her arrow at the centre of his back, only to freeze again.

Sweat dampened her palms, and she adjusted her grip. These men would not respond to a shallow slice of their skin. She would have to inflict real damage—or even kill.

"Watch out." The male voice came from the direction of the road, loud and insistent.

Joss snapped back to her senses and let her arrow fly, straight into the bandit's thigh. He dropped to the ground, holding his leg and moaning, but Joss had no time to dwell on him.

A twig snapped behind her left flank, and a shadow moved in her periphery. She spun towards it, already drawing another arrow. As she shot at the new target—a sixth bandit—something whizzed past her ear and thudded into the man's chest. Her arrow sank into his shoulder a moment later, and he toppled backwards.

A bolt? Where had that come from? She searched for the source and sucked in a breath as she spotted a new man leaping across the fire behind Parker. He landed beside the guard and faced the bandits, and Joss loosed the air caught in her lungs. Not their reinforcements. Someone arriving to help her and Parker.

He pointed at one of the bandits, flicked his wrist up, and a bolt flew from the end of his sleeve and smacked into the man's side. A hidden weapon. Despite the situation, curiosity bit the back of Joss's mind, but she shook it off and raised her bow to search for her next target.

The remaining bandits retreated, crashing through the bushes and disappearing into the forest. Parker chased after them but stopped at the edge of the clearing, breathing heavily.

Sinking to the ground, Joss let her bow and arrow clatter beside her and stared at her trembling hands. Was this what combat felt like?

She had never been in a real fight before. True, she had shot at Luc once, before he and Maddie had fallen in love, but that had only been a warning graze, and even then, no one had known how terrified she had been, how her heart had pounded and her stomach flipped.

This was different. This time, she had been forced to inflict real damage. Her evening meal threatened to resurface, and she clamped her teeth together.

"Are you hurt?" Parker asked, appearing in front of her.

"No," Joss said. Not physically, at least.

She looked up at Parker's outstretched hand, then around the clearing, avoiding the body the bandits had left behind during their escape. The man who had come to their aid crouched at the other side of the fire and inspected something before putting it in his pocket.

Parker pulled her to her feet, then gently gripped her shoulders. "You did well. Stay here while I talk to him."

Donning her serious guard's expression, she walked over to the stranger, who was searching the body. Firelight flickered across dark brown hair and one side of his deeply-tanned face, the lower half of which was covered by a short beard.

Joss followed, despite the instructions to stay back. Whether to remain close to Parker or discover more about the stranger, she could not say.

He stood as they approached and asked, “Are you both all right?”

“Yes,” Parker said. “Thank you for your help.”

“It was nothing. I just happened to be nearby. Besides, you looked like you could handle them without me.”

Something about him seemed familiar, and when Joss placed him, she stepped out from behind Parker, her eyes wide. “You were on the ferry from Tyrrath.”

“Uh, yes.”

An urge rose to question him further. Who was he? Why had he been hiding beneath a hood? How did the weapon in his sleeve work? She opened her mouth to ask, but Parker squeezed her elbow, and she pressed her lips closed without speaking.

“I’m Theo Taskil.” The man’s baritone voice curled into the awkward pause. “May I ask your names?”

“Parker,” Parker said.

He stared at her, clearly expecting more, but she remained silent. “Parker. Is that…?”

“Family name.”

“Then, your given n—”

“Just Parker.”

“I see,” he said, though his tone made it evident he did not. He turned to Joss, his eyes lost in the shadows. “And you are?”

A name. She needed a name. They had agreed she would travel as a peasant outside Tyrrath to avoid attention and keep her safe—and she had no desire to alert anyone to her royal status anyway—but she had not considered whether she might need a different name.

Would Joss suffice? Was it common outside the nobility?

Panic hit as she searched her surroundings for inspiration, all the while aware of the stranger's steady gaze boring into her. In her periphery, she caught the white fluff of a rabbit's tail disappearing into the undergrowth and blurted, "Kit. Kit Parker," before she could think it through.

He glanced between them, straight black brows bunching.

"We're cousins," she added. Her mid-brown braid, dark eyes, and slim frame were nothing like Parker's blonde locks, sky blues, and stocky build, but being only cousins rather than sisters might explain the differences.

Parker lofted one brow at her, and a bubble of amusement tickled Joss's throat. Coughing to hide it, she crouched and searched for her waterskin, which should have been beside the log where they had been sitting earlier.

The man—Theo—held one out to her, stopper already removed and dangling on a cord against the coppery skin of his hand. She reached out to take it from him but paused when her gaze fell on his wrist. A black line swirled out from the cuff of his shirt.

Her eyes widened, jumping to his. Was that the top of an Iskarian tattoo?

He pulled his hand back and tugged his shirtsleeve down, letting go of the waterskin in the process. She fumbled it for a moment but managed to grip the neck before it fell to the ground.

To give herself time to think, she took a long swig, the water soothing the scratch her coughing had caused. Wherever he was from—and she was not completely certain of what she had seen—he posed no threat, had helped them, even. Whatever his reason for keeping his heritage a secret, it was none of their business.

Parker cleared her throat. "We need to go… Kit."

Joss wiped her mouth with the back of her hand, stoppered the waterskin, and handed it back to Theo. She gave him a small nod of thanks and joined Parker, who eyed the dead bandit.

"I'll take care of the body," Theo said.

"My thanks," Parker replied. Then she grabbed Joss's arm and towed her and the horses out of the clearing and back to the road.

They mounted as soon as they cleared the treeline and followed the moonlit road towards the mountains looming over the forest. The only sounds were the dull clops of the horses' hooves, the hoot of an owl that swooped down from a tree ahead, and the squeak of a small animal, which abruptly cut off.

Joss mulled over the name she had chosen as they rode. Kit. It was not a bad name. She could be Kit for the duration of their journey. She glanced at Parker riding ahead of her. Kit and… She frowned. "What's your given name?" she asked. "I've never heard you use it, and I might need to know if we're pretending to be cousins."

"Parker's fine."

"Oh? Now I'm curious." Joss urged her horse to catch up. "What is it?"

Silence.

"Won't you tell me?"

"No."

"I'll keep it a secret."

More silence.

"What if I promise to follow your lead in Aralan?"

Parker snorted, which was fair. Joss would not believe herself either.

"What if I guess it?" She tapped her lower lip with her finger. "Samantha? Fiona? Eloise...?"

When Parker dug her heels in to pull ahead, Joss grinned and kept apace. The reticent guard would tell her eventually, she was sure. They had an empty road and all night ahead of them. And pestering her guard stopped her mind from straying in other, more disturbing directions.

Chapter 7

Theo

Theo watched the women lead their horses out of the clearing in the direction of the road, their silhouettes soon blending into the dark forms of the trees. The younger woman's face lingered in his mind, one corner of her mouth tilted up, her eyes shining in the firelight.

She was older than he had first assumed, maybe only a couple of years shy of his twenty-three. Kit Parker.

"Farewell, Lady Kit." The name rolled naturally from his lips, but he paused. Why had he referred to her as 'Lady' when she was a commoner? He mentally reviewed their brief encounter.

She carried herself with willowy grace and spoke with an eloquence that suggested an extended education, but so did many merchants' daughters back in Jadhe. Besides, her clothing was made of the plain fabrics worn by most labourers, and not even the most rebellious lady he knew would stoop to wearing breeches. Nothing about her stood out that he could put a finger on.

But she was intriguing. It was a pity he was unlikely to see her again.

He turned back to the clearing and the body he had offered to bury. With no one around, he could inspect it more thoroughly. He knelt in the grass beside the corpse, damp seeping through his breeches to chill his skin, and unwrapped the cotton strip binding the dead man's right forearm.

As Theo had glimpsed earlier, the mark of a mage hunter was clearly inked into the back of the man's hand above the clan tattoo curling around his wrist.

Theo stilled as he stared at the mark, his mouth going dry. Mage hunters. In Farling Forest. And not just any hunters. This man belonged to one of the Order's founding clans—the clan whose leaders most often clashed with Theo's cousin.

Cold suspicion prickled the base of his neck. They must have discovered what he intended to do and sent the group to follow him from Jadhe. No wonder they were so far from home, and disguised as bandits.

He had noticed them earlier in the day, once outside Dynnford, and again, behind him on the road. Unsure whether they were following him or simply heading in the same direction, he set an ambush when he stopped for the evening, but they never triggered it.

Then he had heard fighting and discovered the women's campsite not far away. The hunters must have mistaken it for his.

He shuddered, sweat from his previous exertion cooling in the night air and raising gooseflesh across his skin.

A check of the rest of the body unearthed no further clues, but that was to be expected. If the hunters had gone so far as to disguise themselves as bandits, they were hardly likely to carry identifying items on them.

He picked up the man's knife—a long blade, crudely made—and grimaced. The Order's double swords and throwing stars were sharp enough to cut through bone, and their dart launchers could hit a copper coin at twenty paces. If they had been using their usual weapons, the women they had attacked would not have stood a chance against them.

Theo's mind replayed the evening's clash. The pair had skills, especially Parker. Though Kit's reflexes had been equally impressive, shooting both the man behind her cousin and the one sneaking up on her in quick succession.

As for her aim… He studied the arrow protruding from the hunter's shoulder. She valued life, if she had hit her mark.

But she was also observant. Theo looked down to where his own tattoo hid beneath the cuff of his tunic—she had definitely noticed it earlier. Despite being alone, he instinctively tugged his sleeve lower. Maybe he should have wrapped his wrists like the hunters.

He dumped the man's arm wrap on his chest, then stood, brushed off his knees, and hauled the body deeper into the forest. He could have left it where it was. Most who encountered bandits would. But they were not real bandits, and whatever their purpose, he could not leave a fellow Iskarian to rot or be eaten by wild animals.

When he found a suitable spot, he searched the undergrowth for a sturdy branch, stripped the leaves from it, and set about digging a hole. Fortunately, the ground was soft with few rocks or roots to slow his progress. Breath blowing, muscles heating, he soon lost himself in the rhythm of the work, allowing his mind to wander once more.

Maybe he should not have intervened in the fight. The man beside him might still be alive then—his bolt had been the killing blow, after all. But he would not have known mage hunters lurked in the far regions of Garellion, though the reason they might be there troubled him.

He glanced at the body. If they were after him, what—or who—had given away his purpose for coming to Garellion? Could it be…?

No. Speculation was of no use at this point. Focusing on the task at hand, he eyed the depth of the trench he had dug. It would do. He tossed the branch aside, then climbed out and rolled the body into it, adjusting the man's arms and legs until he lay straight with his palms facing up.

Theo sat on the rim of the grave beside the pile of displaced earth and stared down at the corpse. He could have ignored the fight, should have if he wanted to continue unnoticed, but instinct had taken over. And now here he was, burying a man he had killed to protect a stranger.

With a soft sigh, he cut a piece of cloth from the dead man's tunic, soaked it in water from his waterskin, and placed it over his heart. There. At least he had given the hunter a true desert burial, or as close to one as he could manage in a forest. He got to his feet for the last time and spread loose soil over the body.

By the time he finished filling in the grave, dawn was almost upon him, and his whole body cried for rest. He stretched his back, ignoring his muscles' protest, and dusted off his clothing. Then he lowered his head to murmur the song of passing under his breath before returning to the clearing.

A splash of cold water to the face at the nearby stream banished his fatigue, and a breakfast of dried meat and wild berries took care of his grumbling stomach. He retrieved his horse, a skittish thing he had left just off the road, and steered it away from the traces of dawn spreading across the eastern sky.

Not for the first time since he had purchased the colt, he longed for his own mount—Iskarian horses were known for their stamina—but he had stabled Dusk in Tyrrath for fear of drawing attention in Garellion. A snort escaped him, causing the colt to toss its head. It was too late to worry about being noticed if hunters were truly after him.

He needed to get to Aralan and find a way to return his kingdom to life. Then he could stop the Order for good.

Chapter 8

Joss

Joss and Parker slept in a clearing a few miles from the first, and after a fitful rest, Joss woke up late. From then on, Parker insisted on being more careful, stopping at waypoints rather than travelling as far as possible each day, which added at least one night to their journey and left Joss itching to move faster.

They arrived on the outskirts of Aralan five days later, and when they topped the final rise, Joss sucked in a breath at the view. Garellion's capital was unlike anything else she had seen. Spread across two slopes of the mountains' foothills, trees mingled with the wooden buildings throughout, or rather, the buildings mingled with the trees, as if the city were a natural part of the forest rather than man-made. Towering over it all on the crest of the farthest slope stood a giant oak that must have been fed magic to have reached such an impossible size.

She stretched her neck and shoulders, studying the maze of rooftops. "I wonder where the guildhall is."

Parker pointed to the mammoth tree. "Over there, near the palace."

"How'd you know that?"

The guard gave her a look that suggested the answer should have been obvious. "I memorised a map of the city before we set off."

"Oh. Come on, then." Joss urged her horse forwards, eager to find what they needed as soon as possible.

Up close, the city was even more interesting. Instead of a paved street, they walked their horses along a packed-dirt lane with wide grass verges that meandered up the first hill. A brook chattered to one side, and birds' voices joined the sounds of industry around them, creating a sense of natural harmony that soothed the knot in Joss's core.

Smaller paths of flattened grass branched off between the buildings, many of which had been built into or around tree trunks. Leafy canopies formed the entire roof in some cases, and gania vines climbed the walls to splash brightly coloured flowers across the varying shades of green foliage.

But that was not the only wonder. Throughout the city, people used magic as they went about their daily tasks, and Joss's eyes jumped from one incredible scene to the next. A man lighting a forge fire, conjuring roaring flames from unlit logs; a woman coaxing peonies into bloom with the turn of her hand; another channelling air to sweep the dust from her porch.

Not everyone used magic—a group of labourers sawed and hoisted beams for the frame of a new building and a woman washed laundry by hand—but it was clear that mages were an accepted part of the fabric of the city.

In an open area ahead, a young man dropped a bucket into a stone well and held his hand over the opening until the full bucket rose to meet it. Joss gaped as he emptied the water into a jar and repeated the process.

Her feet veered in his direction of their own accord, even as questions bubbled to the surface of her mind. How was he doing that? Had he always been able to move objects? "Does it take a lot of power?"

She did not realise she had spoken the last aloud until he looked up and answered. "All magic drains energy. But this is a small task, so I'll recover soon."

"Oh." She should have known. Closing wounds always exhausted Bronwen, the palace healer back home, and Olivia had to rest for a day or two every time she used her powers.

Parker clasped Joss's elbow and tugged her away. "We should keep going, Milady."

"Yes. Of course."

Joss flashed the youth a brief smile and continued up the second slope.

When they reached the summit, they skirted the palace, which surrounded the giant oak in a sprawling complex, and stopped outside a huge building to its rear. Joss could not help but stare at the façade. This was the guildhall? Twisted vines framed a pair of arched doors that rose to the height of three men. Above them, appearing far more lifelike than the medallions all registered mages wore around their necks, hung the guild's dragon emblem, shimmering gold against the dark wood of the hall.

They handed their horses' reins to a liveried groom who emerged to greet them and walked inside. The entrance hall was as large as the one in Redcairn Palace, the main difference being a desk at one side. A mage with more salt than pepper in his short beard sat behind it and directed a small group of visitors to the upper floor.

Catching Parker's eye, Joss tilted her head in his direction, and they made their way across the hall to ask for the location of the archives.

They were only a few strides from the desk when someone called her name.

"Princess Jocelyn?"

Joss spun towards the cheerful, female voice, her mouth curving into something halfway between a grin and a grimace as a familiar mage hurried towards them. "Ciara. It's good to see you." She glanced around, grateful to find only a couple of people within hearing distance, and added in a lowered voice, "But please, don't draw attention to my title."

"Oh." The young mage aborted her curtsey mid-dip and covered her mouth with her hand, her eyes widening. "Apologies, Your Highness," she said more quietly. "May I ask why you're here?"

"I have a few questions for the librarian. What about you? The last time I saw you, you were studying with Olivia at the guildhall in Tyrrath."

"I came to work with Master Tye. We have similar gifts, so Mistress Nessa wanted me to learn better control from him." Ciara gestured behind her. "May I show you around while you're here?"

Joss glanced at the mage behind the desk and drummed her fingers on her thigh. The need to begin their task tugged at her core.

Ciara followed her gaze. "I can take you wherever you need to go after the tour. It won't take long."

"Can we see the library first?" Joss asked.

"It's right behind the main building, so we may as well start here and go there next," Ciara replied.

She led them along a wide corridor, pointing out some of the paintings of past mages hanging on the walls and opening a door to show them a large lecture hall. They stopped outside the third doorway and were about to peek inside when the door opened and a tall, stocky man emerged from within.

"Dean Orrin," Ciara said, dipping her head.

The man, who was impeccably dressed in a dark green robe, peered down his nose at Joss, then Parker, and pursed his lips. Irked by his appraisal, Joss tried to imagine how their travel-worn tunics and trousers would appear to a mage of high rank but gave up.

Ciara stepped into the gap between them. "Your Highness, may I introduce Dean Orrin, head of the guild of mages. Dean Orrin, this is Princess Jocelyn Dalbot of Tyrrath."

"Princess Jocelyn?" His expression immediately brightened.

Joss gave a single nod. "Dean Orrin."

"Welcome to the Aralan Guildhall, Your Highness." He bowed his head much more deeply than she had. "If

I'd known you were visiting, I would have arranged a reception for you." A nervous laugh escaped him. "Please. You must at least join me for some refreshments—"

"Thank you, Dean, but this isn't an official visit. We're here to do some private research."

His brows collided for a moment, and then he waved a dismissive hand. "Whatever you need, I can have someone help you with it."

Joss shared a look with Parker, who offered a tiny shrug. At this point, they could not easily refuse, and it would be quicker to get help anyway. She turned back to the dean. "I'm looking for information about a mage called Mistress Yarin, from around the end of the mage wars."

"Hmm. Anything in particular about her?"

"Where she lived, whether she left anything behind…"

He handed a small token to Ciara and said, "Did you get that? Go to the library and ask Mistress Melia to find everything she can on Yarin as a matter of urgency."

"Yes, Dean." Ciara bobbed a quick curtsey, cast an apologetic smile at Joss and hurried away.

The dean strode in the opposite direction, almost gliding along the corridor despite his bulk. He walked through the door at the far end and called over another young mage. Whatever he said was too quiet for Joss to hear, but the mage scurried past them and disappeared through an archway she had missed.

“Please make yourself at home, Your Highness,” the dean said as he opened another door at the far side of the chamber and held it wide for them.

Joss crossed the antechamber past a small desk in front of several bookcases and into a much more spacious and comfortably appointed room. Light streamed through two large windows to her right and fell on several loungers arranged around an unlit fireplace to the left. Across from the doorway sat a solid, carved desk twice the size of the one outside before a huge portrait of a woman with twinkling eyes and a flowing robe embroidered with the dragon emblem.

“That’s Mistress Katrin, the first dean of our guild. The paint is retouched every fifty or sixty years, but I like to think it’s still an accurate likeness.”

Joss perched on the nearest lounger, and the dean sank onto the seat opposite. Despite her urging, Parker refused to join them, standing just inside the doorway instead. Joss gave up with a shrug and turned to the dean, who wiped the traces of a smile from his mouth with one meaty hand.

Unfortunately, the drinks arrived before Joss could say anything, though she had no idea how she would have addressed his arrogance had they not. She accepted the cup the young mage handed to her and sipped her tea, trying not to jiggle her leg or tap her fingers on her armrest.

“Are your family well, Your Highness?”

“Very, thank you.”

“I believe King Lucas and Princess Madeline recently returned from Craeick…”

"Yes. That's correct."

He leaned forward and offered her a biscuit. "Then they'll be able to support Garellion in our dispute with Iskaria." The fruit shortbread fell into her tea, but he continued, oblivious. "After all, we have a strong relationship with your family now your sister's discovered her magic, do we not?"

She set her cup down and brushed the crumbs from her fingers. "The guildhall in Tyrrath has certainly helped her, for which we're most grateful to Mistress Nessa."

Pasting a smile across her face, she did everything she could not to look at the door. This was going to be a long afternoon.

The moment she could escape without appearing overly rude, Joss excused herself and all but pushed their guide—Dean Orrin's subordinate—through the twists and turns of the maze-like guildhall to the library. The dean had offered an extensive tour of the grounds, but Joss had wasted several hours conversing with him already. Admittedly, under normal circumstances, she would have enjoyed exploring every nook and cranny of the place, but images of her father lying prone in bed urged her to her task.

They found the librarian halfway up a ladder that leaned against one of the larger bookcases.

"Mistress Melia?" Joss asked.

The white-haired woman dropped the scroll she was studying with a start.

"Yes. May I help you?"

Joss picked up the scroll and held it out. "We're looking for information about a Mistress Yarin. Have you found anything yet?"

"Ah, that was for you." The librarian frowned, a little vee forming between her brows and her lips pressing into a thin line. "Very little, I'm afraid. Most of the books from that period have already been requested. I won't be able to start in earnest until they're returned."

Requested? "Who's taken them? Where can I find them?" Joss asked. Maybe she could convince the person to share, or better yet, return them early.

"I believe it was a young scholar, yesterday afternoon. Some of the texts are original copies, so he'll be somewhere in the library…"

Joss turned to leave before the librarian finished explaining. She stalked down the central aisle, her head weaving back and forth as she searched the rows of bookcases on each side. Eventually, in the farthest corner of the inner archives, a small room full of dusty tomes, she found a figure hunched over a desk laden with stacked books and scrolls.

"Excuse me," she called out.

The figure turned, and Joss ground to a halt. "You."

Theo stared up at her, his dark brown eyes rimmed by thick lashes.

"Kit?" he asked at the same time as she demanded, "Why are you here?"

He stood, fully facing her. "I didn't expect to see you again."

"Neither did—" Joss shook her head to clear it. She needed to focus on what was most important. "You've taken nearly all the books from the time of mage wars. Have you finished with them yet?"

His mouth opened, but he only blinked at her.

"I need those books. How soon can we have them?"

Mistress Melia bustled over and stood between them. "It's against guild policy to limit time to read." Her lips pinched. "And it's not polite to hassle other patrons."

"But I need the information in them urgently, and he's got so many—"

Parker squeezed Joss's arm.

She turned to the guard, then looked around the room. Several people were staring at them, and she winced. Had she been speaking so loudly? She took a calming breath and opened her mouth to argue her case, but Mistress Melia spoke first.

"You arrived in Aralan today, correct?" She linked her arm through Joss's and steered her away from Theo. "Why don't you get settled at an inn, and I'll send a note as soon as I have anything to report. There are several reputable places nearby if you haven't booked a room yet."

"Thank you," Parker said. "We'll do that, won't we, *Kit*?"

With a last glance at Theo, who quickly returned to his reading when their eyes met, Joss reluctantly agreed, and she and Parker walked out of the library. For now.

Chapter 9
Joss

They found an inn a couple of streets away, and as night fell outside, Joss sat opposite Parker at a table in the corner of the inn's main room and watched a maid deliver a roasted chicken and platter of bread to a rowdy group of men by the window. The savoury scent wafted to her nostrils, making her mouth water and her stomach grumble. She instinctively covered it with a hand, though the general hubbub prevented anyone from hearing it.

"Sand-cursed mage hunters!" a man a couple of tables away said particularly loudly. "Most of the Weavers they took were women and children."

The conversations around him quieted to a dull hum, so Joss heard one of his companions ask, "How'd they find them?"

She did not hear the answer, for the couple at the table behind her burst into laughter.

As their merriment died down, a heavyset man with cropped sandy hair said, "Someone needs to teach them a lesson they won't forget."

"That's right," the man sitting next to him said. "They can't keep coming over here and kidnapping innocent people."

"It's about time we fought back," someone else added.

Joss glanced at Parker, who sat with her back against the wall, her eyes roving the inn, alert for any hint of danger aimed in their direction.

"But what about the Weavers?" a thin man with a long, grey beard asked. "Our Sadie was among them, and she's only thirteen."

The ringing statement temporarily silenced the room.

Joss's stomach soured at the image of the young girl in the hands of the hunters. She met Parker's gaze. Everyone knew the fate of those taken by mage hunters—a mockery of a trial in Iskaria followed either by exile across the Eastern Ocean or a swift execution.

"Will we go to war with them, then?" the loud man asked, drawing Joss's attention back to their conversation.

"Iskaria won't give us an option, if you ask me."

"Yeah," the heavyset man said, "and they don't just hate those who have the gift. They hate anyone who supports them too."

"It's not like we ruined their kingdom," the older man said. "That was done aeons ago."

"They don't care. They just want to destroy the guild at any cost."

"Not just the guild—our whole way of life." The large man slammed a meaty hand onto the table, making their tankards jump.

Several men from nearby tables joined the tirade, the sentiments becoming more and more heated until someone shouted, "Cursed mage killers. We should attack them first."

Joss shifted in her seat at the murmurs of assent that rippled through the room. While she could understand the fear fuelling the men, and the longstanding feud between the two southern kingdoms that fed it, Tyrrath would do everything it could to prevent the conflict from spilling into bloodshed.

"Don't get involved," Parker whispered.

"I won't."

The heavyset man stood and headed for the door. He paused beside a table at the far side of the room and said something to the person sitting there. There must not have been a response because the man raised his voice. "I asked who are you?"

Joss could just about hear the reply, and something about it seemed familiar. "I don't want any trouble. I'm just here to visit the guild library."

"Burn it down, more like." The man reached across the table and pulled the person's hood down, revealing a darkly-tanned face Joss knew well by now. The local man turned to the others and pointed an accusing finger at Theo.

"He's Iskarian, look!"

A few of them got to their feet, and Joss eyed them in turn, her fingers tapping the tabletop. When they started moving from their own tables, she jumped up as well. Shrugging off Parker's restraining hand, she skirted the crowd and stepped between Theo and the men closing in around him.

She looked over her shoulder and met his eyes. They seemed to ask the same question that ran through her own mind. He was a stranger, so why had she intervened? She gave a mental shrug. She was here now, so she would defend him as best she could.

Returning her attention to the locals, she lifted her chin. "This man has nothing to do with the mage hunters. Leave him alone."

"Oh yeah? How'd you know that?" the man at the front demanded, a blacksmith if the burns scarring his thick forearms were any indication.

Someone behind him shouted, "Yeah, he could be a spy."

Others added their voices to the swell of accusation, and the candles throughout the room flared together. Had a mage joined the angry mob?

The smith loomed over Joss, his ale-drenched breath striking her face with the force of a hammer and his bulk blocking her view of the rest of the crowd. Fear tickled the back of her neck, and her hand instinctively reached for the bow she had left upstairs, until she noted Parker in her periphery.

One hand on Theo's shoulder, holding him in his seat, the guard rested the other casually on the pommel of her sword as she watched the men around them closely. She would never allow a drunken rabble like this to harm Joss.

Reassured by her presence, Joss straightened and faced the ringleader.

"He helped us drive off bandits on our way here from Tyrrath. Is that the actions of a saboteur?" She leaned around him to glare at the shorter man hiding at the rear of the group. "Or a spy?" Refocussing on the smith, she continued, "Besides, we saw him at the guild library earlier today. He's telling the truth."

At least, she hoped he was.

The smith held her gaze for an endless minute, challenge lurking in his eyes, then he shrugged, the fight draining from his muscles. "If he needs a woman to defend him, he's not worth the effort."

He pushed past her and stomped out through the door, and after a few mumbled insults, the others scattered to their seats.

Joss released the breath she'd been holding and turned to Theo, who was watching her with an expression she could not read.

The silence between them became awkward, especially as the chatter around them returned to a normal level.

She was about to leave when he called out, "Kit?"

It took her a moment to realise he addressed her, but when she did, she turned back to him.

"Why did you do that?" he asked.

Much to her consternation, her cheeks burst into flames. She ignored the heat and answered him honestly. "Because you did nothing wrong, and no one should be attacked by an angry crowd while they're eating their dinner. Even if you did steal my books," she added with a grin.

"Thank you." He leaned back and folded his arms across his chest. "I'm glad it didn't turn ugly. I need to stay in Aralan for a while. Would you care to join me?" He gestured at the bench opposite his and looked to Parker as well as Joss for an answer.

Joss scooted onto it, giving Parker little choice but to sit as well. With an almost imperceptible sigh, the guard waved to the barmaid, gestured for her to bring their meal to the new table, and positioned herself beside Joss so she could see both Theo and the rest of the room.

Joss picked at a whorl in the tabletop, then looked up and asked him, "So, have you finished with any of the books you've been reading?"

"Not yet."

"What?" Her hand flattened against the wood, pressing into the grain. "Why not? I need those books."

His eyes tightened. "So do I."

"Well, can we at least have some of them? You can't possibly read them all at once."

Parker touched her elbow, a silent reminder to remain calm, but Joss paid it no heed.

"The problem is I'm not sure which one contains the information I'm looking for, and I need to verify the details between different accounts." He spread his hands in a helpless gesture. "I'm sorry. I'll be as fast as I can."

"But I don't know how long my father—"

This time, Parker coughed and clutched Joss's forearm, and she clamped her lips together.

He eyed them both through narrowed lids and leaned closer, lowering his voice. "You're looking for a magical cure for something?"

How could she deny it? Fortunately, the barmaid arrived with their stews, giving her time to regroup. When the bowls and platter of bread had been arranged on the table and the barmaid weaved away through the crowded room, Joss glanced up and found Theo still studying her. It was too late to lie or deflect from her slip, so she opted for a version of the truth.

"We need a dragon stone that can break a curse."

"A dragon stone…" His brows scrunched together. "And you say it can break curses?"

"Yes. But we don't know where it is, so we need to find the mage who created it."

"Mistress Yarin?"

"How did you know that?"

He scrubbed a hand over his bearded jaw. "I think we might be after the same thing."

She sat straighter as he continued, "I'm trying to find something she left behind at the end of the mage wars. Something that can reverse magic."

Parker pinned him with a dubious look. "Why's an Iskarian looking for something magical?"

His hand clenched into a fist on the tabletop. "I need to undo a great wrong to stop another war."

"Should we share the books, then?" Joss asked before Parker could question him further and drive him away. "That would speed things up for all of us."

He looked behind her and frowned again, but when she glanced over her shoulder, no one was there. Did he not want to share his resources with them?

"Sorry." His gaze returned to her. "I thought I saw… Never mind. It'd be better for us to search together. That way, when we find the stone, we can both use it."

She stilled. Swapping information was one thing, working together was something else. "Can we trust you?"

"Yes, but you won't know that until you try. So, what do you think? Partners?"

She shared a look with Parker, whose dark expression said she wanted to say no.

Joss met his eyes and said, "Yes."

Chapter 10

Joss

They returned to the guild library the next morning, and Theo brought the texts he had reserved to a large central desk. He picked up a particularly thick tome and angled it so Joss could read as he flicked through the pages.

"See?" He pointed at a scrawled entry about halfway through. "Mistress Yarin is in the general registry. Joined the guild in 914EA from the Free Isles."

"The Free Isles? I didn't think they became mages, only Summoners." Most of them had gifts with wind on water and trained to ease the fleet's voyages.

"Maybe it was different back then." He returned to the entry. "Let's see… She bonded with a fire dragon called Keed, excelled in regeneration and purification magic, took on an apprentice in 907EA called Tammas. But that's all there is. I found a note about her in one of the other early guild records, but the text it mentioned was lost in the great fire. And the only references I found to specific dragon stones both led to dead ends.

But I've only searched about a quarter of the texts from that period so far. If we work together, we should be able to get through the rest in a couple of days. I'm sure we'll find something."

He flashed her a smile and set about dividing the books into three piles.

"None for me," Parker said from the end of the table, where she stood with one hand on her hip where her sword usually rested. "I'm only here to protect Kit." She kept one steely eye on Theo, whom she had told Joss that morning that she still did not trust, and one on the rest of the room.

Theo studied her, his brows pulled low. Then he gave a little shrug, his features clearing, and reorganised the piles into two without a word.

Joss sank onto the nearest chair and stared at the amount of reading set before her. Why had she not brought Olivia along? This was going to take forever.

When he finished assigning the texts, Theo sat opposite her and picked up a scroll from the top of his stack. He unrolled it on the desk and leaned over the ancient script, his forehead furrowing again as he read.

She watched him for a few minutes, noting the angles of his face and the way he rubbed his bearded jaw when he finished making a note. Up close, in the daylight, he was quite attractive. Certainly better than Lord Ealley.

His eyes met hers, and she started. She pulled a random book towards her, cheeks burning as she focused on opening it the right way round. What was she thinking? She was here to find the dragon stone, not swoon over a random stranger. Putting all thoughts of anything else from her mind, she settled in to read.

By the third day, Joss was ready to spar with a dragon if it meant escaping the ancient tomes piled around her. Endless words marched across page after page, the ridges of her chair dug into her back, and the silence was only broken by the occasional swish of a page turning or a murmur of recitation. Even the candle flames barely flickered in the sconces around the room.

She shoved the numbingly dry memoir she had been skimming to one side and stretched her arms above her head. Then she stood and walked over to the nearest window, her gaze drawn to the trees outside. She needed fresh air and sunshine and wide, open spaces, not a stuffy hall with walls that closed in around her.

"Not a fan of research, are you, Kit?"

She spun to Theo, who did not bother to hide his knowing smile.

"How could you tell?"

He pointed to her sheaf of paper, where she had tapped her pen while she read, creating a mess of inky splodges, and to the small pile of tailnut shells she had left on the desk.

"My sister Olivia's more suited to spending all day in a library. I prefer being outdoors. Or at least being able to move around."

Nodding slowly, he held out a piece of paper. "Would you find this book for me? It's mentioned here, and I think it…"

She missed whatever further explanation he offered, having already plucked the slip from his fingers and started skirting the desk in the direction of the archives. He chuckled behind her, the deep rumble warming her gut and making her swivel back to face him.

"Bet I can find this before you finish reading that one," she said on impulse before hurrying on her way.

A brief glance at Parker revealed the guard moving to join her. Joss gave a tiny shake of her head, and Parker returned to her previous position, leaned against the end of a bookcase near their desk. A slight frown tightened her features, but Joss had no time to question the cause. She had a book to find.

It turned out to be a collection of letters belonging to a mage who entered the guild at the same time as Yarin. Joss searched through the index on her way back to the others and found Yarin's name listed as one of the correspondents.

Her feet drew to a halt. Something written by the mage herself? This could be what they needed.

When she found the letters from Yarin, she wrinkled her nose. The first was written in Dracestian, the ancient language of the mages. She turned the page and blew out a breath. Fortunately, there was a modern translation on the reverse.

She skimmed the text until she reached a section towards the end of the fourth letter. '*Keed and I will fly home tomorrow to work on the dragon stone project. We should celebrate our success with a jar of nightingale wine when we return. Pray for all our sakes that day comes soon.'*

Excitement buzzed along Joss's spine. Could that be the stone they were after? It seemed to be important from the way Yarin had described it, and surely even an ancient mage could have only made one so powerful. Joss let out a low whoop that elicited a stern 'shhh' from a nearby mage.

Smoothing her features, she snapped the tome closed and returned to the others.

"Here." She tossed it onto Theo's pile of unread texts and took her time getting comfortable before clearing her throat.

"Bet I can find a clue before you do." She leaned forwards. "And if I do, I get to use the stone first. Deal?"

He studied her through narrowed eyes for a moment, then laughed. "I don't think so. You've already found something, haven't you?"

Could he read her so easily? She frowned for a second, but her earlier excitement soon overpowered it. "Fine. I'll show you."

She reached for the book and started to open it between them, but her elbow caught a pile of scrolls. With a soft grunt, she stood and rounded the table to stand next to him while she showed him the passage.

"See?"

He read the letter in silence, then spun his head up to her. Their faces were so close, their noses almost touched, and she could see flecks of lighter brown in his eyes.

Joss stilled, her mouth dry and mind suddenly blank. He stared back at her, and when he finally blinked, the thick, black lashes failed to sweep the intensity from his gaze.

Parker cleared her throat loudly, and Joss jerked upright, breaking the unsettling connection.

"What do you think?" she asked. "This could be it, couldn't it?"

He rubbed his jaw. "The timing seems right. Lots of mages returned to their home kingdoms towards the end of the war." He looked back at the book. "We should find out more."

Without thinking, she squeezed his arm as she said, "Seems we make a good team."

He stared down at her hand, and she let go like he was a burning hot griddle cake. "We're going to the Free Isles, then."

He shook his head and riffled through the books spread across the desk. "Not yet. We need to confirm…" He tugged an unfurled scroll from under a pile of papers, set it out in front of him, and studied it for a few moments. "Aha. I knew I'd read that somewhere. Look."

He pointed out a passage, but Joss remained where she was and waited for him to explain.

"There's a place in the Free Isles that was set aside for mages at the time of the Third Landing. That must be where she went."

"So let's go there."

"We don't even know if it's still there. We should see if we can find anything else about the stone here first. Let's see…"

He pulled a book towards him, flipped to a page two-thirds of the way through, and started reading. After a few moments, he checked his notes and grabbed a second scroll, opening it beside the book.

Joss drummed her fingers on her thigh while she watched him work, but when he showed no sign of stopping, she braced her hand on the desk and leaned into his line of sight. "I'm going to go buy provisions so we can leave first thing in the morning."

He waved her off without even looking up. But at least they had a lead now. They would head to the Free Isles, find the stone, and save her father.

Chapter 11

Joss

The ride out of Aralan was uneventful, aside from Parker subjecting Theo to several dubious glances, and they were soon on the road south to Garellion's main port in Ravelan. Parker rode ahead at times and dropped behind at others, but Joss stayed beside Theo, asking questions as they occurred to her and avoiding answering his in turn.

The forest thinned as they descended the foothills, and marshland took over when they reached flat ground. It stretched out around them, mauve calidis bushes mixed with rushes and spindle grass, shallow pools and wet, sandy peat. The road wound through it on ribbons of dry ground, and a few stands of trees broke the flat monotony here and there. To the west, a sprinkling of low-lying hillocks partially hid the green haze of Arden Forest beyond.

They rode on, settling into a silence that matched the sombre terrain. As the sun rose overhead, the air grew thick with heat, and swarms of gnats claimed the waterlines, biting Joss's exposed skin. She tried covering her face and hands but soon found it was better to face the onslaught than boil in her own sweat.

A few hours into their journey, they came to a large stretch of murky water crossed by a long, wooden boardwalk. Shadow shied for a moment before stepping onto the uneven planks, and Joss stroked her neck. "Easy, Shadow. It's just like a bridge."

Halfway across, a sharp, high-pitched cry drew Joss's attention to the east, where a bird circled high above the open marsh. It swooped low, skimming the feathery tips of the tall grass, and she reined in to watch it hunt.

"Is that a marsh hawk?" she asked.

Theo shielded his eyes and studied the bird for a mere moment before it twisted midair and dropped onto something hidden in the grass. "Yes. You can tell by the tail."

"Oh. I've never seen one before."

The hawk brought its catch to a small rock nearby, where it proceeded to rip out small pieces to toss down its gullet. A combination of awe and fascination fixed Joss's gaze on the strong claws and sharp beak as it devoured its meal.

Suddenly, its head came up, swivelling from side to side, and it launched into the air, leaving the remaining carcass behind. It winged into the distance with a harsh cry as if bemoaning the hasty retreat.

A moment later, Joss heard the reason for the hawk's flight. Voices. Coming from the far end of the boardwalk. She turned towards the sound just as a group of four or five men rounded a patch of particularly tall spindle grass, heading towards them.

All dark-skinned, all muscular, they walked at a steady pace that suggested they were used to travel and hard work. They wore homespun cotton tunics, most in reddish browns, one in green, and three of them carried large bundles over their shoulders. The last led a mule laden with several packs stretched to breaking point and a collection of long-handled tools.

Parker stiffened and rested her hand on the pommel of her sword, and Joss stifled a chuckle. What did she expect them to do—pull out weapons and capture them as slaves? The guard's eyes traced the strangers' every movement while they drew alongside, exchanged brief greetings, and continued on their way across the boardwalk.

With a click of her tongue, Joss squeezed Shadow's flanks, and they set off again. Parker rode ahead, no doubt checking for more threatening farmers, and Theo eased alongside Joss.

He gestured at the guard's retreating form. "You and your cousin have a pretty strange relationship."

She tried not to wince. "She's always protected me"—true—"and my sister and brother-in-law made her promise to keep me safe on this trip."

He was quiet for long enough that she assumed the conversation was over. Then he said, "I wish I had siblings like that." He looked over at her and added more cheerfully, "I've got a cousin who used to be like a brother, but we don't get to see much of each other now we're grown."

Joss had no idea how to respond, so she offered a weak, sympathetic smile and rode on.

When they caught up with Parker, who waited for them at the end of the boardwalk, Theo said, "We should stop to rest the horses for a while."

Joss stretched her back. "I could do with a break too. Parker?"

"The other side of those trees would be better, if you can keep going."

A large stand of trees straddled the road in the mid-distance. Joss nodded. "We can do that."

They had only ridden a few lengths when a couple of high-pitched cries came from that direction.

"Oh. Another marsh hawk." Joss searched the sky for the bird, but Theo caught Shadow's reins and drew them both to a halt.

"We need to turn back," he whispered, his brows lowered and neck corded with tension.

"What? Why?"

"That's not a marsh hawk. It's a mage hunter's whistle. They've probably set up an ambush in that grove."

Joss only gaped, but Parker levelled him with a narrow-eyed glare. "How do you know?"

The hawk-hunter-whatever cried again.

Theo looked towards the sound then back at them, his expression serious. "I'll explain later, but we need to leave before they see us."

Parker grumbled under her breath but turned her horse around. "Let's go."

She positioned herself at Joss's rear flank and gave Shadow's rump a slap to get them moving faster.

The only sounds as they hastened back to the boardwalk and recrossed it were the thuds of the horses' hooves on the wooden planks and an occasional croak of a frog above the low hum of insects that made the marsh their home. Not until they reached the other side, well beyond sight or sound of the potential ambush, did Theo speak again.

"There's a path ahead that leads to Arlan Forest. We can take it and circle round them."

A few minutes later, he pointed out a narrow trail that branched off the main road towards the west and guided his horse onto it first. Joss made to follow, but Parker blocked her way. A few lengths in, Theo stopped and looked back at them.

"How did you know about this trail?" Parker asked him.

He turned his horse in the tight space and returned to the road. "I memorised a map of Garellion before we left Aralan."

She nudged her mount closer to his and drew her sword, levelling it at his chest.

"So it's not a trap? You're not one of them? Faking an ambush on the main road, then taking us to a remote spot where the hunters are really waiting for us?"

Joss gaped at her guard. She had not even considered that possibility. Her gaze jumped to Theo, who eyed the sword and swallowed. If he did not want it thrust between his ribs, he would need to have a good explanation.

"I promise it's no trap," he said, looking up again. "I'd be in far more trouble than you if they caught us. You'd only need to tell them I'm looking for a dragon stone, and I'd be stranded the first chance they got."

"But you knew to watch out for them."

It was not a question.

He muttered something under his breath, then straightened and faced Parker. "We really do need to get off the road."

Parker did not reply, only studied him with an intense stare, and Joss drummed her leg while she waited for the guard's verdict.

After what felt like half a lifetime, Parker re-sheathed her sword and said, "Very well. I'll trust you, for now." She dismounted and added, "We should reduce our profile in case the hunters have scouts."

Joss and Theo followed her lead, and Joss set out along the path before the guard could change her mind or they started arguing again.

The first section was narrow, bordered on both sides by tall grass, so they travelled in single file, Joss in the lead, then Theo, and Parker at the rear. As they wound westwards, the walls of light green and pale-yellow fronds soon gave way to more open wetland vegetation, revealing dark forested foothills beyond the distant edge of the marsh.

A little over a third of a mile farther, the path split around a large calidis bush. Joss looked both ways and, seeing little difference other than that one side widened, chose the left. Within a few paces, the ground gave way beneath her feet and sucked first one, then the other into the soft silt.

She let out a small cry and attempted to pull her feet loose, which only served to push them deeper.

Her body tensed. What in the…?

Quicksand.

"Stop. Don't follow me." She dropped Shadow's reins, lest the mare follow her into the quagmire, and flung her arms out wide.

Theo drew up behind her and emitted a quiet chuckle. "What are you doing?"

"Olivia told me this is what you do if you get stuck in quicksand."

"When it's deep and you're sinking fast, yes. But it's only up to the top of your boots." He gathered Shadow's reins and handed them to Parker, saying, "Stay back on the path."

Then he eased around to Joss's side, testing the ground before placing his feet, and spoke in a calm tone that reminded her of her elder sister, Maddie.

"First, you need to sit down. The ground's solid behind you, so just lower yourself and sit back as far as you can."

She did, slowly crouching and putting her weight on her arms before transferring it to her rear. Her feet sank a little more with the movement, and she clenched her jaw to hold back a panicked whimper. When she repositioned her hands to scoot backwards, sand clung to her palms.

"Good, now lean back on your elbows so you have less weight on your legs, and gently wiggle your feet to bring them to the surface. Like this." He demonstrated, moving his hands up and down like he was peddling a spinning wheel.

"How do you know what to do?"

He stopped and looked at her. "There are patches of dry quicksand in the desert outside Jadhe. I saw someone escape it once and asked them how they did it."

"Oh."

Again, she followed his instructions. With her feet trapped in the sand, copying his rhythm amounted to little more than tensing and relaxing her muscles, but after a few moments, the sand shifted, and her right foot moved a fraction.

She gasped and spun to him. "It's working."

Shadow whinnied at her sudden cry, and Parker stroked the mare's neck, uttering soothing sounds—until the cry of a hawk behind them was answered from farther along the main road. Too close.

The hunters were searching for them.

Joss strained her leg muscles as hard as she could, pulling against the quicksand, but her feet only sank deeper.

"Don't pull," Theo whispered, his head close to her ear. "Keep going like you were before. We have time."

He was right. The wide bank of reeds and grass hid them from the road. Even if the hunters knew they had retreated to circle around the ambush, the number of tracks left by other travellers would slow down even an experienced tracker. They would be hard pressed to know which trail he, Joss, and Parker had taken.

"Stay with her. I'll see where they are." Parker lowered the horses' reins to the ground and padded back along the trail on silent feet.

Despite her racing heart, Joss slowly worked her feet loose, and when they broke the surface, she scrambled backwards as fast as she could before jumping up.

Parker returned a few moments later and whispered, "They've found this path."

"Then we need to hurry," Theo said.

Snatching up the reins, they led the horses along the winding, ribbon-thin trail, heading for the distant forest as fast as they dared across the treacherous, open marsh.

"I see them," a male voice shouted from behind.

Joss looked over her shoulder as the hunters spewed from the tall grass bordering the road—five dark-clad figures on horseback, shouting and slapping their mounts' rears with the ends of their reins.

"Don't let them get away."

"Quick. This way."

"Hyah!"

Parker, at the rear, motioned for her to keep going, saying, "Move faster."

Instinct urged Joss to ride rather than run, but the hunters dismounted before she could put action to the thought. She smirked. They must have discovered the quicksand.

Her satisfaction was short-lived, however. The hunters chased her, Parker, and Theo across the remaining marsh, seeming closer at times and falling behind at others as the trail twisted around shallow pools, dense undergrowth, and occasional stands of trees. But they were always there, pushing Joss and the others on without respite.

She had just navigated a particularly boggy patch when something whistled past her arm, making her jerk to the side, and caught in a low-lying bush ahead. She stared at the tangled rope and metal balls—bolas—then ducked as much as she could and peeked behind her.

The hunter in the lead was winding up to throw a second pair, but one of the others shouted from farther back, "Don't waste them. Wait till we're on open ground."

Joss swallowed and ran on. At least it seemed they were to be taken alive. And she could focus on where to safely place her feet without worrying about avoiding any more thrown weapons.

Before they reached the first of the tree-covered slopes, another large, waterlogged area forced the path to detour in a wide loop. Theo, in the lead again, broke off and splashed through the shallow water in a straight line towards the forest. There was no time to go around if they wanted to put distance between them and the hunters, but Joss's heart squeezed hard. What if more quicksand lurked beneath the surface?

One of the hunters must have stumbled into some, for there was a cry behind them, followed by cursing, and when Joss glanced back, a man thrashed in the distance, already sunk to his knees. Still, the others did not stop their pursuit, so she pushed her legs to greater speed, tightening her grip on the slick reins in her hand.

At the far side, they climbed up into a bank of reeds and found dry ground once more. Pushing through the stems was hard work, especially while leading a horse, but when they emerged at the other side, the forest stood before them like a blessed haven.

Joss went to remount Shadow, but Theo gripped her arm and shook his head. "We should leave clear tracks into the forest while our feet are wet, then hide in the reeds till the hunters pass by. There's a smaller path farther north that we can take once they're gone."

Joss looked back towards the marsh, hidden behind the wall of reeds, then at Parker, who gave a firm nod of agreement. "All right. Let's do that."

They walked to the treeline, pressing their feet into the soft ground, and backtracked as quickly as possible, ducking into the reeds a little farther along the bank. Then they waited.

Splashing and rustling sounds soon reached them, and Joss peered out from their hiding spot at the first of the hunters to break through the reeds.

"This way," he said to someone behind him. He mounted his horse and followed the tracks Joss and the others had left without a moment's hesitation.

Four more men escaped from the reeds, swung up into their saddles, and raced after their leader into the forest. They soon disappeared among the trees, and within a few minutes, even the sounds of their horses' hoofbeats faded from hearing.

The ruse had worked. Tension draining from her muscles, Joss turned to Theo and grinned. "Let's go before they realise we tricked them."

They skirted the forest for about a mile, then took an overgrown path into the interior, Theo in the lead and Parker at the rear.

"How did you know this was here?" Joss asked him.

"I told you. I memorised a map of Garellion at the guildhall last night."

"Right." He had. Maybe she should have thought of that too. "Where does it lead?"

"There's a river ahead we might be able to follow to the coast. If not, there should be a small bridge over it, so we can keep going to the next river. That one goes to the port of Eindal."

"Perfect."

They rode on in silence, climbing steadily higher until the trees parted to reveal a deep ravine cutting through the hillside in front of them. Water roared down the narrow passage and, along the bottom, churned white around boulders in its path.

Any boat that attempted to navigate it would be smashed to pieces, and following it on foot appeared almost as dangerous.

Parker peered over the edge. "We should keep going."

Joss hummed and studied the suspended wood-and-rope bridge a little way to their right. Weeds hid the bottoms of the support posts, but it appeared sturdy enough. There were no boards missing, at least.

"I'll go first." She handed Shadow's reins to Theo and stepped out onto the first plank before Parker could grab her arm to stop her. Even so, the guard still hissed, "Get back here," which Joss ignored.

The board held.

And, though the rope handrails sagged too much to be of use, so did the rest.

She returned to their side and retrieved Shadow's reins. He balked at the sight of the bridge, so she tied a cloth over his eyes and stroked his neck as she led him out over the gorge.

Aside from whinnying when a sudden gust caused the bridge to sway slightly underfoot, he followed her across without too much fuss, their many years together helping to soothe his nerves.

When they reached the far side, she removed his blindfold, then turned and shouted to the others, "Come on, then."

Theo crossed next, his mount balking several times and nearly tipping him into the ravine at one point. Parker crossed last. Despite her horse following her lead without a single complaint, she muttered several choice curses before joining them on solid ground.

On the other side, the forest was much denser. Thick undergrowth and vines tangled throughout, making it more like a jungle than the woods Joss hunted in at home.

She had assumed it would be cooler under the canopy of the trees than in the marsh, but the tightly packed foliage somehow managed to trap the heat and within half an hour, she was sticky and hot. At least there were fewer gnats, though several scurbugs circled her head like scavengers around ripe carrion.

Her stomach rumbled, adding to her discomfort, and she paused to take stock, wafting the bugs away with her hand.

Once their buzzing receded, her ears caught something rustling in the undergrowth to her left. She turned to the others and said, “I’m starving. Let’s hunt.”

Chapter 12
Theo

Theo studied Kit, whose eyes sparkled in a way that made him want to move closer. A grin lit her entire face, and she added, "Last one to catch something has to build the fire to cook them."

Then she tossed her horse's reins over a nearby bush, pulled her bow and arrows from behind her saddle, and slipped silently into the jungle.

He stared after her, until Parker shifted in his periphery and he snapped out of whatever daze had captured him. "Are you going to hunt too?"

"No. I'll stay with the animals and watch our rear."

"Oh." He pulled a coil of string from his pack, checked the ties on the knife at his waist, and slung a wineskin over his shoulder. "I'll be going, then."

"Mm-hm."

He eased through the vegetation at the side of the path and searched for signs of animals passing. A few lengths in, he found a thin, well-worn trail and followed it until he spotted a good place to set up a trap. He had not been so adept at this when he first left Iskaria, there being little opportunity to hunt game in the magic-ravaged, barren kingdom, but recent experience had refined the techniques he had studied in the texts back home, and he was confident he could catch something before the sunlight waned.

When he finished placing the bait—a piece of apple smeared with the last of his Iskarian nut paste—he eased farther along the trail to set a couple more, then retreated into the trees downwind and hunkered down beside a wide, gnarled trunk to wait.

He soaked in the sights and sounds of the forest, the mulchy smell, even the rough bark digging into his shoulder. So much life squeezed into every inch of land. Was this what Iskaria would have been like before the mage wars? Could it be like this again if he found the stone?

Something moved deeper in the forest, a flash of dark orange between the leafy greens. Kit. He searched the area and caught another glimpse of her stalking through the trees, bow and arrow in hand.

Instinct urged him to follow her, though what instinct that was, he had no idea. Deciding not to question it, he pushed up, and something stabbed his palm. Hissing in a breath, he rubbed the spot and glared at the prickly fern beside him. Fortunately, the damage from the barb was no worse than a large splinter, but he should have paid closer attention to his surroundings, and maybe less to the captivating woman now passing out of sight.

Still, the forest could be dangerous, and she was alone.

He crept through the trees behind her, careful not to make any sound that could disturb whatever prey she had found, and watched from the cover of a stone outcropping as she lifted her bow. She took aim at a young boar rooting through the undergrowth lower down a slope.

It would be a difficult shot, given the angle and the number of trees between them, so he readied for her to change positions. But she did not. A soft twang, and the arrow flew from her bow, straight into the boar's flank, just behind its foreleg.

It squealed once—causing several birds nearby to take flight—and dropped to the ground. A clean kill.

Kit let out a whoop, and he nearly joined in with his own. Her skills were far beyond those of the average soldiers in Iskaria, and his chest swelled for her.

She strolled down the incline, tugged the arrow free, and knelt to gut her catch. Knife in hand, she slashed at the carcass and removed the innards a bit at a time, creating a mess of the animal, the ground around it, and herself. How could one so proficient in hunting be so sloppy in dressing it?

As he moved closer, she swiped her forearm across her brow, leaving a red smear behind. She looked like his apprentice Daevi had as a six-year-old when he tried to copy one of Theo's designs. All innocence and frustration and ink everywhere.

Theo laughed. It bubbled up from his stomach, and he could not have held it in for all the water in Jadhe.

Kit's head jerked up, so he smothered his mirth and stepped out into her eyeline, his hands open and visible.

He walked towards her but, seeing the tight grip she still had on her knife, stopped a couple of lengths away and leaned against a solid tree trunk as casually as possible.

He pointed to her forehead. "You have a little something…"

Fire blazed in her eyes. "You're making fun of me?"

"No." He lifted his hands in surrender. "I'm impressed. I don't know many people who could've taken that shot."

Her eyes narrowed as if she was deciding whether to believe him or not. Then all traces of ire disappeared, and she smirked up at him. "I take it I caught something first."

He stilled.

She clambered to her feet and wiped her hands on a nearby fern. "That means I win, so you can carry this"—she waved her hand at the boar—"back to the horses."

Without waiting for a reply, she set off up the hill, leaving him to deal with the mess she had created.

He looked from her to it and back again, then blew out a chuckle. "Guess that serves me right for laughing."

After making quick work of cleaning the carcass and tying it to a stout pole, Theo also climbed back up the hill. He returned to his traps and sighed when he saw they had not been sprung. It seemed Kit was correct—he would be cooking her kill.

He dismantled the traps, tossed the apple into the undergrowth, and headed back along the trail to the others, her kill swinging from the pole digging into his shoulder. His shirt clung to his back as he walked, and he adjusted his grip on the pole and reached for his waterskin. The remaining trickle at least wet his gullet even if it did not quench his thirst.

Still, Arlan Forest was riddled with watercourses, fed each spring by snowmelt from the Dragonspine Mountains that sought the quickest paths to the sea.

They would surely cross one soon enough and be able to replenish their supply.

They found a stream not too far along the path they had been following and stopped in a small clearing beside it. After they had drunk their fill of the lukewarm water, Parker helped him build a fire, claiming she had also failed to catch anything to eat, and he soon had pieces of the boar roasting on skewers over the crackling flames.

They ate in a comfortable silence, serenaded by the soft sounds of the jungle—rustling leaves, the chirping of insects, and occasional birdsong. When Theo finished gnawing the last of the meat from a bone, he tossed it onto the embers and leaned back on his elbows.

Trees towered around him, their leaves cloaking the sky overhead and vines dangling down from their branches. How different Garellion was to Iskaria. He could not say he missed the windswept wasteland outside Jadhe, the sand stretching as far as the eye could see while the sun baked everything it touched, but the faces of his foreman, his apprentice, and his cousin appeared in his mind, and his chest twinged.

If only they could be here to see this…

His thoughts were interrupted by Parker, who straightened on the other side of the fire and said, "Now that we have time to talk, how did you know about that ambush earlier?"

Kit, sitting beside her, caught her cousin's arm. "Parker—"

"He needs to tell us how he knew those mage hunters were after us and not someone else," Parker said, and Kit turned her eyes on him too.

He frowned down at the ground between his feet, avoiding their scrutiny while he tried to decide how much to reveal. When his thoughts were somewhat in order, he straightened and faced Parker.

"The men who attacked you that first night in the woods weren't bandits. After you left, I found out they were mage hunters." Kit gasped in his periphery, but he kept going. "Then I saw someone in the inn the other day who looked like a hunter I've seen before. I was afraid something like this might happen, so I suggested working together for protection."

"Whose? Yours or ours?" Parker asked in a low growl.

He spread his hands. "Both. Whoever they're tracking—and I can only assume they discovered what I'm doing here and followed me from Jadhe—we're searching for the same thing. I didn't want you to be attacked again."

"So why didn't you tell us about them in Aralan?"

"I didn't want to worry you for nothing if I was wrong."

Parker nodded slowly and asked the one question Theo truly dreaded. "Are you hiding anything else from us?"

He glanced away for a split second, guilt worming deep, but his secrets had nothing to do with their search. He replied firmly, "No. I don't know anything else about the hunters."

Quiet followed his statement, broken by the bone popping among the embers.

"I trust him," Kit murmured, almost too low for him to hear, and the tightness in his gut eased a little.

"Then we should get moving." Parker stood and poured water over the remains of the fire, creating a cloud of hissing steam. "We need to put as much distance as possible between us and the bridge, just in case the hunters backtrack and find it."

Theo stood too, thankful to have something to do with his hands. He refilled the waterskins and packed away his knife and the seasoning he had used while the women saw to the horses.

"When do we start cutting south?" Kit asked when they were ready to leave.

"South?" Parker spun to her cousin. "Surely you mean north."

"No. I mean south."

Their eyes locked, and something passed between them that he could not interpret.

"Excuse us for a moment," Parker said with a tight smile. Then she pulled Kit farther away and, with a quick glance in his direction, muttered something too low for him to hear.

They spoke for a few minutes, the air around them thick with tension, their expressions hard and their gestures sharp.

Eventually, Kit said something that made Parker snap her mouth closed, and they returned to his side. "Well?" Kit asked. "When do we cut south?"

Theo looked between them but swallowed his curiosity. The women probably would not answer any questions anyway. He snapped a twig off a nearby tree and closed his eyes for a moment, bringing to mind the map he had studied in the guildhall. He scratched it into the ground between them, a rough rendition but good enough for their purpose.

"We're somewhere here." He pointed the stick at the centre of his drawing. "And there's a village here. Ilderdell, if I remember correctly." He indicated an upturned V farther to the left and looked up at them. "It'll take a few hours on foot, but we can probably make it there tonight if we push hard. What do you think?"

"Is there anywhere we can make camp before then?" Kit asked.

He pursed his lips and tried to recall more details of the surrounding terrain. "I don't think so. At least, nowhere safe."

"I'd rather we keep going," Parker said with an air of finality. She met Kit's eyes and added, "A village will be safer than the forest."

The same odd feeling about their interaction hit him, but once again, he could not define it.

"Fine," Kit replied.

There were no complaints from either of them as they traversed the forest, even when it grew so dark they could barely see where they were treading. A smile tugged at the corners of his lips. Kit might not excel at dressing meat, but she was admittedly a far better hunter than he was. His spirits lifted. Not only would they not go hungry, but she was also good company.

The thought, however, was swiftly followed by another—eventually, they would part ways.

Unaccountably, his chest twinged, and he lost his footing on a slippery, moss-covered log. Kit's taciturn cousin glanced back, and Theo shrugged. He wrangled his mind away from Kit and the future, back to the present, where they had a forest to navigate, hunters to evade, and a stone to find.

Chapter 13

Joss

Joss's shoulders sagged under the weight of her pack by the time they reached Ilderdell—far later than Theo had predicted. After fighting through jungle that grew more rugged the farther west they travelled and crossing another river on the most precarious bridge she had ever seen, Parker's horse had thrown a shoe. She had packed the hoof as well as she could, adding precious ointment to ease any inflammation, but they were forced to walk the horses the rest of the way to prevent the mare from laming.

Thus, it was well after midnight when they spotted the dark mass of a building concealed among the trees. More emerged from the surrounding forest only when they were within twenty lengths of the first, and Joss almost collapsed with relief. By the time they found one with a light still shining and knocked on the door, her legs quivered, and the only thing holding her upright was sheer willpower.

They had made it. And it would be all but impossible for the hunters to find them in such a well-hidden place.

Theo knocked again, and a bleary-eyed man opened it and peered out at them.

"What is it?"

"Apologies for disturbing you. Is there an inn in the village?"

The man blinked at them like he was trying to decide whether they were real or a dream. "No, but the Elder sometimes puts up visitors." He pointed towards the other barely visible structures, said, "Three down, next to the green," and closed the door.

Joss could not blame him. He was probably half asleep. In fact, she was surprised anyone was still awake at such a late hour.

They trudged along a blessedly clear path past two more inky outlines and found a light shining through the cracks in the window shutters of the next. The yellowy stripes fell on a flattish expanse beyond the far wall that must have been the 'green' the man had mentioned, but Joss had no energy left to investigate.

Theo took the lead again, and when he rapped on the door, it opened straight away. The silhouette of a tall, muscular man appeared in the gap, and a deep voice said, "Yes? What can I do for you?"

"Are you the village elder?" Theo asked.

The shadow stepped forwards. "Yes. I'm Bruno Oftull."

"Theo Taskil, and this is Kit and her cousin, Parker." Theo pointed at each of them in turn. "We're looking for somewhere to spend the night and were told you could help. We'd have arrived earlier in the evening, but one of our horses lost a shoe and the village was harder to find than expected."

"Ah, I see. You must be tired. Please, come inside." The man flung the door wide and gestured them forward. "I'll see to your animals after I get you settled. And we have a smith who can shoe your horse in the morning."

Joss was too tired to protest that she should rub down her own horse. "Thank you, Master Oftul."

"Please, call me Bruno."

She ducked her head in agreement, and they walked into a large main room with a ladder leading to a second floor at one side and a table at the other. A candle in a simple round holder sat on a shelf, casting soft light over the near half of the living space. Only then did she note that he wore a nightshirt.

"I'm sorry if we woke you," she said, averting her eyes.

"Oh, no. I was just about to turn in. Can I offer you something to eat?" He spoke over his shoulder as he headed towards a fireplace on the far wall, where a pile of banked embers glowed faintly.

"No, thank you," Parker said, examining the bars across the window shutters.

Joss sank onto one of the chairs beside the well-used wooden table. "We ate on the way."

"Just somewhere to sleep would be appreciated," Theo said from just behind her.

The older man pivoted towards a door beside the ladder at the other side of the room. "Very well. You and your wife can sleep down here, and—"

"No."

"We're not married."

Joss and Theo spoke at the same time. Her voice came out higher than usual, and she cleared her throat before adding, "We're not related at all," though that sounded somehow worse to her ears. Why would the elder assume such a thing?

"My apologies," Bruno said, an expression of chagrin crossing his features.

"I'll stay with my cousin," Parker said. "Do you have anywhere else for our travel companion?"

"Of course. And sorry, again. I meant no offense."

"None taken," Theo said. Was there a note of amusement in his voice? The thought brought heat to Joss's cheeks.

"If you please, then." The elder pushed the door open and lit a lantern inside.

Joss heaved herself up and plodded into the smaller chamber, followed by Parker, who mumbled something to the elder before closing the door behind them. A water jug and bowl sat on a dresser beside the door, so Joss forced herself to go through the motions of washing, then flopped onto the bed without even pulling back the blankets or removing her outerwear.

Sleep dragged her under as soon as her head touched the pillow.

She woke the next morning to a knocking on the door. A female voice outside it asked, “Are you awake?”

“I am now,” Joss grumbled under her breath. Aloud, she said, “Yes. You can come in.”

A short woman carrying a steaming jug and stack of drying cloths entered. After depositing them on the dresser, she bustled over to the window and opened the shutters wide, letting in enough daylight to pierce even the deepest sleep. “Morning, my dears. You’ll be needing fresh water.”

Joss sat up and stretched as the woman emptied the bowl out the window and refilled it.

“I’m Merriyen, Bruno’s wife. I’ll leave you to wash and dress, but come to me if you need anything.”

She left with a single nod and the lingering scent of freshly baked bread.

Joss’s stomach rumbled in response, and she threw off the blankets, then paused. She did not recall getting into bed the previous night. Had she crawled under them in her sleep? On closer inspection, her boots and belt were missing too.

“You’re welcome.”

Parker’s voice came from a chair in the corner of the room. Joss glanced at the pillow beside hers, which was untouched.

“Why didn’t you sleep in the bed? We could’ve shared.”

“You kick in your sleep.”

Oh. “Sorry.”

Parker shrugged and stood. “Better for me to stay here anyway, just in case.”

Just in case the hunters tracked them down and attacked while the village slept. Joss shuddered despite the already warm day and leaped from the bed. “You should take the bed next time.”

When Parker looked like she would object, Joss met her eyes with all sincerity. “After everything we’ve been through together, you’re more than just a guard to me. You’re my friend.”

She made quick work of her morning ablutions and hurried out to the main room.

Theo and Bruno were nowhere in sight, but Merriyen sat at the table shucking a mountain of corn. She looked from Joss to the pile and said, “We’re having a gathering tonight.” Waving a cob at the fireplace, she added, “There’s plenty left for you to break your fast.”

A pan of bacon sizzled over the fire, and Joss’s stomach rumbled again. She helped herself to two servings with a thick slab of bread and a cup of some kind of tea. While she made room for her plate on the table, Parker downed a cup of water and asked, “Where are the men this morning?”

“They’re working on the central pulley. Been at it since dawn.”

“Then if you’ll excuse me, I’ll go and join them.” With a nod to Joss, Parker took a round of bread and slipped outside.

Joss sat down opposite Merriyen. She devoured the bacon in no time and washed it down with the herby tea.

Rested and sated, she cleared her plate and excused herself to join the others.

In the daylight, the village was a wonder. Many of the structures sat high in the trees around the central grassy clearing, and swinging bridges connected them like a web. No wonder the place had been difficult to find in the dark.

As in Aralan, several villagers openly used magic—one speeding the growth of a row of pepper bushes, another lowering a barrel from one of the treetop dwellings without ropes or touch.

She found Theo with a couple of men, bent over a complex pulley beneath a high wooden platform with bridges on three sides. "Good morning," she said as she approached them, making eye contact with Theo when he looked up. "Did you sleep well?"

He straightened, and the corners of his mouth tipped up. "Yes. You?"

"Mm-hm." She nodded at the other men as well and asked him, "Have you seen Parker this morning?"

"Bruno took her to get her horse shod." He wiped his hands on a rag and walked closer. "He's offered to arrange passage on a barge heading downriver if we can wait a day or two. I said I'd discuss it with you, but it'll be faster than trekking through the forest."

It certainly would. And far less exhausting too. They would have to find a way to repay Bruno for his many kindnesses.

"That would be wonderful. Where are they?"

He pointed deeper into the forest, where a cluster of roofs peeped out between the bushes.

“Thank you.” She dipped her head in farewell and followed a path through the undergrowth to the nearest building, which turned out to be a smithy. Bruno stood beyond the open side with Parker’s horse and a burly man a little shorter than Joss who wore only a leather apron over his trousers.

Within moments, Joss could understand why. Heat spewed from the forge in billowing waves that dried her skin and blew wisps of her hair away from her face and neck. She lifted a hand in silent greeting but stayed as far as possible from the forge while she looked around for Parker.

The guard emerged from one of the other buildings with Theo’s mount and a little girl who barely reached her hip. The girl climbed onto a nearby log, and Parker led the horse alongside, handed the girl a comb, and said something Joss could not hear.

She eased closer and watched them for a few moments. Parker was surprisingly patient, explaining how to groom the horse and untangling the comb when it got caught in the mane. Huh. She was never so gentle back home.

Bruno’s voice startled Joss from her observation. “Mistress Parker tells me you’re an expert archer. Would you be willing to offer my eldest some guidance? He’s been begging me to ask since daybreak.”

From the corner of her eye, she spotted a group of youths fidgeting by the path from the main clearing. Two carried bows, and the others held what appeared to be slings.

Parker looked over and gave her a firm, if slight, nod. “I’m needed here, but you should go.”

Why would Parker allow this? She must have put other provisions in place. Trustworthy locals, or maybe a hunting ground only accessible from the village. Regardless, this was an opportunity Joss would not miss. She turned to Bruno and beamed. “In that case, it would be my pleasure.”

When she returned to the village in the early evening, with three kills and five new friends in tow, the green was already filling with people and the scent of roasting meat indicated that the feast would soon begin.

She had learned that afternoon that the village had no meeting hall. Instead, they gathered in the clearing under the stars, only retreating to the trees during the worst storms when their water-controlling mage could not shield them from the rain.

Bruno waved at her from a knot of youngsters at the edge of the green, so she said goodbye to her fellow hunters and walked over to him.

“How was your hunt?” he asked.

She held up her catch in reply, and he took them from her.

“Thank you.”

“You’re welcome.” She peered around the area. “Have you seen my cousin?”

He rubbed his chin. “I think she’s helping Merriyen prepare the food.”

Parker—in a kitchen? A grin tugged at Joss's lips as she pictured the no-nonsense matriarch stuffing the elite guard into an apron and setting her to chopping vegetables. This, Joss had to see for herself.

"I'll go and find them."

She headed towards the elder's house but spotted Parker turning a spit over a cooking fire between two elderly women. Changing course, Joss wove through the growing crowd towards them and was just within teasing distance when a cheer rose. She started as everyone scrambled to sit on logs placed around small unlit bonfires dotted throughout the open space.

Merriyen appeared beside her and directed her towards a seat in the middle of the green with Theo, Bruno, and a handful of important-looking people.

"It seems you returned just in time," Bruno said in an undertone as Parker joined them.

He stepped up onto a solid log planted on its end, and a hush spread around them in an expanding circle until all eyes were on him.

"It fills my heart that we can gather today to welcome our new friends to Ilderdell," he said, his voice seeming louder in the stillness. "However short your stay, we're happy to have met you. To new friends."

He lifted a cup high, and the villagers chorused, "To new friends."

As they tipped back their drinks, Joss searched for her own cup, and Theo passed one to her. It contained a soupy, orange liquid that smelled sweet and tasted like ale mixed with some kind of fruit she could not identify. Her throat stung slightly when she swallowed it, but the sensation lasted only a moment and left her feeling refreshed and full of energy.

With the toast made, Bruno sat, and the villagers dug into the platters of food spread over a couple of tables beside the cooking fires. A few youths prepared dishes for the elders, and one of them handed Joss a plate piled high with meat, glazed vegetables, and dumplings.

The party was soon in full swing, people frequently leaving one circle of logs and joining another as they talked and ate. Children played to one side of the green, their squeals of laughter seeming utterly carefree. Joss gazed around her as she nibbled a corn cob and let out a contented sigh. What a life these villagers had.

Halfway through the meal, the little girl that had followed Parker that morning ran over and plopped down on the log beside Bruno. Her face crumpled, her eyes swimming with moisture.

He tucked her against his side and asked, "What's wrong, Little Pea?"

"Leyya won't let me play with them. She says I'm too little. But I'm not, Papa. I'm big now I'm five." A giant tear rolled down her cheek, and she swiped it away with the back of her hand.

"I'm sure she didn't mean to upset you." Bruno stroked the girl's hair. "Hush, now. Play with your brother in future. He'll never let you be bullied. That's a brother's job."

"Really?" The little girl straightened. She looked over at Theo, sitting on the next log. "Do you look after your sisters?"

"I don't have any," he said to the ground in front of him.

She gasped, and her eyes rounded. "Not even one?"

Sadness passed across his eyes. "No."

Joss's heart squeezed. "I've got two sisters," she said before the girl could ask anything else that might cause him distress. "One older, one younger. We tease each other, but we're very close. And we definitely look after each other."

"Ooooh."

The girl turned to Parker, who lifted one shoulder. "I've a large family. Seven of us last time I heard from my Da. All girls. No one would dare bully them when I'm around."

Joss stared at her. That was the most information Parker had ever shared about herself, and without prompting too. Eager to hear more, Joss shuffled closer and spoke in an undertone so Theo could not overhear. "I didn't know you had siblings. What are they called?"

Parker threw a twig on the fire and swigged from her cup. She would not reveal anything else, so Joss returned her attention to the others. The little girl stood on her tiptoes and kissed Bruno's cheek, then raced off into the crowd as one of Joss's fellow hunters appeared with a jug of the fruity brew.

She accepted two more refills in the next half hour, and by the time Bruno lit the bonfire with a wave of his outstretched hand—he was a mage too?—her insides were pleasantly warm. Sparks danced around their group like fireflies, and as the sky deepened to navy and then black, all the worries coiled in her heart melted away.

Sometime after nightfall, a group of musicians started playing, and several young women pulled partners into an open area on the other side of the fire. A couple tried to get Theo to dance with them, but he waved them off with such finality that they moved onto local men.

The dancers wove around each other, stomping their feet and twirling in pairs every so often, and Joss was soon bouncing her leg to the beat. She jumped up to join them, but her head spun so much she dropped straight back onto the log. Why was she dizzy? And hot too. She tugged the neck of her tunic and looked at her cup. How strong was that drink?

Theo's fingers lighted on her arm, and he asked, "Are you well?"

"Yes. I'm fine." But why was his face so blurry? She reached out and touched it. "You're so nice, and handsome too. You have lovely eyes."

He stilled, then sucked in a breath and straightened, breaking the contact between them.

Hands gripped her shoulders, and Parker forced Joss to meet her gaze. "How much have you had to drink?"

"I'm sorry," Bruno said. "I should have warned you our wine is stronger than it seems."

"'S delicious." Joss lifted her cup for a sip, but Parker tugged it away from her mouth. She tightened her grip. "No. Give it back."

Wrenching it away from the meddling guard, she gulped a mouthful and smacked her lips. "Much better than the wine at home. And so is the village. Only stupid lords in Faerstolmere trying to curry favour and—"

"I apologise for my cousin," Parker all but shouted over her.

"You're not my—"

"She just needs to sleep it off. Come on, Kit." She emphasised the fake name, but someone had stuffed Joss's head with cotton, so she could not grasp why.

Parker gripped her arm and tried to tug her up. Why? Did she want to take Joss back to Redcairn Palace? Something about that did not ring true, but Joss could not take the risk. She flung off the guard's hand, scooted closer to Theo, and wrapped her arm around his bicep. If she held onto him, she would be safe.

"I'm staying here. With Theo."

A whisper in the corner of her mind warned that she was not thinking clearly and would regret her actions, but she could not bring herself to care. She had never had this much freedom at home and did not want it to end. Besides, Parker could not force her to leave.

Theo gently removed her arm from his and stood. "I'll take you back to your room."

He offered her a hand up, which she gladly accepted, but when he pulled her to her feet, she overbalanced and stumbled into him, landing against his chest. His muscles felt solid beneath her palms, and without thinking, she rested her cheek there too, lulled by the steady thump of his heartbeat.

Clearing his throat, he stepped to her side, forcing her to straighten, though the green continued to swirl around them.

"Thank you," she mumbled as he supported her under her arm and led her to the elder's house.

When they got to her sleeping chamber, he opened the door and said, “Rest well.”

She gazed at him, a smile stretching her face. He was so kind and strong, and gracious. Or was it generous? She frowned. Why were her thoughts so sluggish? Either way, she needed to show her appreciation, but a search of her pockets revealed she had nothing to give. What should she do?

Ah. Leaning forwards, she planted a kiss on his cheek. His bristles prickled her lips, and she immediately pulled back and rubbed her face. “Ugh. Scratchy.”

“That wasn’t me,” he said in a panicked voice.

Behind her, Parker’s calm voice replied, “I saw. Leave her to me.”

Arms guided Joss inside and across to the bed, where she flopped face down, and muffled voices spoke behind her again. She could not determine what they said, though, for a thick fog blanketed her mind and blackness took hold.

Chapter 14

Joss

The next morning, Joss found herself sitting aboard a barge tied to a small pier in the nearby river. She had vague memories of the previous evening's feast—and of being woken up before dawn, shoved into clean clothes, and half carried to the riverbank—but she could not recall anything clearly. Every sound pierced her skull, and her stomach lurched with each sway of the deck.

She squeezed her eyes shut, curled into the handrail, and rubbed her temples. Something must have died in her mouth, for her tongue was coated in fuzz and stuck to the back of her teeth. Where were her chew sticks? Or her waterskin?

A blind search of her surroundings found nothing but the large crate on which she sat, a basket of leathery strips that smelled of smoked venison, and further punishment to her aching head when she bent to feel the deck around her feet. She moaned as she straightened, and a moment later, footsteps approached.

"Am I still good-looking this morning?"

She cracked one eye open and found Theo grinning down at her.

It took her sluggish mind a few moments to decipher his question, but when it did, her cheeks heated and she covered her face. What had she said to him the previous evening while in her cups?

"Don't worry. I don't take advantage of drunken women."

Embarrassment tightened its hold. She had never been so drunk before—and never would again. How could she ever face him after this?

He crouched in front of her and lowered his voice. "But I liked seeing what you really think of me."

She peeked at him, and his expression appeared more sincere than teasing, which only added to her mortification.

"Here." He held out a handful of leaves. "Bruno said to give you these. Apparently, chewing on them will ease your bottle ache. He also asked me to apologise again for giving you such strong wine without warning."

Gingerly, she plucked the leaves from his hand and pushed two into her mouth. They tasted of malt and earth, but her headache receded almost instantly. She straightened, looked at the remaining leaves, and added another for good measure.

"Working?" Theo asked, shifting to sit beside her.

"Mm."

He pointed at the cabin. "Why don't you go inside and get some more sleep?"

She glanced at it and suppressed a shudder at the tiny, enclosed space. Shaking her head, and wincing at the movement, she said, “I prefer to be outside.”

“Well, I’d better get back.” He stood and walked across the deck to the short pier, where Parker, one of the youths Joss had taken hunting, and another gangly young man were carrying various loads of cargo aboard. A broad-chested man with a wide-brimmed straw hat pulled low over his greying hair watched them closely as they worked.

They led the mounts on last and hobbled them at the stern beside a water barrel. Then the hunter hopped onto the pier, and at a command from the older man, the second youth bent to untie the ropes that held the barge in place.

Joss stood and, once steady on her feet, joined Parker and Theo, who were bidding farewell to Bruno and a few of the other villagers who had come to see them off.

As she approached the boat’s handrail, Bruno moved opposite her and said, “I hope you’re feeling better now, Kit.”

“I am, thanks to your leaves.” She held them up. “Thank you for all your help these past two days. I don’t know how we can ever repay you for your kindness.”

“Just pass on the blessing to the next person you meet.”

The barge juddered and eased away from the pier, and Joss steadied herself before calling back to him. “I will. I promise.”

They waved to the villagers, such lovely people whom she would never forget, until they passed around a bend in the river, and then Joss finally took a good look around her.

The flat-bottomed barge was split into two main decks by a simple cabin that stood in the centre with walkways on either side. Netting and ropes secured the small mountain of crates, barrels, and baskets that filled the foredeck, and Theo leaned over one of the stacks, sketching something on a sheet of paper.

To the aft, Parker practised with her sword in the open space behind the cabin. She swung the blade through a series of arcs, each one smooth and controlled until the barge swayed just as she spun on one foot. Planting both feet, she dropped the point of the sword to the deck and bent slightly, closing her eyes. Was she well?

"Not got your river legs yet?" the captain called out. He left the tiller to his deckhand, jumped down from the short platform, and walked forwards between the horses on his right and more piles of crates to his left.

Unlike his crew member, who scowled at them before turning away, a wide smile creased the captain's weather-lined face as he joined Parker. "You'll get used to it soon enough. I have a tonic if you..."

She shook her head and said, "I'll be fine." Blowing a long breath through her mouth, she sheathed her sword and picked up her waterskin.

"Keeping your eyes on the river ahead helps. I have a fishing line, if you want something to pass the time."

He pointed at a couple of poles strapped to the base of the railing opposite Joss and clapped Parker on the shoulder. Then his eyes landed on Joss, and he lifted a hand.

"Ah, good morning." He walked over and sat beside her on a crate. "How're you feeling now?"

"Better, thank you…" What was his name?

He must have noticed her discomfort, for he touched his hat and said, "R.C. Butts, but most people just call me Captain." He pointed at the deckhand. "And that surly lad's my son, Lewen. Don't mind him. He's young and full of ideas for making our fortune. But this is still my boat." He said the last sentence louder, and Joss got the impression it was part of an entirely different conversation. "Anyway, I'd have introduced myself sooner, but you didn't look too good when you first came aboard."

She winced, then more so at the stab of pain it caused. Could she have more of the leaves yet? "I'm sorry about that," she said. "And thank you for taking us downriver."

"You're welcome. Last night's feast was worth setting off a few days early." He patted a small barrel beside him. "And Bruno gave me some of his prized ryllfruit wine for my trouble."

Nausea rose at the reminder, and Joss wrinkled her nose.

He chuckled. "I heard you had a little too much. It's potent stuff, especially if you're not used to it."

"Yes. I'm aware of that now." She gave him a lop-sided smile.

He rooted through his waist pouch and offered her some leaves, but she held up her hands to stop him. "Thank you, but Bruno already gave me some."

"Ah." He returned them to his pouch. "Doesn't surprise me. He's a good man, that village elder." He slapped his knees and pushed to his feet. "Well. I'd better get back to work. Lewen can't move this thing on his own for long."

She studied the captain's son, who held the tiller with one hand but angled the other towards the water behind them. They used magic to navigate the river? A glance at the prow confirmed what she had missed earlier—no tow lines attached to horses along the bank and no crew with poles to propel them through the slow-moving water.

In fact, though they stayed within striking distance of the riverbank, they floated past the forest at a speed they could never match on foot. Thank the creator Bruno had secured them passage.

Joss looked down at the water, which was too dark to see anything of interest, and back at the trees lining the bank. Some reached out to offer pockets of shade while others trailed their leaves in the current like they were cooling off from the heat emanating from the dense interior.

The river widened after a while, and the sun came out, bouncing off the water as well as beating down from above. Her head throbbed under the onslaught, and she closed her eyes against the piercing light that tried to stab through her lids.

A few more leaves could not hurt. She chewed them as fast as she could and slumped in relief as the pain abated. A shadow passed overhead, and she peeked up at branches that were much closer, and moving much slower, than they had been before.

"Gather around," the captain said, appearing beside her. "We have a decision to make."

As soon as Parker and Theo joined them, he continued, "There are rapids ahead."

"Rapids?" Joss glanced at the glassy surface of the river beyond the prow of the barge. She had heard of the white waters from her friend Aitha but had never seen them herself.

"Yes. The river splits after the next bend. The left fork is gentle but longer. It'll add an extra day onto our journey. The right is faster, but it goes through a series of rapids. We'll need to dose the horses and strap them down if we go that way.

Joss looked at Shadow. "Is it safe?"

"Perfectly. I'd never harm an animal. But passengers sometimes prefer to go round, so I'm giving you the choice."

She turned to the others.

"I vote for the rapids," Theo said.

Parker gave a shrug, leaving the decision to Joss.

"We'll take the rapids."

"Very good." The captain returned to Lewen, and together they fed the horses something that looked like balls of grass, guided them to lie down, and strapped them into harnesses attached to the deck on both sides.

When they finished, they used their powers to increase the barge's speed again, and as it rounded the next bend, they steered it to the right.

"Hold on," the captain called out. "It's going to get a bit bumpy."

Before Joss could respond, the barge rocked suddenly. She gripped the rail and peered ahead, where little crests and eddies appeared on the previously still surface. So that was what rapids looked like. The barge dipped again, and water splashed across the deck.

She searched for Parker and found her sitting on a bench just inside the cabin's doorway, her hands clamped around the jamb. The guard appeared a little ill, her face pale, eyes closed, and jaw clenched tight.

Concerned for her friend, Joss shouted back to the captain, "How long will it be like this?"

"Don't worry. I've spent most of my life on this river and know it as well as my own mother. We'll be through soon enough."

Time seemed to slow, the seconds passing like hours as the barge wove through the rapids, tilting first one way, then the other. The roar of rushing water grew until it drowned everything else, and frothy spray hit Joss's face almost continually. Eventually, the churning torrent spat them out, and they glided into another wide, calm stretch of the river.

She let out a whoop and spun to the captain. "Are there any more?"

"No. That's the last of them," he called back.

"If there are, please knock me out along with the horses." Parker slowly straightened and muttered something that sounded like a prayer.

On the foredeck, Theo rose from behind the wall of the cabin and immediately checked the ropes securing the cargo in place.

"Ah, good lad," the captain said from beside Joss. He stretched his arms and padded over to the cabin. "I must be getting old. That took more out of me than it used to." Lying down on the bench Parker had just vacated, he dropped his hat over his eyes and was soon snoring softly.

Joss checked on the horses, who were still asleep and appeared none the worse for their trip through the rapids. "They're fine," she told Parker and Theo, who had both walked over as well.

While the captain napped and his son took over the tiller, Parker sharpened her various blades and Theo returned to measuring and sketching, leaving Joss to her own devices once more. She cleaned her bow, then offered to help Parker, but her friend shooed her away. With nothing else to do, she paced the deck and watched the sun creep unnaturally slowly across the sky.

Fortunately, Lewen woke his father after only a half hour or so, and they declared it was time to eat. The pair left the barge to drift along the slow current on its own and brought a basket of provisions from the cabin. Lewen spread a cloth on the open deck, and the captain unpacked a slab of roasted meat, some oddly-shaped pies, several rounds of flatbread, a pot of greenish paste with red flecks, and enough fruit to last a week.

Joss plopped onto the deck between Parker and the captain and picked up one of the pies. The meat inside was spiced, and her tongue tingled with each bite. She devoured it like a starving woman and reached for a second.

The captain chuckled. “Good?”

“Mm-hm.”

Theo finally joined them, bringing the papers he had been working on with him. He sat beside the captain, folded his long legs in front of him, and helped himself to a spiky, brown jellos, which appeared overripe to Joss’s untrained eye. Setting the usually sour fruit aside without taking a single bite, he turned to the captain and said, “I have a gift for you.”

“Oh?” The captain handed Joss a piece of flatbread he had wrapped around a slice of meat and some of the paste, saying, “Try this,” before meeting Theo’s gaze.

She swallowed what was in her mouth and bit into the offering while watching the two men. Sweet, sharp, and savoury flavours danced across her taste buds, and she could not help humming.

“It’s a design for a loading device,” Theo said. “If you build it on the foredeck, you’ll be able to lift larger items on and off more easily.”

Lewen’s head shot up. “Really? Let me see.”

Theo passed him the papers, and Lewen studied them for a long time, flicking between them every so often. Joss had already made herself a second serving of the meat-and-paste-filled flatbread when he looked back at Theo with the first smile she had seen from him lighting his face.

"This could make a huge difference to what we can carry. Where would we put it? And how quickly can it be made?"

"A good carpenter should be able to get it done in less than a week. And I'd put it at the prow, here." Theo leaned across and pointed to one of the pages.

"Hmm. Will that be stable?"

Doubt seeped through Lewen's voice, but Theo answered with utter confidence. "Of course. Come, I'll show you."

He snatched up a flatbread and some of the meat the captain had sliced—but not the paste, for which Joss could only pity him—and stood.

Lewen jumped to his feet as well, then turned to his father. "Are you coming?"

The captain waved them off. "No, no. I'll leave all that to you youngsters."

"Very well, then."

They nodded and headed for the foredeck, Theo talking quietly and gesturing around them, Lewen looking from the plans to where Theo pointed and back again.

A flash of appreciation brought a smile to Joss's lips. Theo was a generous man, able to make even the grumpy deckhand happy. She soon lost interest in the finer points of their discussion, though, and returned her attention to the spread before her.

She frowned. Taking a third flatbread would be impolite, and stretch her stomach beyond its capacity, so she opted for a handful of berries and washed them down with a cup of water.

When she finished, she helped Parker and the captain clear the remains and took the opportunity to relieve herself in the privacy of the stern. Then she leaned against the handrail and watched the forest pass by, drumming a random rhythm on the sun-baked wood.

For the first time since setting out from Faerstolmere, homesickness crept in. Too much time with nothing to do left her feeling cramped and confined. Even the scenery, at first exciting for its differences from home, now only reminded her of her absence. She paced the deck from side to side, then around the cabin and back.

The barge was too small to practise her archery, and she did not want to leave holes in the deck with her throwing knives. Besides, the temperature rose as the day wore on, even on the water, and she was nearly as uncomfortable as she had been in the midst of the jungle.

A sudden downpour forced her, Parker, and Theo to take shelter inside, which only added to the pressure building in her body. It needed a release. She needed a release, or she would surely burst.

The wall of rain outside did not last long. It disappeared as quickly as it had started, leaving the barge glimmering wet in the afternoon sun. Steam rose as the wood dried, and the air became hot and sticky again.

"Why don't you try catching some fish," Parker suggested at one point.

Joss grimaced at the thought of sitting still for so long.

"Or write a letter to your sister?"

Another pang of homesickness hit as an image of her sisters curled up in their library formed in her mind. "I'll do that later," she snapped, forcing it away, then mentally winced. She should not take her frustration out on Parker. "Sorry," she threw out. "I just need to be moving."

"You're making me dizzy," the guard grumbled under her breath, but Joss refrained from commenting.

"Don't tell me you're bored?" Theo said from behind them, making Joss jump.

"Not exactly."

He nodded slowly and sank onto a nearby crate. "Then let's talk. We can get to know each other a bit better."

Curiosity sent a zing through her, and she hauled herself up to sit on a stack opposite him. She was deciding what to ask first when he spoke again and made her freeze.

"You live in the palace in Faerstolmere?"

She shot a look at Parker. What had she let slip the previous night?

Parker gave a tiny shake of her head and said, "What makes you think that?"

"You talked about lords clamouring around the royal family. I assumed…"

Ah. "We work there," Joss said. Strictly speaking, it was not a lie.

"It's the same way in Iskaria too." He seemed not to have noticed their exchange, and her tense muscles relaxed. "The noble houses are always vying for power, and they've been using the return of magic over the last few years to gain even more influence in court."

He peered at her from beneath his lashes with an expression she could not decipher, almost as if he were testing her somehow.

Joss grimaced. "People like that"—an involuntary shudder shook her—"are sickening."

"You're not interested in using your position in the palace to get ahead?" Again, she got the impression he was more interested in her answer than his relaxed posture suggested.

"No. I just want to be free to make my own choices."

"I suppose working at the palace would give you that."

If only it were true. She pressed her lips together and her palms into the rough wood beside her.

"Did you have to give up your position to leave and look for the stone?"

She shifted on the crate. Why did he ask so many awkward questions? "They allowed me to come. But what about you? Why would you risk so much to find it?"

He did not answer immediately, only rubbed the back of one hand with the thumb of the other. When he spoke, he met her eyes fully, and sincerity shone in his gaze. "I've spent my entire adult life trying to help the people of Iskaria—building aqueducts and pulley systems to make their lives a little easier—but until our land's healed, we'll never be free of the shadow the mage wars cast over us.

"Now that magic's growing stronger throughout the kingdoms, the majority of the Iskarian nobles want to attack Garellion to wipe out the seat of the guild for good."

"They won't actually do it, will they?" Joss asked.

He leaned closer. "It's an impossible goal, but they'd destroy thousands of lives trying to achieve it." His hands fisted. "I'll do everything in my power to stop that from happening. The story of a mage offering to restore our land has been passed down through my family for generations. I thought if I could find out how they meant to do it, maybe I could help my people and stop the war."

The urge rose in Joss to do all she could to help him, as strong in that moment as the one to meet her own needs. "That's a worthy cause."

"What about you?" he asked.

"I need it to save my father. He's everything to me and my sisters. We need him, and without the stone, he could… he could die." She choked on the words but managed to force them past her lips.

"Why? What's wrong with him?"

She took a steadying breath. "He's been cursed by magic. We don't know who did it, or exactly when, but none of the healers we've seen can do anything about it. Not even the mages.

"My sister found an old record of the stone, and I set out to find it. It's our last hope."

Neither of them spoke again, and the birdsong and lapping water that had faded into the background while they talked seeped back into Joss's awareness.

“Then we should do everything we can to find the dragon stone,” Theo said at last, steel entering his eyes as he met her gaze again and something indefinable passed between them.

Unnerved by the moment, she looked away and spotted an opening in the foliage along the riverbank ahead. “Oh, what’s that?”

She jumped down from the crates and ran over to the starboard rail for a closer look. Theo came to stand beside her but Parker… Where was Parker? She scanned the barge and spotted the guard sitting between two barrels on the foredeck.

With a shrug, Joss turned back to the forest just as they pulled alongside the open area. Only, it was not open. A cluster of grassy mounds filled the clearing, many with a tangle of flowering vines growing over them. Skylarks flew high above it, hovering to sing before descending in lazy spirals, but the area was otherwise still and quiet. It appeared almost mystical, as though imbued with memories of a time long forgotten by the world beyond the forest.

“What is that place?” she asked the captain.

He removed his hat and mumbled something under his breath before answering. “It’s an ancient burial ground. From back when mages ruled the land.”

So far from civilisation? Or were entire mage cities buried beneath the greenery?

They passed it in silence, and Joss tried to imagine traipsing through the jungle—or rather, walking behind a mage who parted the undergrowth for them—to lay a loved one to rest. She shuddered at the thought, painfully reminded of what would happen should she fail to find a means of breaking her father's curse.

Her hand gripped the railing tighter. She should be focusing on her mission, not enjoying the sights of the neighbouring kingdoms.

"Captain?" She strode to the stern, where he redonned his hat.

"Yes?"

"Will you tell me about Eindal."

He scratched his jaw. "It's not as big as Ravelan, but if it's a seafaring vessel you're looking for, the Free Isles gathering means you should find passage easily enough."

Joss calculated the dates in her head. He was right. The free folk should be on their way to the isles for their summer gathering.

Good. The sooner they got to Yarin's home, the sooner they could find the dragon stone.

Chapter 15

Joss

They arrived at the river dock on the edge of Eindal mid-afternoon and, after helping unload the cargo, bid farewell to Captain Butts and his son. Though not as charming as Bruno, the captain was a friendly fellow, and Joss appreciated his willingness to adjust his plans to help them.

She also appreciated his knowledge of the town. They stabled their horses at the inn he had recommended—a well-kept establishment with a stable hand who promised to look after Shadow well until their return—and followed his directions to the port without any trouble.

As they approached the bustling waterfront, a cacophony of voices and the pungent scent of seaweed and fish assaulted her senses. They turned the last corner, and the port opened before them.

A stone quay stretched along the seafront, lined by warehouses on the left and a handful of boats moored alongside on the right. Beyond that, the bay curved around into a natural harbour, and Arden Forest blanketed the hills above the town.

Men laboured wherever she looked, loading cargo onto a row of carts, hauling baskets of fish from several of the smaller boats, and climbing rigging overhead. A few clung to knotted ropes off the stern of a large ship nearby, repainting the name *Sea Sprite* emblazoned below the windows.

Only that and one other of the moored vessels appeared large enough to safely cross the sea, though Joss would admit the extent of her knowledge of boats ended at knowing port from starboard. She looked at Theo and pointed to it, and he nodded in reply.

They wove through the crowd in search of someone to ask about passage, and Parker moved ahead of Joss, one hand on the hilt of her sword. She need not have, for no one so much as gave them a second glance in their travel-worn state.

A stocky woman with coral beads threaded through her multiple braids stood on the dockside beside the ship, shouting instructions to the men working on the stern. Joss veered in her direction.

"Excuse me." She had to tap the woman on the shoulder to get her attention. "We're looking for passage to Firstport."

The woman looked her up and down, then tsked. "We'll not be leaving till the end of the week. Had a run in with pirates and had to put in for repairs."

She jerked her head behind her, causing the beads in her hair to clack together.

Joss looked past her to where more men on ropes fixed new boards over a gaping hole farther along the hull. They dangled precariously close to the waterline between the ship and the wall of the quay, and an image of them being squashed between the two flashed in Joss's mind. She shuddered and turned back to the woman.

"Oh. I'm sorry."

"You didn't do it." The woman grinned, until her eyes flicked back to the men working on the stern. "Careful of your ropes, Fawley. The captain'll have my hide if your wound reopens." She rubbed the back of her neck and muttered, "Knew I shouldn't've let you on the work crew." Gesturing at them, she called, "Harden! Get Fawley inside, now."

She stomped away, leaving Joss mulling their options. The prospect of wasting four days in port bowed her shoulders.

"Better try the next one," Theo said, reading her mind.

They spoke to a man cleaning the deck of one of the smaller vessels, who told them none of the fishing boats could make the crossing and to try the *Sea Sprite*. Which left them with only one option—the last ship in the port.

As they continued along the quay, a group of five or six people emerged from between two buildings ahead of them. The party headed straight for the nearest of the ship's two boarding ramps and a wiry, grey-haired man sitting behind a small desk beside it.

"When do you sail?" one of the young men called out while they were still a few lengths away.

"With the evening tide," the old sailor said without looking up.

"Then I'll book passage for six."

"The *Evening Star*'s a cargo ship." He stopped a couple of crewmen and recorded their loads before allowing them up the ramp. "We're not set up for passengers."

"But my father said we'd be able to hire a ship here."

"Not this one."

One of the women in the group pushed the leader's arm, though without much force. "Milord. You promised us an adventure."

"And you'll have one." He bent and kissed her fingers. "I'll speak to the harbour master."

They bustled off in the opposite direction, presumably to complain about the lack of options for young lords seeking to impress women, and Joss stifled a snort. This was exactly what she hated about having a title.

But her heart sank as her mind circled back to the reason for the group's disappointment. How would she and the others get to the Free Isles? She glanced back along the dock. Would they have to wait a week for the *Sea Sprite* to be repaired after all?

She tossed a last look at the *Evening Star* and caught sight of a familiar figure ambling down the second ramp. Tall, lean, cropped hair and beard, gold glinting from his ear. The same easy gait as his sister, Aitha.

"I can get us onboard," she said, gripping Theo's arm without thinking.

At the same time, he turned to her and said, "I might be able to get us passage on this ship."

"What?"

"You can?"

Their eyes locked, and something in Joss's gut fluttered. It ignited a spark of excitement that burned through her body until she could barely contain it. "Want to make a bet? Whoever gets passage first gets to use the dragon stone first when we find it."

"Not another bet," Parker groaned. "What if one of you doesn't get onboard?"

"Then he can cross on the *Sea Sprite*, and we'll meet up later," Joss replied without looking away from Theo.

He studied her for a long moment, the same, indefinable emotion flitting through his eyes as when they had talked on the barge. Then the corners of his lips curled up, and he brought his face closer to hers. "Deal."

With that, he spun and walked away, not in the direction of the ship but between two buildings into the town. Where in the world was he going?

Joss shook the question from her head. It did not matter, for she would win their bet, regardless. She headed for the nearest ramp but paused as an even better idea popped into her mind.

She ducked behind a cart piled high with grain sacks, pulling Parker down beside her, and studied the ship.

"What are you doing?" the guard asked in a whisper.

"Stowing away." Joss eased around the cart to the far side, scattering some loose grain as she moved. She swept it aside with her toe and kept going.

Behind her, Parker muttered, "Can't we just use the boarding ramp like normal people."

Joss turned back to her. "We could, but this'll be more fun."

"And what happens when they catch us?"

"Nothing." She waved a hand through the air, but the creases between Parker's brows only deepened. Joss pointed in the direction the captain had gone. "Didn't you see whose ship this is?"

"No."

That explained it. "Noa Malz. Aitha's older brother." She shrugged. "Dax is probably somewhere out there too."

Parker blinked once, then rolled her eyes.

"So can we stow away now?" Joss asked.

"If we must."

Joss peered around the end of the cart and eyed several large crates that were being winched one by one over to the ship and down through a hole in the deck to the hold. Could they…? No. Removing enough of the goods to hide within one would be nigh on impossible, especially with the netting encasing them. They were bound to be caught.

She searched for another way onboard, and her eye caught on a stream of sailors descending the far ramp. They collected bundles of what appeared to be animal skins from one of the warehouses opposite the ship and carried them back up the ramp. At least a handful of them were women, providing Joss the opportunity she was looking for.

Quickly, she spread her cloak on the ground and wrapped it around her pack, bow, and quiver in the approximate shape of the sailors' loads. Parker followed her lead, and when they were ready, they scurried out from their hiding place and joined the end of the line.

With the amount of activity around the ship, no one paid them any heed, so Joss picked up a bundle when her turn came and hefted it onto her shoulder atop her own belongings. The additional weight nearly caused her to stagger, but she adjusted her grip and gritted her teeth. It would be worth the effort to see the look on Noa's face later. And Theo's.

They passed in front of the man tallying numbers, and Parker was about to set foot on the ramp when he called out, "Wait."

Joss froze. Had he noticed the sword sticking out from the end of the guard's pack? Parker stopped and turned slightly, keeping her face hidden from his view behind her load.

"The rope on those skins is coming loose," he said, allowing Joss to breathe once more. "Make sure you secure them properly when you get them inside."

"Yessir," Parker mumbled.

She followed the others onto the ship, her steps heavy enough to tell Joss she would be receiving a tongue-lashing as soon as they were alone.

Joss kept pace behind her until they came to the hatch down to the hold. It gaped like a giant mouth waiting to devour them whole. She swallowed. Maybe she should have boarded as a normal passenger after all, but it was too late to change her mind now.

The crewman behind her nudged her forwards. She hesitated for only a moment before reminding herself if was just a hold—not too dark, not too tight. Drawing a breath, she stepped onto the ladder.

In the hold, they deposited their loads with the rest, but instead of returning to the deck, they slipped behind one of the partitions and hid between some large barrels and a pile of grain sacks.

It was not as cramped as she had feared. Only a few rows of cargo had been stacked at the back, leaving plenty of open space in the middle. Light filtered down from the grilled hatch overhead and from a couple of lanterns near the ladders.

Joss leaned her pack against the hull and felt around in the semi-darkness for something on which to sit. Her hands found a crate, and she sank onto it, cross-legged, and bounced her knees.

"Now what?" Parker asked from atop a grain sack farther along the wall.

"Now, we wait."

"Mm-hm. And how will we know if Theo makes it onboard?"

Joss stilled. She had almost forgotten about the bet in her rush to surprise Noa. She climbed over the grain to one of the ventilation hatches near the ceiling. Fortunately, they had chosen to hide on the side of the ship that faced the quay. "We can watch from here."

The view was not the best, but she could see most of the ramps if she angled her head just so. Where *was* Theo? She was certain he had not boarded before them.

Noa returned some time later, accompanied by a well-built, handsome man wearing an embroidered tunic and trousers.

It took Joss a moment to realise it was Theo. Where had he got those clothes? And how had he convinced Noa to let him aboard? Had he offered to make a loading device for the *Evening Star* as he had for Captain Butts?

She sank back onto the pile of sacks but immediately straightened again. It did not matter—she had made it onboard first.

A smile tipped up the corners of her mouth. She had won. Whatever happened next, when they found the stone, she would be the first to use it.

Chapter 16

Joss

They set sail in the early evening, and Joss knew the moment they left the harbour, for the ship rocked with the swell of each wave on the open sea. She climbed onto the pile of grain sacks, braced herself against the inner hull, and settled in to wait for someone to discover them.

Hopefully, it would not take too long—her empty stomach growled to be filled.

Parker's apparently gurgled for a different reason. Her already pale face turned ashen as the ship moved farther from the shore, and she sucked in a deep breath when they crested a particularly tall wave and dropped into the trough.

"Would you feel better on deck?" Joss asked her. "Fresh air might help."

"Probably."

They crept from their hiding place and were halfway to the stairs when the hatch over them opened. For half a heartbeat, Joss stalled, considered ducking behind the water barrels beside her, then relaxed. They needed to be caught to win her bet with Theo.

A bare foot descended from above, followed by loose, calf-length trousers held up by a fabric sash, and a bronzed, hair-smattered chest. The face that appeared was blessedly familiar—a short beard in twin braids, crooked nose, small silver hoops in both ears, and a bald head.

Noa's first mate, Dax, started when he saw them but recovered quickly. "Well, well, well. What have we here? A couple of stowaways?"

"Surprise," Joss said.

The ship rolled again, and Parker moaned.

"No vomit in my hold." Dax rushed forwards, grasped her bicep, all but holding her upright by it, and tugged her to the stairs. "Up you go. Let's see what Noa thinks of you stowing away," he said to Joss over his shoulder.

She followed them up onto the main deck and closed the hatch behind them. Dax hauled Parker to the starboard side of the ship and urged her to take several deep breaths, after which she appeared a little better. Then, leaving her leaning against the railing, he marched Joss over to the captain's cabin and rapped twice on the door.

"Found a couple of stowaways, Captain," he called through the wooden panel with a wink at her.

Unseen, Noa replied from within, "You know the rules. Throw them overboard."

“Aye, Captain.”

Dax offered a helpless shrug and hauled her by the arm over to the port side. She trailed behind him without protest. He would never follow through.

A few nearby sailors stopped what they were doing to stare. Their wide eyes told her they genuinely believed he would toss her into the water, but they did not know their captain and first mate as she did. She suppressed a grin.

When she and Dax reached the railing, he paused and studied the water below. “Not a bad night for a swim.”

She looked down into the churning depths, then out at the distant coast sitting on the moon-flecked ocean’s surface like a thin, dark ribbon. If she had truly been about to face it, the swim to shore would have been intimidating. “I suppose not.”

“This’ll teach you not to sneak aboard the Evening Star,” Dax said, loudly enough to attract the attention of the one or two sailors on deck who had not already noticed them.

Joss waited for him to cave in, but instead, he bent and scooped her up. Before she knew it, she was in his arms, her legs dangling over the side of the ship.

Her mouth dried. He wouldn’t—would he?

His grip loosened.

A squeak escaped her, and she threw her arms around his neck and held tight. Her gaze darted across the deck to Parker, who struggled to her feet and lunged towards them. She would not make it in time.

Joss opened her mouth to plead for mercy.

“Stop.”

Dax’s arms tightened, and he looked over his shoulder.

Theo stood outside the captain’s cabin, his arm raised. “Don’t throw her overboard.”

Everyone froze, even Parker.

Harrumphing, Dax swung Joss back over the railing and set her down.

“They’re not stowaways,” Theo said. “They’re with me.”

Noa strolled out beside him and took in the scene as if he were perusing fruit at a market. His eyes landed on Joss, and his lips pressed together into a thin line, though whether with displeasure or to suppress a grin, she could not tell.

Theo said something to him that Joss could not hear, and Dax whispered, “Now look what you’ve done. Even the Iskarian lord’s trying to save you.”

She gaped at Theo. He was impersonating a nobleman? He could be executed for that. And while Noa put up with her and Aitha’s shenanigans, he would not tolerate real crime. She would have to play along to protect him and pay whatever he had promised Noa later.

“Bring them here,” Noa said. “And the rest of you, back to work.”

Activity resumed around them, men climbing the rigging and unfurling another sail, others doing something with ropes that Joss did not care to understand. Dax caught her arm again and looked at Parker, who had slumped against the rail.

"You'd better stay there," he said to her.

She glared at him and pushed herself upright before asking Joss, "Will you be well without me?"

"Yes. Just breathe."

Dax escorted Joss back across the deck to the cabin, where Noa gestured for Theo to precede him inside.

As they entered, Theo cleared his throat, drawing her gaze. He gave her a look that pleaded for her to follow his lead and turned to Noa, who leaned against the front of a large desk with his arms folded across his chest.

"They're my maid and guard. The ones I told you about," Theo said.

"Is that so?" Noa looked from him to Joss, one brow raised.

She gave Noa a tight shake of her head behind Theo's back, hoping he would understand not to reveal her identity. "Yes, captain. We, um, we got lost when we boarded and ended up in the cargo hold."

"I told you to gather our things and meet me on the deck, Kit, not wander around the ship." Theo dipped his head slightly towards Noa. "I apologise, Captain."

"Sorry, Milord. Captain," Joss added.

Noa straightened and addressed Theo. "Please make yourself comfortable while I see to them. We don't normally have servants on the *Evening Star*, so I'll need to ensure they don't get in the way of my crew."

Theo glanced at her, clearly reluctant to be separated, but she needed to speak to Noa in private. Before he could object, she bowed to him, then Noa, and said, "Thank you, Captain."

Dax and Noa escorted her outside, collected Parker, and headed to the upper crew's quarters.

"Lord Sakanin's taken my cabin, so you can have the sailing master's bunk," Noa said. "It's the next best. It's also the closest to his, so it'll be easier for you to 'serve' him." He opened a door partway along the short corridor and ushered them all inside.

The moment the door closed behind them, Parker slumped onto the narrow bunk, and Joss rounded on Dax. "Were you really going to throw us overboard?"

He waved a casual hand in the air. "I'd've fished you out straight away."

"But it would've taught you a lesson," Noa added.

She studied him, the pieces sliding into place in her mind. "You knew it was us."

"Of course I did. Do you think anything happens on this ship I don't know about? Dax saw you scuttling out from behind that cart while we were loading the furs. Had to force old Caff to let you up the ramp so we could see what you were up to." He shook his head. "Tch, tch, tch. Do you think we don't know our own sailors?"

Ugh. She really should have just asked for passage.

Noa perched on the chest at the end of the bunk. "But now Lord Sakanin is involved. Do you know him, or is he just taking pity on you?"

"We know him. I swear." Joss sat in one of the chairs opposite his. How could she explain without giving away Theo's real identity? "We met in Aralan. Parker and I were posing as commoners for safety, but we had a few run-ins with bandits. He suggested we travel together, so we offered our services for the duration."

The captain crossed his arms. "Why were you in Garellion in the first place? I'd have thought King Lucas would want you in Tyrrath, away from the trouble."

"He tried," Parker said.

Joss glared at her friend, who had closed her eyes again, and tapped her thigh. If Noa or Dax knew anything… No, better not to involve them. Besides, Noa never paid attention to anything beyond his ship. He only returned for the gatherings under duress.

She forced a laugh. "We're on a quest."

Dax snorted, but Noa rolled his eyes and muttered something about Aitha and her being a pair. Then, he asked more clearly, "So why were you hiding?"

"I wanted to warn you not to reveal my identity, so we hid until I could speak to you privately." She sighed. "We probably should've just walked onboard."

There. Almost the truth.

"You land-tied are something else."

Joss flinched at his use of the derogatory nickname. "Don't call us that."

"I'm sorry. You know I don't mean it. But seriously, you've got yourself into a real mess this time. I don't know what you're up to, but leave me out of it. I can't afford to offend the Iskarians." He stood and pointed a finger at her. "For the rest of this trip, as far as I'm concerned, you're his maid."

Parker groaned. For a moment, Joss thought she was complaining, but the poor woman rolled with the motion of the ship and held her stomach.

"Do you have anything that can help her?" Joss asked Noa.

He glanced at her prone friend and nodded. "I'll send something over when I get back to my cabin."

"Thank you. And I'll make all this up to you next time."

"I've no idea what you're talking about. *Kit*. Now let me get out of here before I change my mind and toss you in the sea myself."

Dax followed him out but paused in the doorway. "We've no Summoner at present, so we'll not get to Firstport until the day after tomorrow. Can you be a maid for that long?"

Joss narrowed her eyes at him. Aitha always complained about her brother being late to the gatherings so he could keep his ship on the periphery. Whether coincidence or by design, Joss could handle an extra day aboard. "I'll manage," she said, then added at another groan from Parker, "But Parker will need that tonic."

When Joss ventured outside later, Theo was waiting for her, pacing the deck. He tugged her over to the railing, away from prying ears, and said, "Stowing away? That was your grand plan? How reckless."

A twinge of guilt stabbed her chest at deceiving him, but it was too late to turn back now. "Yes, well. I can't believe you brazened your way onboard pretending to be a noble." And not just any noble. A Sakanin. She checked over her shoulder to make sure they were alone, then looked down at his wrist. He had wrapped it in a cloth bracer. She lowered her voice. "Did you alter your tattoo? You'll swing if they find out."

He grimaced and muttered, "I'll pay the fee later."

No, she would cover it. Not that she would tell him that. It would probably take him months to earn however much he had promised Noa. She peered at him, at the callouses on his hands, the defined muscles that could have only come from hard work. How difficult it must be to be born without means…

Tilting her head to the side, she tapped her fingers absently against her thigh. She had never considered that before, only longed for freedom without considering the price that came with it. What would commoners risk to trade places with her?

Theo turned to watch the ocean, his brow furrowed. Apparently, a lot.

Resolve settled in her gut, and she straightened. She would do everything she could to keep him safe. "I suppose I can be your maid for a day or two, especially as I won the bet."

His head jerked up. "What do you mean, you won?"

"I made it onto the ship first. I saw you walking up the gangplank with N—the captain from the hold."

He folded his arms across his broad chest. “The bet was for who secured passage first, not just made it onto the ship. That was me.”

She opened her mouth to argue, then closed it. Technically, he was correct, though she could claim she had been the one to secure their place by covering for him.

He grinned, and she dropped all pretence of sulking. Another day onboard might not be so bad after all.

Chapter 17

Theo

Late the next afternoon, Theo sat on a water barrel by the main mast, out of the way of the sailors who were readying the ship for the evening's festivities. Though they would not join the gathering until the following day, it appeared the presence of passengers warranted an early night of revelry. The deckhands scrubbed the deck, polished the railings and brasswork, dragged the captain's desk out to serve as a top table, and placed the gangplank atop several barrels for the rest of the crew.

If the preparations were anything to go by, it would be a night to remember.

The savoury scent of fish stew drifted up from the open hatch to the lower decks, and someone shouted, "Which one of you scurvy dogs moved my reed pipe?"

The man's tone suggested it was good-natured ribbing, and Theo chuckled, reminded of his own workmen back in Jadhe.

Unlike those around him, he had little to do but wait for Kit to emerge from her cabin. He doodled a half-baked design on a scrap of paper and glanced occasionally at the entrance to the upper crew quarters.

He still could not believe she had stowed away. Did she ever think before she acted? The corners of his lips twitched up even as he shook his head with a huff. All the same, there was something about her that drew him in.

The door swung open just as the ship's bell rang for the crew to gather, and Kit walked out. She wore the same dress she had appeared in that morning—claiming she should look the part if she were to serve as his maid—and had done something to her hair that made it shine. Did it feel as silky soft as it looked, swept over her left shoulder and tied with cord?

Theo leaped off the barrel and sidestepped a couple of the crew heading for the tables. "You look lovely this evening," he said. "Where's Parker?"

She stabbed a thumb over her shoulder. "She's still not feeling well, so she's going to stay in there. I'll take her something to eat later."

Poor Parker. Not everyone was suited to travelling by sea.

"Probably for the best. Shall we?"

He offered his arm, but she did not take it. Instead, she looked at him with her brows scrunched together as if figuring out a puzzling mechanism. He did his best not to squirm under her scrutiny.

"You shaved," she said.

"I thought it was time for a change." He stroked his bare jawline, recalling her complaint in Ilderdell that it was scratchy, and asked as casually as he could, "Is it better like this?"

She studied his face, tilting her head first to one side and then the other, and shrugged. "The beard suited you more."

He stared at her, then laughed and muttered under his breath, "I wish you'd make up your mind."

"What?"

"Nothing. Let's go and eat."

The grin she gave him as she slipped her fingers around his elbow made his heart beat faster. He took a deep breath and escorted her across the deck.

Captain Malz waited for them with the rest of the upper crew at the desk-turned-dining table. "Ah, Lord Sakanin. Please, sit." He gestured for Theo to take the seat on his right, and Kit pulled it out for him, much to his discomfort. She took the place beside his once he was settled and poured them both a cup of ale.

There were no toasts or speeches to start the feast. In fact, the only nods to formality were that the men joined the women on the crew in wearing shirts with their trousers, and the captain was served first.

After that, everyone dug into the cheese, flatbread, and salted beef as soon as each platter arrived, calling for bowls of stew from a couple of the youngest sailors who ladled it into bowls. It was simple but hearty fare, and the atmosphere across the deck was relaxed, more like a family meal than a formal banquet.

The crew took turns telling stories while they feasted, laughing and cheering equally at accounts of battling sea monsters, getting tangled in the rigging while inebriated, and the day one of them got their first pair of earrings—the mark of the free folk's seafaring life.

"I've never quite understood that tradition," Theo said as the proud woman showed off her three sets of piercings. "What do they mean?"

Dax leaned forwards, pointing out his own three pairs. "We get our first set when we join a crew at sixteen, then another every ten years."

"Or swapped when we're promoted." Captain Malz fingered the gold in his right lobe.

"And we only remove them when we're landed by age or injury," Dax added.

Grinning, the captain slapped the older man's back. "If you're not stripped of 'em for insubordination first."

"I see." Theo hid his smile behind a sip of ale. That explained the differences in their adornments.

When the meal was finished, only crumbs and piles of bones left, a few of the crew produced instruments and began playing while the young pair cleared the tables. The others clapped or stomped their feet in time, and soon the deck was a mass of twirling dancers.

There were no courtly bows to start or set steps to take. The free folk moved with wild abandon, leaping, skipping, and spinning as the mood took them.

Beside him, Kit watched the revelry, her eyes alight.

"Do you want to dance?" he asked her.

Warmth spread through him when she immediately replied, "Yes."

They joined the throng, linking their arms together and gambolling along the deck and back, then holding hands to spin around and around. Every touch felt intimate, despite the lively tune and crowd around them, and when Theo lifted her into the air as several other couples were doing, his body thrummed at the contact.

The tune came to an end all too soon, and before he could decipher his reactions, Captain Malz appeared beside them.

"Can I have a turn?" he asked Kit, who stood bent over, her hands propped against her knees.

She straightened and grinned at him. "Of course."

A twinge pierced Theo's chest, and his hands clenched. He returned to his seat but could not pull his eyes from Kit as she danced with the captain, the pain growing with each of their easy smiles and casual touches. Why did it bother him so much?

The answer sent a jolt through him, and he shifted uncomfortably in his chair. He liked Kit. More than liked her. He was falling for her. Hard.

She was not like anyone he had met before—bold, fearless, skilled, and independent, with keen intelligence and sharp wit. But most of all, she was not interested in pursuing power, unlike the last woman he had considered. If Kit agreed to be with him, it would be for him, not his position.

"Strand me." What was he thinking?

But it was too late to doubt. He drew a hand over his jaw and huffed. If he were not serious about her, he would not have shaved, not that it had done him much good.

What to do about it, then?

When the dance eventually finished, she murmured something to the captain and wove through the crowd to the side of the deck. Locks of her hair, escaped from its plait, fell in beautiful disarray around her flushed face as she fanned herself with a hand, and her smile was luminous in the fading light.

She leaned on the railing and gazed out at the ocean, her back to the revellers crowding the deck.

Farther along the ship's rail, a group of sailors stole glances in her direction while whispering among themselves. They pushed one young man towards her, who blushed and slapped their hands away but did not retreat.

The youth sucked air between his teeth and spat over the railing into the sea. Then he tightened the sash around his waist, stuck out his chest, and walked forwards.

Theo did not think, just reacted. He jumped up and strode over to her before the young sailor could seize the opportunity. "May I join you?"

"Of course." Kit glanced up at him with a bright smile before returning her attention to the sea.

He relaxed beside her, noting in his periphery the sailor retreating to his friends. Good.

Looking out towards the horizon, Theo allowed the sweeping brushstrokes of orange and pink painting the sky and reflecting in the water to soothe the frayed edges of his heart. His gaze strayed to Kit, to her silky hair and the soft skin of her nape. The dress's neckline dipped lower than her usual tunic, exposing a band of paler skin across her chest. Averting his eyes, he swallowed hard and whispered, "You're killing me, sikani."

She turned to him. "What did you say?"

"Oh, um. Have you enjoyed yourself tonight?" Why had he said that out loud? At least he had used the old tongue and not entirely given himself away.

"Very much. But I'm looking forward to getting to Firstport and finding the stone."

Words popped into his head, and for the second time in less than a minute, he spoke them without thinking. "Then let's make a new bet. Whoever finds the next useful piece of information gets to ask one thing of the other."

"One thing." She tapped her fingers against the railing in the adorable way that seemed to indicate thinking. "What sort of thing?"

He leaned in closer, partly to keep anyone from overhearing them, partly because he could not resist. "Well, if I win, I'm going to ask you to spend more time with me."

She blinked. Then her eyes widened and her mouth fell slack. "S-spend time with you?"

"Yes." He closed the remaining gap between them, paused a mere hair's breadth from her lips to give her the chance to pull away, and when she did not move, sealed his over them.

His fingers dug into the wood of the railing beside her, but he kept the kiss soft and tender, just long enough to show her he was serious. Then, after far too short a time, he forced himself to straighten and smile. Could she hear the pounding in his ears?

He caught her stunned gaze and shrugged one shoulder. “Think about it. I’ll see you in the morning.”

With that said, he turned and strode to his cabin, praying that no one noticed the tremor in his hands and that she would not reject him. What broken cog had caused him to speak so rashly? And then to kiss her?

No, the kiss he would not take back. He could not have stopped himself for all the water in Egrea. Besides, it was too late now for regret. He needed to get off that boat and find the mage’s home, if it still existed. And before Kit.

Chapter 18

Joss

They arrived at Firstport the following afternoon, and Joss towed Parker over to the railing. "Look at all the ships."

A forest of masts speared the sky between the three main islands, a handful of larger vessels clustered off-centre with a mixture of different-sized ships around them.

"Aitha told me there'd be a lot here, but this…" Joss let out a low whistle. Her friend had not been wrong when she had said every Free Isles ship that could make it returned for the twice-yearly gatherings.

Noa took the *Evening Star* around the main group to the port, where the crew unloaded the bulk of the cargo under the watchful eye of an elderly port master. Eager to continue her quest, Joss interrupted their labours to bid Noa and Dax farewell.

She could barely look Theo in the eye as they disembarked and walked along the jetty towards the shore. What had she been thinking, letting him kiss her?

Her hand rose to touch her lips, but she forced it back down. At least she was back in her trousers now, though how that offered any protection from the warring emotions storming through her mind, she could not say.

"Feeling any better?" she asked Parker.

"A little." The pallor in the stoic guard's cheeks and the way she swayed slightly as she walked made a lie of her response.

Joss wiped the sweat from her brow and squinted up into the clear, blue sky. Where were the clouds when they needed them?

She pulled the port master aside and asked where they might find any historical records, or anything about past mages from the Isles.

"Nothing like that here," the man said. "We free folk pass down our history by word of mouth. And we don't have mages either, only Summoners, and they're all aboard ships."

She didn't let her shoulders slump. "If you—"

"I'm busy," he interrupted before pivoting and walking away.

Joss stared after him. "Now what?"

"We should probably find an inn first," Theo said.

She looked up at the township ahead, fully taking it in for the first time.

A shipyard, warehouses, several taverns, and a smithy made up the seafront, and behind them, more buildings nestled against the slope of a hill. People of all ages milled about the cobbled streets in both directions.

It all seemed so… normal.

"Ma!"

A girl of around eleven or twelve ran in front of Joss to a woman in her early thirties, who dropped the bundle she was carrying to hug her child. After a long embrace, the woman pulled back and looked her daughter over. "You've grown."

"Granny Kealy says I'm over three arms tall now." The girl lifted one hand above her head. "That's nearly tall enough to take a berth."

The woman grinned and tousled the girl's hair. "Four more years, my love. Will you try out for the *Warbler*?"

"Mm-hm."

"It's a good ship to live on."

Picking up her belongings, the woman held a hand out to her daughter, and they continued their conversation as they walked up one of the lanes into the town.

Joss stared after them. So, it was true that, among the free folk, only children and the elderly lived on land. She rubbed her chest and set off again. What must it be like to be separated from family for most of the year?

"Are you all right?" Theo asked, falling into step beside her.

"Just thinking."

According to Noa, there were only three reputable inns to choose from. The first was full, so they made their way up the hill to the second, which looked like several buildings had been knocked into one. A low hum of multiple voices emanated from within, proving its popularity.

As they approached the entrance, a stocky man with no rings in his ears and a bitter expression etched into his face stormed out. He pushed past them, knocking Joss into Parker and eliciting a growl from the guard, and stomped down the cobbled street to the beach.

"Someone isn't looking forward to the gathering," Joss muttered.

They ducked inside to the scent of fragrant stew and a main hall that was pleasantly cool after the baking heat outside. Tables filled the area to the left, two thirds of them occupied, and a staircase rose to the upper floor on the right. The room managed to feel both bright and cosy.

A woman looked up from a counter along the back wall, more creases on her weathered face than one of Joss's dresses. She wiped her hands on a cloth and limped over to greet them. "Welcome to the Captain's Rest."

"Do you have any rooms available?" Joss asked. "We'll need two. And I'll be sharing with my cousin." She flapped a finger between her and Theo. "We're not married. Or a couple."

Theo chuckled, making her cheeks burn even more. Why had she blurted all of that?

Fortunately, the innkeeper ignored her rambling. "Don't you worry. I've plenty of space upstairs." She glanced at a handful of young helpers dotted around the hall, but they were all busy serving people, so she gestured to the staircase rising along the right-hand wall. "I'll show you up."

The second step creaked under her weight and then Theo's, so Joss hopped over it to the next. When they reached the upper floor, they turned left, and the innkeeper hobbled over to a door halfway along the hallway.

"This is yours," she said to Joss and Parker, opening it. "And the one next door will serve for your companion."

Parker walked inside and, after only a cursory inspection, dumped her pack against the wall and sank onto the nearest bed.

"You don't look too well, m'dear," the innkeeper said. "Rough crossing?"

Parker only nodded.

"You need Old Sty's special tonic. We all swear by it. Works a treat."

Joss would pay whatever was asked to ease her friend's suffering. "Where can we get some?"

The innkeeper pointed over her shoulder in the general direction of the street. "Three doors down. Can't miss it."

Joss made to leave, but Parker stood. "I'll go. I could use the walk anyway."

"Are you sure?"

The guard rewarded the question with her typical long-suffering look and slipped out of the room before anyone could argue.

"I'll take my leave as well," Theo said. He turned to the innkeeper and asked, "Is there any water for washing in the room?"

"Yes. On the dresser by the window, and clean towels in the chest."

"Thank you."

He strode down the hallway, and the innkeeper addressed Joss. "I'll be downstairs if you need anything. Food's served till ten, and the door's barred at midnight."

She closed the door behind her with a soft thud, and for the first time in what felt like forever, Joss was left alone. She flopped across her bed, closing her eyes before she hit the mattress, wriggled into a more comfortable position, and listened to the sounds floating up from the main hall below.

A short while later, a rap on the door was followed by Theo calling, "Kit? Are you hungry?"

Joss groaned. She should have given him her real name. "Coming."

When she joined him in the hallway, he glanced behind her and asked, "Is Parker not back yet?"

"No." Joss shrugged. "She's probably exploring the town." Or memorising escape routes.

"Ah. Shall we?"

They walked along the hallway and were about to descend the stairs when Theo stiffened. He pulled her back around the corner out of sight, put a finger to his lips, and whispered, "The mage hunters are down there."

Joss wrinkled her nose. Surely, he was mistaken. "How'd you know it's them?"

"I saw them. The one at the front was in Garellion."

She pushed out of his hold to see for herself. Stealing around the edge of the stairwell, she peered down into the main hall, where three men blocked the entrance while they talked to the innkeeper.

They wore plain, belted tunics and trousers, but their hunter tattoos were no longer covered. All three carried an array of weaponry that would have been impressive had they not likely been searching for her. The man at the front was speaking, and Joss angled her head, filtering out the general hubbub to hear what he was saying.

"…not seen them? Two women and a man? One's pale and blonde. The other's tanned with brown hair. The man's Iskarian."

Eyes widening, she spun back to Theo, who motioned for her to retreat farther along the hallway. She followed him and whispered, "How are they here?"

"I don't know. Maybe they decided to intercept us here when they lost us in Garellion."

"So persistent."

The inn's front door banged open, and Joss met Theo's eyes and crept back to the stairs, Theo right behind her.

Unfortunately, the hunters had not left. Another of them had joined the group and appeared to be reporting in. "…not at either of the other inns. Are we sure they're in Firstport?"

"Yes," the leader said. "My informant said they arrived on the *Evening Star* this afternoon."

"What if they went to another island?" one of the others asked.

"Better to search everywhere here first. We can't afford to lose them."

"I don't see why." The man with a bald head and full beard curled his lip in disgust. "They're not even mages."

The leader stepped close and leaned forwards until their noses almost touched. His lowered voice was hard to hear over the distance. "The artefact they're looking for is extremely dangerous and could be used as a weapon against Iskaria. Do you want to be responsible for the next wasting of our kingdom?"

"No sir," the other man said, swallowing hard.

"Good." The leader stepped back and addressed the newcomer. "Find out if that drunkard knows anything else." Then he turned towards the stairs.

Joss and Theo ducked out of sight, and her mind reeled. No wonder they were pursuing her and the others with such determination. They thought the dragon stone was a weapon. But who in the world had told them that?

She glanced at Theo, but his face showed no reaction to their discovery.

When the second tread creaked a moment later, they ran, keeping their steps as light as possible on the ancient flooring.

Theo charged into the nearest of their rooms, paused long enough to fling his gaze around, and tugged her over to the wardrobe.

Yanking the doors open, he turned to her and said, "Quick. Get in."

She stalled, staring at the empty mahogany interior—so small, so dark.

"There isn't anywhere else to hide."

She scanned the chamber, but he was right. There was nowhere else to hide. Swallowing hard, she climbed in and shuffled to one side to make room for him.

He closed the door just as someone down the hallway yelled at being interrupted in the middle of their bath.

The innkeeper must not have told the hunters which rooms were theirs. But she had not stopped them from searching either. It seemed the free folk's neutrality between the other kingdoms held.

Another door banged open, closer.

Joss's heart pounded wildly, and sweat stuck her tunic to her back and made her palms clammy. What would happen if the hunters found them? Would they be taken to Iskaria? Tortured? Killed? Even if Parker were with them, she would not be able to prevent their capture alone.

The air in the wardrobe became thick, stifling, and the walls closed in around her.

Fear of a different kind took hold as she fell into memories of the past. Her stern-faced governess. The cramped cupboard. A padlock's click. Then relentless, suffocating darkness and screams ripping from her throat. The voice told her anew that she must learn to be still and silent—a proper princess like her sister.

Her limbs began to shake. The fine tremor spread uncontrollably, rattling her soul as thoroughly as it did her body.

Until a man's voice whispered in her ear, "I'm here. I've got you."

Theo.

His hand found hers, trailed up her arm, rubbed her shoulder. Joss leaned into the comfort he offered, focusing on him and blocking out all else lest she return to the nightmare.

His breath feathered her neck, and strong muscles flexed against her side with each of his movements, the heat of his body and his gentle touch melting the tension in hers. He shifted closer, and for the first time since she turned six, the confined space did not defeat her.

Slowly, she pried her eyes open. A sliver of light slipped through the crack in the wardrobe doors and fell across his face. His eyes, swimming with compassion, found hers in the darkness.

And the doors swung open.

"There you are."

Joss blinked in the sudden light, her mind taking a moment to catch up with reality. Instead of the hunters, Parker stood between the doors, one brow raised and her lips twitching up at the corners as her gaze bounced from Joss to Theo and back again.

Why was she here and not…? Joss darted a glance around the room. Where were the mage hunters?

"Are you getting out or not?"

"Yes." She sprang away from Theo and scrambled out, nearly falling over in her haste. He shot out an arm to steady her, and she muttered an incoherent thanks.

In her periphery, he unfolded himself from the wardrobe, closed the doors, and faced Parker squarely. "What happened to the hunters?"

The amusement in her eyes melted away, replaced by a tight expression. "I saw them searching the inn and paid the lad across the street to say he'd seen us walking down to the beach."

Bless Parker for not commenting on what she had just witnessed. Joss straightened her tunic and studied her friend. "How are you feeling now?"

"Much better. That tincture really works." Parker's brow furrowed. "But we have more important things to discuss. If these mage hunters are so persistent, is it safe to keep going?"

Theo slammed his hand down on the dresser, scowling like a thunderstorm about to break. "Strand them. I should've known they had an informant here."

"Strand them…" He had said that before. "What does that mean?" Joss asked.

He glanced at her, his expression still distracted. "Criminals in Iskaria are taken into the desert and left there. If they can make it back to civilisation, they're considered forgiven."

She gaped. "Even for minor offenses?"

"It's mainly used in special cases. There are other punishments for minor crimes." He exhaled heavily. "The seriousness of their crime determines how far out they're taken and whether they're given food and water. Most are never seen again."

"In that case, there are a few people I wouldn't mind stranding," Parker said.

Joss sent her an incredulous look, which the guard batted away with a flick of her hand. She squared her shoulders before continuing. "What I want to know is what we do now. I don't know about you," she looked at Theo, then at Joss, "but we should leave."

"What? No," Joss cried.

"It's my job to keep you safe, and this isn't safe."

"Your *job*?" Theo's face wrinkled with confusion. "Surely that's taking it a bit far."

Joss bit her lip. How she wished she could tell him the truth about her identity. She had grown to hate lying to him, but it was too late to say anything now.

She had no choice.

She faced her guard and said, "It's no less safe now than it was an hour ago."

A single eyebrow climbed Parker's forehead again. "You were hiding in a wardrobe."

Joss cleared her throat. "Yes, well. They're gone now, and we can—"

The door opened, and for a moment, Joss's heart stopped beating. But a boy of no more than ten pelted into the room and skidded to a stop in front of Parker.

"I led those men away like you said, and they're headed for the docks. If you want to leave, you should go now before they find out I lied to them and come back."

Chapter 19
Joss

"We can't leave now," Joss said. "Not without finding"—she glanced at the boy—"what we came here for."

Theo stepped closer, said, "I'll leave you to talk," and padded from the room.

Turning to the boy, Parker dug through her waist pouch and tossed a coin to him. "Will you wait for us downstairs?"

His eyes rounded on the silver, and he nodded hard enough to rattle his brain inside his skull. He tucked it inside his belt and ran out as fast as he had entered, leaving Joss and Parker alone.

Joss straightened and spoke before Parker could. "You're right. We should leave this inn. But not to go home. I want to find the dragon stone." Parker opened her mouth, but Joss raised her hand to forestall whatever she might say. "The hunters will think twice before touching us if we reveal my identity, and if they find us again, that's what we'll do. But we have a chance to finish what we started now, and I'm going to take it."

Parker studied her for what felt like a long time. "You sound different."

"I suppose I am." Joss glanced at the wardrobe. Squeezed in that hiding place with Theo, the walls had not crushed her, the darkness had not broken her. She had allowed fear to control her earlier, but now, even if only for a moment, she was ready to fight back.

"So, what's the plan?"

"Find out where Mistress Yarin lived. Find the stone. Save my papa." She prayed it would be that simple, though she knew in reality it would be anything but.

They gathered their things, and when they opened the door, Theo was waiting for them in the hallway, arms folded, his pack resting at his feet.

"Where to?" he asked.

Joss grinned as Parker replied, "We keep going."

He picked up his pack and gave them a single nod. "Good. Let's go then."

They found the boy leaning against the wall at the bottom of the stairs, and he straightened as they joined him.

Parker glanced around the main hall, tilted her head towards the front door, and walked outside. Joss followed behind her, mouth sealed shut. There were too many ears inside for them to talk freely.

When they reached a quiet section of the lane, Parker stopped and turned to the boy. "We need to find out where any mages might have lived in the past. Can you help us?"

"There's an islan—" He bit his lip and looked at them, wide-eyed, as if checking whether they had heard his answer. None of them spoke, and after a moment, he continued, albeit in a lower, more cautious tone. "We're not supposed to talk about it with outsiders."

An island specifically for mages? Joss suppressed a whoop for fear of spooking the boy, before meeting Theo's, then Parker's gaze. That would be the perfect place to hide a dragon stone. There were plenty of smaller islets to choose from, with hidden bays and rocky shorelines to keep people away.

"Those hunters could find it on their own," Parker said to the boy. He whipped his head towards her, and she spread her hands. "They only need to visit every island in turn. They'll find it eventually if they keep looking. Please. Help us get there before them. We can warn anyone there to hide, if that's the problem."

He looked out across the rooftops, to the mass of ships gathered offshore and the humps of scattered islands beyond, and rubbed the back of one ankle with his other foot. "I suppose you're right." He gave each of them a stern look. "You won't do anything to hurt the summoners."

Theo squatted down and met the boy's eyes. "I promise. We're just looking for something left by one of the ancients."

The boy's lips pursed, a vee forming between his brows. Then it cleared, and he blew out a breath. "The island doesn't have a name, but when the guardian took my friend there to train as a summoner, he told her they were going to Whistling Cove. He said only those with the most talent get chosen to go there and she'd be learning skills passed down from the first summoner." He leaned closer.

"I shouldn't know any of that, but I listened in from the attic."

The fine hairs on Joss's arms stood on end. This was it. It had to be. "Where is it? Can you take us there?"

He nodded, then set off down the hill at a pace that took her by surprise. She hefted her pack higher on her shoulder and followed his lead, Parker and Theo close behind her.

"I'll get my brother to take you out to the fleet," the boy said over his shoulder. "It'll be quicker to cross the boards than sail around now that everyone's here. And if you tell the rowers at the other side that you're visiting the guardian, they won't try to stop you."

Joss had no idea what he meant by crossing the boards, but at least they were moving again.

The boy's brother pulled the rowboat alongside the nearest ship, and Joss and the others climbed the ladder to the deck. After straightening her clothes, she looked around and let out a low whistle. The ships were anchored much closer together than they appeared from Firstport, some so close they were almost touching.

When she walked across the deck, without anyone stopping her or even giving her a second look, she saw why. A plank rested on the railing at that side, its other end propped on the rail of the next ship, joining the two together.

"This is incredible."

She looked out at the rest of the tightly packed ships. A web of walkways connected the entire fleet? That must have been what the boy meant by crossing the boards. No wonder he had said it would be quicker than sailing around the fleet. She climbed up onto the plank, ran across the short distance, and dropped onto the next deck with a thud and a huge grin stretching her cheeks. That was fun.

A group of the free folk sat around the ship's central hatch, chatting and drinking, and as Joss walked towards them, a handful more appeared on the other side of the ship. There was no plank visible where they jumped aboard, so she changed direction to take a look.

As she approached, a straggler arrived with two large bottles slung over his shoulder on a piece of string. He loped across a narrow rope ladder from a ship off the bow, balancing on the cords as easily as if he were strolling a wide path on solid ground.

Joss grimaced and searched along the port railing for a sturdier crossing. The ladder would be impossible for Parker, given her tendency for seasickness. She found a plank hanging across a wider gap from ropes at both ends just as Theo and Parker joined her.

"Let's go."

Taking the lead once more, she swung her legs over the railing, leaned out, and stepped across the short gap onto the wooden board. Thick and solid, it remained fairly steady under her weight, so she scurried across and repeated the process at the other side.

She ran across the third deck, which was empty save for a couple on watch, and found a board taking them farther into the centre of the fleet. But when she glanced behind her, the others were still crossing the previous board. She leaned against the railing to wait for them, bouncing one leg when they took forever.

"Come on," she called when they finally made it. "What are you doing?"

"Steady your ropes, sikani," Theo replied.

Another term she did not understand. "What does that mean?"

"Um, nothing." He ducked his head, avoiding her gaze, so she folded her arms and stared at him until he answered. "It means impatient one."

Parker snorted as Joss huffed.

"Well, you're as slow as a tortoise," she countered.

"I'm careful. I don't want any of us falling and getting crushed between the boats."

A glance over the railing revealed a narrow channel of water tossing white-flecked spray against first one hull, then the other. When he put it like that… she waited while he checked the plank was secure before stepping onto it.

They traversed ship after ship like that, crossing the fleet in as straight a line as possible. Parties gathered on many of the decks, the free folk moving from one to the next like the ebb and flow of the tides they lived by, calling greetings, sharing food and wine, and singing and dancing as the mood took them.

All seemed to be going well until Parker gripped Joss's arm while she was inspecting a potential board, saying in an undertone, "We're being followed."

Pretending to weigh her options, Joss turned just enough to be able to see the far side of the deck from the corner of her eye. Two men leaned against the railing some distance from the rest of the crowd onboard. While one wore a hooded cloak that completely hid him from view, the other was dressed all in black with the bulge of a hidden weapon beneath his long sleeve. Mage hunters.

She grimaced and forced herself to turn away and not look for those she remembered from the inn.

"Are there any more?" she asked Parker.

"Just those two so far." The guard scanned the nearby vessels. "We can lose them on one of the bigger ships."

Theo joined them. "What's the matter?"

"One of the hunters found us," Joss whispered. "Follow me," she said louder and climbed up onto the board.

She headed towards the nearest of the huge ships, keeping track of their unwanted shadows and noting that the hooded man peeled off from his companion a few crossings from her intended destination. Her lips curved into a satisfied smirk. If he had left to fetch reinforcements, she and the others would be long gone by the time he returned.

They had to climb a ladder to reach the deck of the *Cerennia*, but it was worth Parker's increased queasiness. The ship was packed with revellers, and they dove into the crowd, quickly losing sight of the ladder's ropes.

"There." Theo led them to a staircase down to the lower deck and ushered them ahead of him.

Two more staircases and half the ship's length later, they found a sturdy board connecting it to a smaller boat on the far side. With a quick but thorough check of their surroundings to ensure the hunter was nowhere within sight, they hopped over the railing and resumed their trek across the fleet.

While Theo kept pace with Joss, Parker frequently lagged behind, waving them on and saying she would catch up. They waited for her, despite her protests, and Joss winced every time her friend clutched whatever surface was to hand when the ships rolled.

"Have you got any of the tonic left?" she asked.

Parker shook her head.

Theo lent her an arm as the deck beneath them rose and fell over another wave. "Do you need us to stop for a while?"

"No. Keep going. I'll be fine once we're on land again." She glanced at Joss and added, "Just don't tell anyone about this."

Joss lifted her hand in a solemn vow. "My lips are sealed."

They only had a few boats to go when she came to another wider gap bridged by a plank tied at either end with thick ropes. She sat on the railing, swung her legs over, and hopped across to the wooden board. Halfway across, it tilted as a particularly large swell lifted the ship ahead.

Joss wobbled slightly and extended her arms to regain her balance. As soon as she felt steady, she dashed along the remaining length and leaped onto the next deck. She turned to warn Theo to be careful and found him leaning over the railing, holding the far end of the plank.

"Thank you," she called across to him.

He lifted an arm, and she felt the warmth of his smile, despite the gap between them. "You're welcome," he shouted back. "We make a good team."

Something inside her chest expanded at the thought, but she brushed it aside. She needed to focus on their goal. While it was true that the dragon stone could be anywhere in Egrea, her heart told her they were close. She knew it like she knew her sisters faces, could almost feel the stone in her hands. She just needed to keep going a little longer.

When they reached the far side of the gathering, they searched the sea beyond for a rowboat to take them to shore. Several moved between the fleet and the islands in the near distance, but they were too far out to call for a ride.

Parker walked along the railing and stopped a few lengths away. "There," she said, pointing down at the water between the ships.

Joss ran over and spotted a small boat floating alongside the ship beside theirs. She leaned over the railing and waved to the teens manning it. "Hey there. Can you take us ashore?"

They waved back, then fitted their oars and made quick time crossing to the ladder dangling from the deck not far from Joss and the others.

Theo scrambled down first and held it for her and Parker. When they were all aboard, the teens pushed off the hull and rowed out into open water.

"Where to?" the one on the left asked.

Joss glanced at Theo and said, "Whistling Cove. We're going to visit the guardian."

The boys both stalled at her reply, casting suspicious glances at them all, but one nudged the other in the side, and they kept going.

Digging through her waist pouch, Joss asked, "How much do—"

"No need to pay," the same boy said. "Rowing people ashore is our job during the gatherings."

She let go of the coin she had picked up. "Thank you, then."

It seemed to take forever to get to the island. The small craft crept across the sea at a snail's pace, and Parker grew more ill as the boat tossed about in the waves. Twilight overtook them, the stars slowly waking overhead. With no lantern on board, the night sky seemed bigger, the moon closer than Joss had ever witnessed. In other circumstances, it would have been idyllic.

But she itched to be on land again, continuing their search, and her leg bounced against the hull in a fast rhythm. She needed a way to pass the time and so turned to the pair at the oars, studying them as she thought of something to say.

They looked to be about sixteen, so she asked them, "Are you trying out for a berth at the gathering?"

The one on the left shook his head. "I'm not old enough till the winter gathering, but Mal here's going for a place on the *Dauntless*."

Aitha's ship. Joss looked at the other boy, whose muscles bulged with each smooth pull on the oar. He ducked his head and said, "If I can pass."

She did not know enough about the sea trials to be able to judge his chances, but if the strength in his arms was anything to go by, he should do well. "Good luck."

"Thank you." Though he did not meet her gaze, the corners of his mouth curved into a shy smile.

Finally, the island grew closer, rising from the sea in a single hill as they drew near. They were within swimming distance of the shore when Parker leaned forwards and grabbed the oars.

"Stop for a moment." She jerked her head at the beach, and Joss looked over.

Another boat lay on the sand, pulled half out of the water. Several lamps lit the area around it, one of which was carried by a vaguely familiar man. Where had she seen him before?

"Ugh, Faran's here," the younger of their rowers said.

His friend Mal clenched his hands around his oar. "He'd better not be causing trouble again."

Distracted by their reactions, Joss started when Theo murmured, "Isn't that the man who bumped into you outside the Captain's Rest?"

"Hm? Oh." Of course. That was why she knew his face. "Yes. But what's he doing—"

Four more men emerged from the treeline, and her blood ran cold. The hunters. He must have been their informant—and he had brought them here.

"Can we land somewhere else?" she asked the boys.

The younger of the two shook his head. "The rest of the island's surrounded by rocks."

The hunters pushed their boat off the beach, splashing into the shallows until the water reached their thighs, and jumped aboard one by one. Then they rowed away from the island in a different direction from where Joss and the others floated, hidden in the dark.

She frowned. If the hunters planned to ambush them here, why were they leaving? Roving her gaze over the bulk of the forested island, she caught a faint orange glow at the base of the slope. Her mouth dried as realisation sank in.

"Quick," she told the boys. "Get us to shore."

The hunters had set fire to the island.

Chapter 20

Joss

As soon as the prow of the rowboat crunched onto the beach, Joss leaped over the side, Theo close on her heels. She turned to help pull the boat higher up the sand, but the younger boy said, “We’ll do it.”

Parker also waved her ahead, dropping to her knees on the dry ground and sucking in deep breaths.

Joss squeezed her shoulder and sprinted into the trees in the direction of the fire. A dirt path wove through the woods, and she picked up speed on the solid ground, Theo keeping pace at her shoulder.

When they emerged into a clearing, she staggered to a halt. A timber-framed building burned in the centre, its walls crackling as the flames engulfed them, clouds of smoke and heat billowing out around it.

She felt Theo’s presence at her side, but neither of them spoke. There were no words to say, nothing that would convey or ease the reality they faced. The house was already beyond saving. They could only pray it was not the one they were there to find.

Movement to the left brought Joss's head around, and she shielded her eyes from the intensity of the inferno as she searched for the source. What had at first appeared to be a pile of rocks or mound of earth shifted again, resolving into a person lying prone at the base of some steps leading up to the side of the building. An arm reached out, and Joss dashed towards him.

"Wait—"

Ignoring Theo's warning, she shielded her face with her arm and plunged into the dense smoke. The fire spat and hissed, shooting sparks at her like tiny flaming arrows. Heat stung her eyes and seared her lungs when she sucked in a breath.

She crouched beside the old man, suppressing a cough, and shouted, "Here. Let me help you."

Theo appeared at his other side, and between them, they dragged him farther away from the fire.

When they settled him against a tree trunk at the edge of the clearing, he moaned, and Joss asked, "Are you hurt?"

He lifted a shaking hand to the side of his head, turning it so that the light of the flames fell on a vicious gash in his scalp. Dark, sticky blood matted his white hair and trickled down his neck, soaking into his shirt like roses blooming against a stone wall.

Damn those mage hunters.

Theo let out a more explicit curse. He pulled a square kerchief from his pack, soaked it with water from his waterskin, and pressed it against the wound. The man hissed but did not flinch away.

“This might need a stitch or two,” Theo said, searching through his pack.

“Jus’ ban’age…” the man slurred. “’ve ha worse a’ sea.”

While Theo cleaned and dressed his cut, Joss watched the fire consume the house. A beam in the roof collapsed with a crash, and she clenched her fists at her sides. If only they had arrived sooner.

“Did the hunters do this?” she asked, despite already knowing the answer.

The man’s lip curled up in disgust. “Faran brought them. Tch. He should’ve been banished from the Isles years ago…” He trailed off as if lost in memories of whatever Faran had done to deserve punishment, then tutted again and looked up. “After he left, they forced me to bring them here and started ransacking the place.” He looked down at his hands. “I tried to stop them, but I’m not as strong as I used to be.”

Joss glanced at the top of his head, neatly bandaged in a strip of cloth, no blood in sight. Theo had done a good job. The man already sounded more clear-headed too.

“Anyway,” he said, recalling her attention to his story. “Faran came back again not long ago and said something to their leader about having ‘found them’. Creator only knows what they were after, but they stopped then, quick as lightning, and the leader ordered them all back to the boat. Only he must’ve changed his mind because he turned back, glared at the ancestor’s house, and told them to burn it just in case.” He looked up at the blaze and let out a long sight. “Been here since the mage wars, it has. When I tried to stop them, they knocked me out and… Well, you can see the result."

Joss slumped to the grass beside him. If the mage hunters had burned the house, it must have been the one they sought. She picked at the soft tufts of grass by her leg as any remaining hope turned to ash in her mouth. A wrinkled hand covered hers, and she turned to find the old man studying her.

"What brings you to Whistling Cove?" he asked.

She glanced at Theo, who gave her a slight nod, and explained—without revealing the stone's exact function—what they were looking for and how their research had led them there. "…but it's pointless now," she finished, "because there's nothing left to find."

"Hmm. Wait till the morning." The man patted her hand and winked, which caused him to wince. "You'll see."

The words 'see what' rose to her lips, but with Theo's help, the old man was already climbing to his feet. He clutched Theo's arm and said, "I think I'll need your help getting back to the training compound."

"Of course."

He looked between them. "There's plenty of room for you to spend the night with us."

"Thank you, but I'll stay here for a while," Joss said.

For a moment, Theo looked like he would argue against it, but he pressed his lips together and said nothing.

The old man gave her some directions that she only half listened to, and Theo said he would tell Parker what had happened. She lifted a hand in farewell but could not bring herself to reply to either of them.

They left together, the man leaning heavily on Theo, and she sat and watched the house slowly collapse in on itself piece by piece.

The next morning, Joss woke to light warming her face and something prickling her cheek. Grass. She must have fallen asleep in the clearing. Her eyes stung when she peeled them open, and the acrid stench of smoke lingered in her nose and throat.

Nothing remained of the house but a small section of wall in the far corner. The rest was a tangle of charred beams, chunks of plaster, and piles of rubble. Tendrils of smoke rose here and there. Ash coated everything, turning the entire clearing a dull grey.

She sat up, coughed, and looked for her waterskin. Drat. In her haste to reach the fire the previous evening, she had left it in the boat along with everything else.

Theo appeared at her shoulder, silently offering his, which she gladly accepted. He crouched beside her while she drank, the cool liquid washing away the aftertaste of the smoke, and behind him, she spotted his notebook lying beside the trunk of a nearby tree.

How long had he been sitting there before she woke?

Stoppering the waterskin, she stretched out the kinks from a night spent on the hard ground and said, "Thank you."

"You're welcome."

"Have you seen Parker this morning?"

"She's at the beach. Said something about standing guard in case the hunters come back."

Oh. That made sense. Still, with the mage's house in ruins, they were not likely to return.

Joss stood and wandered over to the rubble for a closer look, but Theo grabbed her arm and held her back.

"Let me make sure it's safe first."

She started to protest but remembered that he designed things and was good with structures. Closing her mouth, she nodded for him to go ahead.

He walked around the smouldering remains, his eyes narrowed and a look of intense concentration on his face. He stopped here and there to prod a section of plaster or upright beam with the toe of his boot but eventually returned to her side. "It's safe enough, but be careful."

"Yessir."

Joss did not know what she was looking for, or whether mere curiosity or something more drove her to search, but she picked up a stick and used it to poke through the debris. She had to cover her mouth against the smoke several times. Avoiding the area still giving off too much heat, she inspected the rest as carefully and thoroughly as possible.

After four or five piles with nothing to show for her efforts but a cracked lantern, the remnants of a fireplace, two cooking pots, and a blackened knife, she tossed the stick aside and kicked at a piece of rubble. It skittered into a slab of plaster and timber beam leaning on something in the far corner of the ruins.

She tested the beam's weight and, finding it impossible to budge, stepped back. Soot coated her hands, and for want of a better place, she wiped it on her trousers while she called, "Theo? Can you help me move this?"

He clambered over to her, and together, they heaved the collapsed wall out of the way. Beneath it, the rounded lid of a chest appeared intact. With a shared look, they cleared the rubble around it, and Joss sat back on her heels when the rest was fully exposed.

She brushed a thick layer of ash from the wood, only for a cloud of it to puff up into the air. Coughing and waving it away, she squinted at the chest and blew out a disbelieving breath. "It's untouched."

"Let's take it over there," Theo said, pointing to where she had slept.

"Mm."

They carried it between them to the side of the clearing and, after wiping it down with some grass, studied it anew.

"How did it survive when everything else is cinders?" Joss asked.

"I don't know."

He stroked the wooden panels as though the secret might reveal itself through his touch. His hand paused on the clasp, and he turned to her, his eyes alight with hope.

"Open it," she said.

Cautiously at first, he lifted the lid, and when nothing ominous happened, he opened it all the way until the top rested on the grass.

Inside was a collection of odds and ends—a seashell necklace, a woman's shawl, some letters, an embroidered waist pouch—no doubt filled with precious memories for those who stowed them but of no value to anyone else. They pulled them out, one after the other, stacking them neatly beside the chest.

Close to the bottom, beneath a collection of maps, Joss found an old leather-bound notebook. She turned it over, inspecting the front and back, but the plain cover revealed nothing of its origin.

Theo watched while she unwound the leather thong tied around it and opened it to the first page. The writing scrawled across the paper looked to Joss like a mixture of a toddler's scribbles and an animal's claw marks. Her shoulders sagged—it was written in the old tongue. She passed the book to him.

A moment later, he straightened. "Kit. I think you've found something."

"Really?" She leaned closer and studied the page again.

He pointed at the illegible words. "It was written by Yarin's apprentice, Tammas."

Her eyes flicked up to his. "Are you sure?"

He thumbed through a few pages, stopping at an annotated map and then some sort of list. "Yes. We did it. We found a solid lead."

Joss cheered and threw her arms around his neck, her heart bursting, every inch of her body buzzing. His hands slid around her back, pressing her to him, and before she knew what she was doing, she was kissing him.

Their breath mingled, the shared excitement of the find spurring them on. Tingles flooded her body as his lips moved against hers.

When she could no longer draw air, she broke away, panting—and reality washed back in like a wave of icy water. What was she doing?

She launched herself to her feet and pivoted on the heel of her boot, but Theo caught her arm.

He did not grip it firmly enough to stop her had she been determined to escape him, but it was enough to bring her to a halt.

"Don't run," he whispered from behind her. "Please."

Slowly, she turned and looked at him, her heart racing and her palms turning clammy. His eyes begged her to stay, and she swallowed hard.

"I like you, Kit." He stepped closer. "In fact, if I'm being honest, I think I'm falling for you."

Panic hit, and she blurted, "You'd be better suited to my sister. She loves to read, and—"

"I'm sure she's lovely, but I can guarantee I'd have no interest in her."

"How can you know that?"

He lifted her hand and pressed it against his chest, his eyes holding hers unwaveringly. "Because my heart pounds for you."

She could feel the truth of his statement beneath her fingers. A soft, steady beat that called her own heart to match its rhythm. What would happen if she let it?

She leaned into him. He was safe. Not like the men back in Tyrrath who only wanted to control her or use her to gain more power and influence in court. They would trap her in a gilded cage, but with Theo, she could be free.

Maybe… Something released deep inside her, and warmth spread through her body. Was this what love felt like?

"I—" Why could she not say anything? Her words would not form around the knot in her throat.

"Kit…"

And there it was. The wall between them. She needed to tell him who she really was, but so many things held her back.

She sucked in a breath. Not anymore. "There's something I—"

A twig snapped, and they both spun towards the sound, Theo dropping her arm like a burning ember.

At the edge of the clearing by the path, a middle-aged woman looked between them from one eye—the other was covered by a patch. Her left arm cut off below her shoulder, but she lifted her right hand in an apologetic shrug.

"Sorry to interrupt, but our midday meal's ready."

"We'll be right there," Theo replied.

Joss glanced at him. Had he met the woman the previous night? Her stomach rumbled, and she thought back to the last time she had eaten. Not since noon the previous day.

But what about the stone? She looked over her shoulder at the journal, and the woman said, “Bring the chest with you.”

Good, because Joss had questions. She glanced at Theo. So many questions.

Chapter 21

Joss

"I'm Rown Fordin, Water Summoner," the woman said as they walked down the path. "I train the youngsters with Master Garell now that I'm landed again." She lifted her stump and glanced down at it.

Joss adjusted her grip on the handle of the chest, which she and Theo carried between them, then asked, "Is that the man we met last night? Is he well?"

"He's resting. Whether he wants to or not."

"Then maybe you can help us," Theo said. "Why didn't this chest burn like the rest?"

Mistress Rown stopped walking and studied them, then looked at the chest with a reverence Joss had only seen in the friars.

"It's magically protected. Passed down through the generations since ancient times, so the story goes. Nothing can touch it, not fire, rain, or even an axe."

Not even an axe? Joss studied it anew but saw nothing remarkable about it, other than the fact that it had survived the fire without even being singed.

They set off once more, taking a second path that split off from the first, and walked along it in silence until they reached another clearing. Three timber-framed buildings made a U-shape around an open area in the middle, where Parker sat at a long table with a handful of children ranging from six or seven to about fourteen.

"We're back," Mistress Rown said.

Joss and Theo left the chest in the shade of the trees edging the clearing and headed for the table.

Parker looked up and raised one brow. "He certainly let you sleep long enough."

The memory of Theo's kiss danced in Joss's mind, and she ducked her head to hide the heat that sprang to her neck and face as she slid onto the end of the bench beside her friend. Parker glanced at Theo and chuckled.

Seemingly oblivious to their exchange, he took the place opposite, set the journal on the table, and filled Joss's cup and then his with water from a jug in the middle.

One of the younger children asked, "Mistress, are we going to practise summoning after lunch?"

The older woman grinned at the little boy from the head of the table. "Yes. I promised, didn't I?"

"Yay."

They ate quickly—a simple, delicious fish soup and piles of flatbread. Then the children cleared the table and gathered around Mistress Rown, who stood between two barrels at the side of the clearing. Theo opened the journal and continued reading, and Joss and Parker watched the summoner demonstrate moving water from one barrel to the other with her power. It flowed in a high arc that caught the sunlight like glass and fell without a single splash or drip.

After watching the children practice for a while, with varying degrees of success, Parker stood and said, “I’m going back to the beach.”

“What about me?” Joss asked.

“Something tells me you’d rather be with Theo.”

Joss gaped at her, and the guard’s lips twitched. She walked towards the path to the shore, and Joss scrambled after her.

“What makes you say that?” she asked when they were beyond the others’ hearing.

Parker stopped and gave her an assessing look. “You actually make a pretty good team. And I trust him to keep you safe and out of trouble.”

Joss’s face burned as hot as the fire the previous night.

Eyeing Theo, her friend leaned closer. “I walked over to the other clearing last night and saw him standing guard while you slept.”

He had? Joss stared at him, bent over the journal, his hair tousled where he had raked his fingers through it too many times. Were those smudges beneath his eyes? Why had she not noticed them earlier?

By the time she turned back to Parker, her friend was disappearing down the track to the beach.

Joss considered her guard's words. She and Theo did make a good team, and she liked him more than any other man she had met. Why had she not admitted it earlier? She needed to tell him, but with the journal to translate and so many others around, now was not the time.

She wandered over to the chest and knelt to inspect the contents more thoroughly. Picking up the shawl, she shook it out, and a small stone fell from its folds onto the grass by her knees. Red veins shimmered under the smooth, black surface, which had the outline of a half-risen sun etched onto it.

Joss's breath caught.

A dragon stone.

Could it be the one they were looking for? Her insides fluttered at the thought, and her breath whooshed out.

Carefully, she picked it up and called out, "Theo. I found a stone." She carried it over to him at the table and held it out on her palm for him to see. "What do you think?"

His eyes rounded. "I've never seen one before." He studied it, traced the etching with his finger. "I've seen this symbol somewhere, though."

"You have?"

"Yes, but I can't remember where." He shook his head after a few moments. "I don't think this is the stone we need. Look."

He flicked to a page towards the end of the journal and showed it to her. A sketch of a dragon stone covered most of the page with a few notes at the side. It appeared to be quite large, though size was difficult to judge in a drawing, and it was also less flat and more uneven in shape than the one she held.

"Oh."

Mistress Rown appeared at Joss's shoulder, making her jump. She took one look at the stone and said, "That's the master's key. Where did you find it?"

"In the shawl in the chest."

"The last time I saw it, I was just a trainee here." Her face softened, clearly lost in memories of her time on the island as a girl.

"It's a key, you say?" Theo asked.

She looked over at him. "Yes. I don't know what it opens, but it's been passed down through the guardians of Whistling Cove for generations. Master Garell would be able to tell you more."

Holding out her hand, palm up, she said to Joss," I'll take it back to him now."

So. Definitely not the stone they needed. Joss dropped it into the summoner's palm and returned to the chest with a hollow feeling in her gut.

Theo continued to read as the afternoon dragged on, making occasional notes on a piece of paper. After finding nothing else of interest in the chest, Joss practised her archery, aiming at a ryllfruit she placed on the lid.

When he finally looked up and called her over, she set her bow aside and plopped onto the bench opposite him.

"I think I've figured out what happened back then," he said. "It all started at the battle of Kasrkan—the one that destroyed Iskaria. Apparently, Yarin wasn't involved, but she felt sorry for the impact the mage war had had on the kingdom, so she decided to find a way to fix it. And that's why she created the dragon stone we're after."

"The same reason you want it." Joss met his eyes and smiled. "Then you should use it first, to honour her memory."

"Thank you." He reached across the table and squeezed her hand, then looked back at his notes. "Where was I… Ah, yes. When she and Tammas took the stone to the battleground, they were ambushed before they could undo the damage. Yarin was already weak from making the stone, and she sacrificed herself so he could escape with it, but he was badly injured too.

"To throw the enemy off his trail, he went north, instead of home, to an old friend of his called Vaan. They hid the stone together, and Tammas returned here."

Vaan. Another ancient mage, no doubt stripped from the Iskarian records long ago. Joss slumped, but Theo leaned forwards, his eyes twinkling and the corners of his mouth twitching.

He spread the journal between them as he had before, but this time a rough map covered the double page. Theo pointed at a mark halfway down the right-hand side. Above the original annotation, someone had written 'Vaan's retreat'.

"The name means nothing," Theo said, "But I know this place. It's just an old ruin now, out in the forbidden zone." He twisted his neck to view the page from her angle and pointed at another mark lower down on the left. "But if this is Kasrkan, the location matches."

The energy that had drained from Joss poured back through her like the water the children were dumping into the barrels. "So we know where it is?"

"I want to keep reading to see if it was moved later, but yes. I think we do."

"Yes!" Joss thumped both hands on the table and leaped to her feet.

One of the children cried out, and she spun around to see them all staring at her, the youngest doused with water.

Joss winced. She had not meant to disturb their practise. Lifting a hand in apology, she called, "Sorry."

When she turned back to Theo, his gaze swam with a combination of affection and amusement. A mock glare wiped the grin from his face, and he focused on the journal in front of him.

"I'll see if I can find anything about how to use it." He looked up at her again, and she gave him a firm nod.

But there was no way she would be able to sit still while she waited. Snatching up her bow, she headed for the treeline and called over her shoulder, "I'm going to hunt something for dinner to celebrate."

By the time she had shot three flightless birds, her thoughts had settled, the excitement a whisper corralled in the corner of her mind. She returned to the training compound, and found Theo waiting for her, a deep vee gouging the space between his eyebrows.

He stood when she emerged from the trees, clutching his notes in his fist, and walked towards her. A look of anguish crossed his face, and his jaw clenched.

"What's wrong?" She dumped the birds on the ground and reached out to him, but he stopped short of her touch.

"It's the stone." His voice cracked, and he cleared his throat, avoiding her gaze. "Tammas wrote at the start of the journal that they only had one chance to use the stone in Iskaria. I assumed that was because of the war, but I was wrong. The stone was the reason." He shifted his weight, crushing his notes in a white-knuckled grip. "It can only be used once."

Joss's mind balked, and the world around her muffled, as though she had plunged into the deepest forest pool and heard everything from underwater. "What do you mean?" she asked, though the twisting ache in her stomach said she already knew the answer.

A look of anguish crossed his face, but his eyes locked on hers. "If we find it, if its power isn't depleted… Only one of us can use the dragon stone."

Chapter 22

Theo

Theo's heart twisted in his chest as a myriad of emotions crossed Kit's face like a sandstorm in the desert. Each one blew over her features and left devastation in its wake. She turned away from him, her fists clenched, a tremor rocking her shoulders.

He lifted a hand towards her but dropped it to his side. What could he possibly say? The woman he loved was crumbling in front of him, and there was nothing he could do about it. Worse, he was the cause of her pain. From now on, they would have to work against each other.

Unless one of them gave up on the stone.

For a single heartbeat, he considered letting her take it, but there was more at stake than the two of them. An entire kingdom depended on him retrieving the dragon stone. The conflict between Iskaria and Garellion, the lives of thousands, mages and regular people alike. Everything could change if he could heal the land as Yarin had intended.

He could not choose her over the task he had set for himself, no matter how much it destroyed him.

She paced the grass, back and forth, back and forth, her lips caught between her teeth, her eyes shimmering with unshed tears. "It's not fair," she muttered at last. "We've come so far, and now… Why can't we both use it? None of the other stones I've heard of can only be used once."

Did she know she was speaking out loud? He stepped in front of her and waited until she focused on him. "It seems Yarin made it that way on purpose, with just enough energy to undo the catastrophe."

"What if we break my father's curse first? That can't take up too much power. And my sister can… There'll be lots left to heal Iskaria." Her voice wobbled like a lost child's, and Theo had to force himself not to embrace her.

"Why?" she asked. "Why make it like that?"

"I don't know. Maybe to prevent her enemies from using it afterwards?" The war was still going at that point. Maybe she had not wanted the Iskarian mages to be able to take down the shield protecting Aralan. Either way, only one of them could use it now. "Can't you—"

"Don't," she said. "I won't try to convince you to give up, so don't ask me to either. We both know what that stone means to each of us."

"But if we stay together…"

He read the rest of his sentence in her eyes. If they stayed together, they would have to decide which of them got to use it, or worse, fight for it, and that would break them both.

“Then, we’ll have to go our separate ways from here,” she said, her voice stiff, her eyes missing their usual spark. She turned to leave.

He caught her arm, unable to let her go, despite everything that now stood between them.

“At least stay till morning,” he said, desperation coating his voice. “Till I finish reading the journal. We found it together, after all.”

She looked blankly around the compound, and although she nodded, he knew he had already lost her.

Chapter 23

Joss

The next morning, before a hint of light touched the horizon, Joss and Parker slipped out of their borrowed room and headed for the path to the beach.

As they crossed the clearing, Joss spotted Theo asleep at the table, his cheek resting on the open journal, a quill dangling from his fingers. Had he been trying to find a way for them both to use the stone? An urge rose to brush the hair from his face, but she squashed it and kept walking.

When they emerged from the trees onto the sand, a low whistle came from their left. Mistress Rown waited for them beside a small boat at the water's edge.

"Get in," she said as soon as they joined her.

Parker took the bench at the bow, averting her eyes from the ocean. She stowed her pack at her feet but clutched her sword as if the weapon could somehow protect her from the effects of another boat ride. They would have to find her some more of the tonic when they reached the gathering.

Joss clambered past her to the stern, and the moment she was seated, Mistress Rown hopped over the side and stood in the middle.

"Do we need some of the teens to row for us?" Joss asked.

The older woman grunted. "I was Water Summoner on the *Voyager* for nearly two decades. I think I can handle a small rowboat."

She stretched out her hand, and the surf around them surged up the sand, turned it with a curl of her fingers, and it lifted the boat and carried it out into deeper water. Aside from the small jolt of the hull leaving solid ground, the whole process felt smooth and effortless.

Under her magical command, they turned and glided across the surface of the sea without a single tilt or sway. Other than the wind brushing their faces and hair, it felt as though they were not moving at all. Joss had never seen anything like it. And the only signs of the summoner's strain were the tightening of her jaw and beads of sweat forming along her hairline.

Parker, who had been gripping the bench on which she sat, eased her hold and even managed a smile.

Joss, though, could not force one to her lips. She looked back at the island slowly shrinking into the distance. Guilt pricked her for stealing away like a thief without bidding Theo farewell. Guilt, and something else she did not want to identify.

Hardening her heart against it, she faced forwards and asked the summoner, "Do you miss living on the sea?"

"Not anymore. It's been a long time since I removed my earrings and returned to the land. I'm used to it now. And I have the youngsters to train." She lifted her face to the breeze. "It's nice to sail like this once in a while, though."

She left them at the edge of the gathering, on a ship farther north than the one the boys had picked them up from two nights prior. After waving her off, they set out to find Noa.

Under normal circumstances, Joss would have sought out Aitha instead, but the *Dauntless* was trapped in the middle of the gathering near their father's ship, and Joss needed a quiet place to think. Her options hounded her thoughts without respite, circling her mind and biting at her calm.

They found the *Evening Star* on the northern periphery of the fleet. Noa was talking to some of the crew when they crossed the final gangplank and dropped onto the deck, so Joss crept up behind him and tapped his shoulder.

"What is it?" He spun around and started. "Joss? I mean, Kit. What're you doing here?"

The handful of crew behind him scattered.

She swallowed, praying the stinging in her eyes would not turn into tears. "Need to get away from the crowds for a while. And maybe leave early, if you're willing."

Noa glanced behind them. "Lord Sakanin not with you this time?"

"No."

When Joss's voice faltered, Parker filled in, "We parted ways."

"Ah." He dipped his head in a polite bow. "Does this mean I can go back to calling you Princess Jocelyn?" His grin evaporated when she did not respond. He looked at Parker, who made a cutting motion in Joss's periphery. More questions rose in his eyes, but he blinked, and they were gone.

"Oh." He clicked his fingers as if recalling something. "By the way, Aitha has a letter for you."

He whistled a sharp, two-tone note, and a few seconds later, one of the youngest on his crew scrambled up out of the hatch to the lower deck, still pulling on his shirt.

"Yes, Cap'n?"

"Run over to the *Dauntless* and fetch a letter from my sister for me. She'll know which one I mean."

"Aye, Cap'n."

The lad sprinted across the deck, over the rope bridge to the nearest ship, and was soon lost to sight.

Noa turned back to Joss. "Apparently, the messenger couldn't find you in Firstport—probably because of that false name you've been using—so they gave it to Aitha in case you went to visit her. I was going to send someone to find you this morning if you still didn't show up, but now you've saved them a trip." He jerked a thumb over his shoulder. "Jaks'll be right back with it."

Joss offered him a weak smile as thanks.

"Captain, the summoner's here," one of the older crew called.

A moment later, a slight young woman jumped from one of the rope walkways and landed on the other side of the deck. She swung a pack from her shoulder and looked around. A single set of silver rings glinted in her ears.

Noa lifted his arm to her and said to Joss, "I need to show our new summoner to her quarters. Just shout if you need anything."

He jogged across the deck, picked up the summoner's pack, and led her over to the upper crew's cabins.

"That's good." Joss pointed after them. "Dax said they wanted to find a decent summoner at the gathering. Now they can extend their trade routes down to the southern continent."

Parker leaned her elbows on the ship's rail beside Joss and looked out across the tranquil water. Neither of them spoke for a few minutes, but eventually, the guard straightened and asked quietly, "Where to next, Milady? Home or Iskaria?"

"I don't know."

It was true. The prospect of fighting Theo for the stone sickened her—and she might have to now, if she kept going—but she did not want to give up either, not when it could save her father's life.

But saving one man, even if he was her father and king of Tyrrath, seemed insignificant compared to an entire kingdom and thousands of lives. She considered returning home. After all, Theo was fulfilling the original purpose behind the stone's creation.

But there was no guarantee that healing the land now would stop the conflict or rid the Iskarians of their hatred of magic. And what happened to her father also impacted an entire kingdom.

Her mind warred with itself, round and round until she wanted to scream with frustration. She pushed off the railing and paced the deck. Whatever she decided, someone would be hurt.

The young sailor, Jaks, appeared beside them, holding out a sealed letter. When Joss took it, he dipped his head and scurried away, leaving her and Parker to read it alone.

It was addressed to *Jocelyn Dalbot, at the Mage Guildhall, Aralan* in her sister Maddie's handwriting. Sent some time ago, then. Joss tore it open and skimmed the contents, then froze and read it more thoroughly.

Dearest Joss,

I pray you're well and making good progress with finding Mistress Yarin's stone. We're all in good health here, and Papa is settled with no more breathing difficulties.

Unfortunately, I have difficult news I must share. I don't know how, but some of the lords on the council have discovered the truth of Papa's condition. They worry that he could deteriorate and... Well, they want our second cousin, Lord Tuftridge, to replace him as king.

You might not remember him—he's been living in Brunland for the last fifteen years—but he's a greedy, unscrupulous man. It would be a disaster for the kingdom if he took the throne.

Fortunately, they don't have the whole council on their side, so we have some time to find a solution. I'm trying to reason with them, but they're claiming that now I'm married to Luc, I'm the queen of Craeick before Princess of Tyrrath and have no right to interfere.

Good news from you would go a long way to easing their concerns. Please write if you've found anything we can use to stop them.

Stay safe.

Your loving sister, Maddie

Joss lowered the letter and looked out at the ocean that separated her from home. How could the lords be so… so…? Words failed her, and she fisted her hands, crumpling the letter in their grip.

"What is it?" Parker asked. "What's happened?"

"Some of the council want to replace Papa as king."

"What?" The guard gripped the handle of her sword as if she wanted to strike the traitors down right there.

"We need to break his curse." Joss would not let a corrupt distant relative and a group of rabid councillors destroy everything her father had built. "Noa?" she called.

He stuck his head out of his cabin door and answered, "Yes?"

"How soon can you get us to Iskaria?" she asked. "I'll pay whatever it takes."

If they hurried, they could get to the dragon stone first, and she would not have to see Theo. Or fight him for it.

An image of them facing off against each other, weapons drawn, flashed into her mind, and nausea stirred in her gut. No, there was no way she could stomach that. She would have to reach the stone before him.

Chapter 24

Joss

While Noa prepared the *Evening Star* to set sail, Joss scribbled a quick reply to her sister and, at Parker's prompting, a note for the innkeeper in Eindal asking him to return their horses to Tyrrath. She passed the missives to Dax, who arranged for someone to send them at the first opportunity.

That done, she spent the rest of the time until they sailed drawing as much as she could remember of Tammas's map and the description of the stone.

Noa procured some sleeping powder along with the provisions for their journey, and after taking a large dose, Parker lay down in the same cabin she and Joss had borrowed on their outward crossing. She fell into a deep slumber before Joss could even cover her with a blanket, which relieved some of Joss's worry. At least this way her friend would be sharp-minded when they arrived in Iskaria the following evening.

Joss returned to the deck and watched the crew dismantle the walkways binding them to the rest of the fleet, stow the gangplanks, and raise the anchor. They used the ship's eight-man rowboat to manoeuvre the *Evening Star* away from the gathering, cutting through the water slowly until they were clear of the other vessels. The moment they reached open water, some of the crew hoisted the rowboat aboard while the rest climbed the rigging to unfurl the sails and Dax pointed them towards the mainland.

The more distance they put between them and the Isles, the less Joss thought of Theo. Or so she tried to convince herself. She did not think of him when the summoner walked to the middle of the deck, planted her feet, and raised her hands to the sky. Nor when the wind answered her call, growing from a light breeze to a steady gust that filled the sails and pushed them to greater speeds.

He was not on her mind when she talked to a blushing young sailor, or when she ate a meal of stew and flatbread. And he especially did not haunt her memories when she stood at the railing and watched the sea throw wave after wave at the hull, each one tossing spray up the sides of the ship before falling away.

Only when the lookout spotted ominous clouds ahead did she briefly wonder if it was retribution for betraying him.

"Do we need to sail around it?" Noa asked the summoner.

She studied the approaching storm, tilting her head to one side and extending an arm towards it. "Doesn't feel too big. I think I can take us through."

"Batten everything down," he called to the crew, who responded with a collective, "Aye, Cap'n."

They leaped into action, and Noa walked over to Joss. "You might want to go inside, Your Highness."

She shuddered at the prospect of being cooped up in the cabin for who knew how long. Still, she could not cause more work for Noa or his crew. "I will when it gets rough. I promise."

"Good." He clasped her shoulder, gave her a firm nod, and went to oversee the sailors adjusting the sails.

They hit the edge of the storm within the hour. A patter of rain at first, then heavy sheets fell around them while the waves attempted to toss them this way and that. The summoner kept them on course, though, creating a little pocket of calm air around the ship as they headed into the heart of the tempest.

She held out for hours, far longer than Joss would have expected of one so slight of frame, but as she weakened, the storm only grew in strength. Much worse than it had seemed at first, it pushed them farther and farther out into the ocean.

Joss staggered back to her cabin and barred the door to prevent it flying open with each lurch of the ship. She checked on Parker, who slept peacefully in her bunk, held in place by netting one of the crew had fixed over her. Assured she was safe, Joss sat by the window, braced herself against the wall, and watched the battle between man and sea unfold.

The wind, once freed from the summoner's power, lashed at the crew's exposed skin. Rain hammered their heads and hid the world around them from view. Waves battered the ship until the wood creaked and groaned, and lightning and thunder rent the air in all directions.

Joss's stomach heaved as the ship climbed and fell over each crest, and she wished she had taken some of Parker's sleeping draught. She clutched the hidden pocket where she had tucked the rest away in case they needed it later.

Eventually, the storm blew itself out. The sky returned to uninterrupted blue, and the sea shimmered in the sunlight like a flat mirror.

The crew emerged from wherever they had hunkered down to ride out the tempest, and Joss joined them on the deck. While they inspected the ship for damage, swept water from the deck, and unfurled the sails again, the summoner reported to Noa, her entire body drooping with fatigue.

"Apologies, Captain," she said. "I underestimated the strength of the storm."

He studied her for a moment before speaking. "It would've caught us even if we'd tried to go around it. You did well."

She lifted her head a fraction. "I did?"

"Yes. You stayed calm and got us through the worst of it. That takes skill, and you'll improve even more with experience."

A weary smile spread across her face.

"But you look exhausted, so go rest."

"Aye, Captain. Thank you."

With visible effort, she turned and trudged towards the upper crew's cabins, and Dax took her place beside Noa. "No major damage to report, Captain," he said. "A couple of broken barrels that weren't lashed down properly—I've put the lads responsible on the bilge-pump and withheld their tot for a month—and Marus managed to put another dent in his skull. Nothing else that won't keep till we can put in for repairs. Shall we head for Iskaria?"

Noa stretched his neck to the left then right and looked up at the clear sky. "Aye."

Joss bit her lip and tried not to think about the delay. Surely Theo must have been caught in the storm too, if he had left the island yet. She still had a chance to reach the stone first.

Mid-afternoon the next day, the lookout called, "Land ho!"

Joss ran to the bow and searched the horizon. A strip of pale yellowy-orange hovered between the darker and lighter blues of sea and sky. It expanded as they sailed towards it, coalescing into a jagged, rocky coastline. No gentle slopes or forested hills rose from the shore, only sheer cliffs with barren headlands.

When they drew closer, she spotted the dark slash of a gorge in the cliff face. Closer still, and more details appeared—structures built into both sides of the gaping maw, a long jetty jutting out from the base of the cliff into the sea, several vessels tied alongside it.

“Welcome to Dekarat,” Noa said beside her, making her jump.

“Dekarat?”

He winced. “Sorry. We passed Akkia in the storm. This was the closest port we could get to.”

Joss tried to recall the maps of Iskaria she had studied with Maddie, but they were a blur of distant memory. She grimaced. Why had Tammas not included the edges of the kingdom in his drawing?

Noa anchored the *Evening Star* several lengths from the end of the jetty, explaining that many rocks hid in the shallow water beneath the cliffs, and sent her and Parker ashore on the rowing boat.

A group of Iskarian guards blocked the far end of the jetty. Four flanked the stairs up to the city while a fifth sat at a table to one side with another standing at his shoulder who had the aura of a leader.

Joss and Parker veered towards the table.

“Names?” the seated guard asked without looking up.

“Kit and Ven Parker,” Parker answered.

Joss spun her head to her friend. Ven? That was not a name she would have guessed. Parker elbowed her side, and she focused on the man’s next question.

“Purpose of your visit to Dekarat?”

Their purpose. What could she say? “Ah, just passing through.”

The record keeper frowned but noted it down.

He did not ask anything else, so they started to leave, but the heavyset guard behind him said, “Wait.” He pointed to their packs, and one of the others walked over and searched them. "Where did you say you'd come from?"

They had not, but Joss answered, "The Free Isles."

The guard who had been riffling through their packs handed the leader the drawing she had made of the map and the dragon stone, and his thick eyebrows lowered.

"What's this?" He looked from the paper to them, his lip curling in disgust. "Seems we've found ourselves a couple of mages."

Chapter 25

Joss

The guards refused to listen to Joss's pleas that they were not mages. They surrounded her and Parker, took their bow and sword, then bound their hands. The two of them were marched up the steps and into the city, the leader in front and a guard on each side of them.

Parker started to speak more than once, but Joss stopped her each time with either a shake of her head or a forbidding look. She could easily guess what the guard wanted to say, but revealing their real identities would be the end of their search for the stone.

Joss could not allow that to happen, not with the throne of Tyrrath as well as her father's life at stake. She drew in a deep breath, filling her lungs with air no longer tinged by salt but by dry heat and fine sand.

"I'm telling you, there's been a mistake," she said for the third time. "We're not mages. We were just curious about some of the stories we've heard on our travels."

"Be quiet," the leader snapped. "Unless you want to be gagged."

Joss clamped her lips together. That was the last thing she wanted. She growled low in her throat. First the storm, and now this. Did the creator himself not want her to find the dragon stone?

Or had Theo arrived before them and arranged for them to be captured so he could get to it first? The thought flitted through her mind, evaporating as quickly as it had formed. He would never do such a thing, even if they were working against each other now.

Besides, the chances of him also landing in Dekarat instead of Akkia were slim.

She straightened and lifted her chin. This was a misunderstanding, easily resolved. She would answer whatever questions the Iskarians had for them, skirting the truth where necessary, and then they could do what they had come here for.

"Say nothing," she murmured to Parker.

The look Parker gave her said she understood exactly what Joss meant, and that she was debating defying the order. She would never be so lax with Joss's safety under normal conditions, but if the Iskarians discovered Joss was a princess of Tyrrath, they would no doubt arrange a royal escort and plan every moment of her stay. She would never be able to search for the stone if that happened.

Fortunately, Parker dipped her head after a few moments, assuring Joss that her lips would remain sealed unless they faced imminent danger.

With her mind somewhat eased, Joss was finally able to take in the city around them. Or more accurately, above them. It climbed up both sides of the gorge, level after level of walkways clinging to the walls beside dwellings hewn into the rock.

She followed the lead guard deeper into the city, peering at the mixture of simple homes and shops with goods of all descriptions and colours on display. The spicy scents from one stall tickled her nose, and a waft of frying dough made her mouth water, until the stench of discarded offal from a butcher's brought bile to the back of her throat.

Few Iskarians braved the early-afternoon heat, to stroll the lower walkways or sit in the shade at the bottom of the gorge. Their conversations cut off when Joss and the others neared. She tried not to react. Two foreign women being marched through the city by armed guards must have been an unusual sight, after all.

The lead guard stopped at a seemingly random point along the path, and she looked up when a few eddies of sand floated down from above. A rope-and-pulley lift descended, creaking to a stop beside them, and he lifted a wooden safety bar from the opening at the front.

"Get on," he said, and the two guards behind her and Parker prodded them forwards.

They squeezed into the square cage, and as soon as the bar was back in place, one of the guards tugged on a cord in one corner of the wooden contraption. Moments later, they were hoisted into the air, the ropes creaking again as the cage clattered past level after level of walkways.

The view changed as they rose higher. The sand-dusted gorge floor was soon lost in the shadows far below while more ornate archways and large courtyards bathed in sunlight opened within the rock walls around them. With the light came more intense heat, and Joss licked her dry lips.

The lift jerked to a stop beside a bridge that connected the two sides of the city, and the lead guard lifted the bar at the rear for them to step out onto the walkway.

They marched a short distance along it before turning into a wide archway with several columns on each side, across a narrow open area, and through a door to what appeared to be the city's guardhouse. A row of pikes rested against one wall with two open chests of armour beside them. Several doors lined the rear wall behind a long table with a collection of recently used platters and cups strewn across it.

The lead guard led them to a door opposite the weapons and rapped three times.

"Well, well, well. Look who it is." A vaguely familiar man walked towards them from the back of the room, and Joss blinked. The hunters were here too?

"These are them?" the guard who had caught her and Parker asked. "I thought they matched the description you gave me."

That explained their capture then, and left Joss with more to worry about.

The hunter stopped in front of her and leaned forwards, his minty breath wafting over her face. "I'm going to make sure they strand you," he whispered, then straightened and glared at her.

He would not, but Joss refrained from responding. She still needed to get the stone.

The door beside them opened, and a middle-aged man with ink staining his fingers said, "I said to come inside."

"Sorry, sir."

The guard pushed Joss forwards, and she entered a room lined with bookshelves and a map of Egrea across one wall. Parker walked in behind her, and the lead guard followed them in and closed the door.

"Caught these mages sneaking in at the docks. They're the ones the hunters were tracking, and they had this on them." The lead guard stepped forwards and spread Joss's map on the desk while the other man rounded it and sat.

"Let me see…" The superior pulled it towards him, squinted down at it, and then up at Joss and Parker. He leaned back in his seat and laced his fingers together across his stomach. "Did you search them for weapons?"

A flush of red crept up the guard's neck. "Um, we took a sword and a bow along with their packs."

His superior sighed and eyed them both. "Hand over any other weapons you have on you."

Parker remained motionless, and Joss hesitated, her hand creeping protectively towards the dagger Maddie had gifted her.

"I can have my men search you if you'd prefer."

He motioned towards the guard, and Parker removed the knife from her hip and dropped it onto the desk with a dull clang. Next came one from her left boot, then her right, a thin blade from her left forearm, and two more from the back of her belt.

She paused, and the seated man raised his eyebrows but said nothing. Muttering under her breath, she withdrew a narrow sheath from her cleavage and tossed it onto the pile.

He turned to Joss, and she added her throwing knives and, more reluctantly, Maddie's gift. He narrowed his eyes and tapped his middle finger on the desk, so she held up her palms in surrender.

"That's all I have. I swear."

"Well then. Now we can begin. I'm Commander Daww, and I'm responsible for the security of Dekarat. And you are…?"

"Kit Parker, and my cousin, Ven Parker," Joss replied.

He nodded slowly. "And why have you come to Iskaria, Kit and Ven Parker?"

She glanced at Parker, who jutted her chin for Joss to explain, then fixed her attention on the commander. "We've been travelling across Egrea. This is my first time outside Tyrrath, so Park—I mean Ven. We usually call her Parker. She came with me. We visited friends on the Free Isles and were on our way to Akkia when we were caught in a storm and wound up here instead."

"I see." He pointed at the map and notes. "What's this, then?"

She licked her dry lips. "Our friend said that place was worth visiting, and my sister has always been curious about different legends, so when we heard about a mage who made dragon stones, I jotted it down to tell her when we get home."

Joss offered him an innocent smile. Those were not bad answers, all things considered. With luck, they would be able to brush the accusation off as a misunderstanding and be on their way.

"I see." The commander looked at the guard and said, "Take them to one of the holding cells while I decide what to do with them."

A holding cell? "Didn't you hear me? This is all a mistake. We're not—"

The guard clacked his boots together, said, "Yessir," and dragged her and Parker from the room by their upper arms. "Holding cell," he said to the guards waiting outside.

They took over from him and marched Joss and Parker across the room, through the middle door and down a long corridor that presumably led to the cells. Bronze mirrors perched at intervals along the walls, angled to catch the sunlight pouring through a shaft near the ceiling and cast it about the windowless interior.

They passed several rooms but kept going. The floor angled down, deeper into the cliff. Torches replaced the mirrors. The flames flickered in the wake of their passage, and a stale note sneaked into the air.

As they turned a corner, a row of barred doors appeared on the right. They stopped in front of the second and one of the guards swung the door wide.

"In you go, then," the other said.

Joss's feet froze in place. It was too dark inside, the walls too close, the ceiling too low. Her heart sped, her mouth dried, and she fisted the hem of her tunic in both hands.

The guard grabbed her by the arm and dragged her forwards, his grip digging painfully into her bicep, and she spun to Parker, frantic, the edges of her vision blurring.

She had been wrong. They would not be able to clear their names and continue their search for the stone. They should have revealed their identities from the start.

Chapter 26

Theo

Theo walked along the second to top level of Dekarat's southern wall towards his grandmother's home. He needed to read the letter that had been passed down through their family to know whether his suspicions were correct. Then he could travel overland to Vaan's retreat, find the stone, and restore his kingdom.

He refused to allow his mind to think of anything else.

Three or four houses away from his destination, the woman ahead of him ducked through an arch in a balustraded colonnade into a mid-sized terrace. As he drew level, she said, "You'll never believe what I just heard, Ama. The guard have caught a couple of mages."

His steps faltered, and he steadied himself on one of the smooth stone pillars. In his periphery, the woman stepped closer.

"Are you well?" she asked.

"Yes. My apologies." He straightened and attempted a smile. "If you don't mind me asking, what were you just saying?"

"Oh, the whole city's buzzing with the news. The guards down at the port caught two Tyrrathian women trying to enter the city with—"

"Two women from Tyrrath?"

Theo gripped the top of the balustrade.

"Y-yes." The poor woman looked like she wished she had never engaged with him. She pointed hesitantly towards the northern wall. "They've taken them to the prison."

He turned and ran, throwing a "Thank you" over his shoulder.

She called something behind him, but the blood pounding in his ears muffled whatever she was saying, and he did not stop to ask. In his haste, he almost missed the first bridge across the gorge but managed to catch hold of the anchor post as he skidded past it. He swung himself around and propelled himself across the wooden slats to the other side, looking for the nearest lift to the lower levels.

While part of him ached to see Kit, a voice in the back of his head warned, even as he ran towards her, that she had left for a reason and meeting again would only cause them both pain. But he could not leave her in the hands of the mage hunters. He knew too well what they did to those they suspected of using magic.

By the time he reached the guardhouse, his breath came in burning gasps, and his legs felt like water. He should have waited for the lift instead of taking the ramps, but it had taken too long to arrive.

"Where are… the women who were… just brought in?" he asked the first guard he found.

The stocky man looked him up and down with a half-sneer. "Why? Are you a friend of theirs?"

Another walked over, saying, "They'll probably be stranded in the morning, and good riddance."

Theo gritted his teeth. The man talked of stranding before there had even been a trial. That would change when Theo found the stone and proved magic was not evil. He swore it. Lifting his right arm, he pulled back his sleeve to reveal his tattoo.

The men's eyes widened, and for the first time in his life, Theo was grateful for his rank. Who cared if others tried to use him to get ahead or to meet his cousin if it meant he could save Kit?

"I-I'm sorry, Milord," the first one said, dropping a hasty bow. "What can I…?"

"The women. Take me to them."

"Right. Yes. Um, this way, Milord."

He led Theo along a corridor that became a tunnel, deeper and deeper into the rock of the canyon wall. The sounds of a scuffle drifted to them, the voices harsh and urgent, and Theo pushed past his guide.

He turned a final corner and spotted Parker fending off two guards ahead, Kit cowering beyond her. The terror in her expression cut him to the marrow. He lifted his hand and opened his mouth to call off the guards, but Parker pulled something from the neck of her tunic, silver flashing in the torchlight as she held it aloft.

"This is Princess Jocelyn of Tyrrath, and I have orders from King Lucas of Craeick to cut down anyone who touches her. His wolf seal is my proof."

Theo stopped cold.

He stared, unblinking as the guards froze. Parker tucked the token back inside her tunic and said something to Kit.

One of the guards prodded the other. They muttered to each other, heads bent together, and Theo ducked against the wall out of sight.

Had he heard that right? Kit was a princess?

A princess… How had he not seen it? He snorted. No wonder her relationship with Parker had seemed strange. She was Kit's personal guard, not her cousin. They had lied to him. Yes, he had lied to her too. But that did not lessen the sting.

She was a princess.

Which meant even more stood between them now than before. He dragged a hand down his face. Even if they had not been forced to work against each other for the stone, he would never be worthy of her. A princess needed someone with equal power, and he had forsworn what little he had a long time ago.

His chest constricted.

It was best to let her go.

He turned and strode back up the tunnel, the guard running to keep up.

"Find them lodgings in the best inn available, and give them free access to the city," Theo ordered. "Then get the best horses from my grandmother's stable and arrange a reliable escort to take them back to Tyrrath in the morning."

Half an hour later, Theo bowed before his grandmother in her private chamber, right hand over his heart with his clan tattoo visible. "Hello, Ama. I'm sorry it's been so long since my last visit."

"Theo, my sweet boy," she said, a warm smile wreathing her weathered face. "Come here and let me look at you."

He stepped forwards and dropped to his knees, picking up her hand and rubbing his thumb over her soft skin. She lifted her fingers to his face, felt his brows, his nose, his lips. "You're well?"

"As always."

She patted the lounger beside her. "Come sit and tell me all about your adventures."

"I will, Ama, but first, I have a favour to ask." He looked into her rheumy eyes. "Can you show me the letter? The one you said was passed down through the family that you let me read when I was a boy."

Her white brows gathered together. "Sands. Why do you want to see that old thing?"

"Please? Just let me see it?"

She squeezed his hand. "For you, my sweet boy, anything."

He helped her to her feet, and she shuffled over to the far wall, which was lined with bookcases.

"You know, it should have stayed with the main branch of the family, but they weren't interested in relics from the past, so when your father asked me to save it during a purge… Well, you know the rest." She ran her hands over the various wooden boxes on the lower shelves. "Ah, this is the one." She picked up a small, plain cube and held it out to him.

"Thank you, Ama."

Theo kissed her cheek and took it over to a table with several chairs tucked around it. After pulling one out for her, he sat and popped the box's lid. A single folded parchment sat inside, atop an assortment of jewellery.

Opening it as carefully as he could, he ignored the faded contents and studied the emblem stamped at the bottom. His breath hitched. A half-risen sun.

He drew the keystone Master Garell had given him from his pouch and compared the two, confirming what he already knew—they were the same.

"What's that?" his grandmother asked.

"It's called a keystone. A Free Isles summoner called Master Garell gave it to me—after I answered a million probing questions about my intentions." A distant smile stole over his lips at the memory. "Apparently, it's been handed down from guardian to successor since the mage who wrote this letter."

"Oh?" She leaned closer and gently stroked the stone's surface, the veins glowing brighter at her touch.

"Yes. He said it was originally kept here in Iskaria, but when no one responded to this"—he nudged the missive—"the friend who had been guarding it for

Tammas sent it back to the Free Isles. Or so Master Garell's master told him when he passed it on."

Which meant Theo was on the right path. He read the letter, pausing here and there to decipher a particularly faded word or phrase. The gist of it matched what Tammas had written in his journal, but at the end of the letter, beside the emblem of Yarin, was scrawled: *Iskaria's restoration lies beyond the sunrise*.

"Well? Did you find what you were looking for?" His grandmother prodded his arm, recalling him to her presence.

A grin spread across his face, and he cupped her cheeks in his hands. "Yes. And it's going to help me save the kingdom."

Chapter 27

Joss

Night still had a firm hold on the strip of sky above the gorge when Joss and Parker joined a young guard outside the inn. One of the trio who had taken them to the commander, he had apologised for their mistake several times since and ducked his head whenever Joss looked at him.

They took one of Dekarat's rope-and-pulley lifts down to the lowest level and crossed the gorge floor to a large stable, where several more men in guard uniforms waited while the grooms readied their horses.

Two of the guards stood to attention when Joss approached. They were both burly men in their late twenties with neatly trimmed beards, one with a scar through his left eyebrow. The third, older and more wiry, stepped forwards and offered a curt bow.

"Your Highness. I'm Captain Silutar, and I'll be responsible for escorting you back to Tyrrath." His sharp gaze roved their surroundings, and Joss immediately knew he would be the most difficult to handle.

"Good morning, Captain."

An elderly man appeared beside them and said in a soft voice, "If you'd come this way, Your Highness, I've got a fine gelding for you to ride."

Joss followed him to a healthy-looking bay whose coat gleamed red in the torchlight. "What's his name?"

"Vale, Your Highness."

She offered a slice of dried apple, and Vale gobbled it up and nuzzled her shoulder. "You'll do well, won't you, Vale?" she said, stroking his neck.

Stepping around to his side, she brushed her hand along his flank, then tied her pack and the wine she had prepared to the back of the saddle. She tested the bindings and, satisfied everything was secure, turned to the rest of the party.

Parker, wearing a long headscarf around her neck, stood beside a large dun to her right, asking a young groom about the wrappings around the horses' feet. Beyond her, their escort busied themselves with their own mounts, and a couple of supply horses waited at the other side of the yard.

Affecting a worried expression, Joss clasped her hands together and addressed the old groom, who appeared to be in charge of their departure. "Are you sure we have enough water? What if something goes wrong in the desert? Oh, I'd hate to be thirsty or run out altogether."

He glanced at the bulging waterskins tied to the supply animals. “Two skins each will get you to Jadhe, Your Highness.”

“Please.” She gripped his sleeve and forced her voice to waver. “I’ve never travelled through a desert before, and I’m so worried about the heat. Is there any way we could take more with us?”

Parker eyed Joss over her saddle but, thankfully, said nothing about her odd behaviour.

The groom covered her hand with his, gently patting. “There’s no need to worry, Your Highness, but if it’ll put you at ease, we can add more.”

He walked over to Captain Silutar and muttered something, then headed for the stable, calling for one of the younger grooms to load another horse with waterskins.

As soon as it was ready and tied to the others, the escort mounted, and the head groom rejoined Joss. He handed her a headscarf that matched the one Parker had now pulled up over her head and mouth. “This will help with the heat and sand.”

“Oh. Thank you.” She tucked it into her saddlebag but, at his deep frown, pulled it back out and wrapped it loosely around her neck and face a few times. Then she allowed him to boost her into the saddle and graced him with a watery smile before taking the reins he held up to her and following Parker out of the stable yard.

The burly pair took the lead, riding with the confident ease of seasoned guards. Joss and Parker came next, and behind them, the shy young guard led the line of supply horses beside the captain.

They followed a steep path up the northern side of the gorge, heading inland from the city, and emerged into the surrounding desert as the first pale fingers of dawn touched the eastern horizon.

There were only two words that adequately described Iskaria's interior, Joss decided after a few hours of riding across it—hot and desolate. The merciless sun only grew more diligent in its attempt to scorch the earth as it climbed towards its zenith. It baked the desert surface and stole the moisture from her mouth.

Even her eyes felt gritty, though that could have been the sand whipped up by every stray breeze. The fine grains had worked their way into places about her person they had no right being.

No wonder the Iskarians resented magic if this is what it had done to their kingdom. Joss could only imagine growing up in such bleak conditions. The only blessing was that she was outside instead of crammed into an airless, underground cell.

"Will we reach some shade soon?" she asked. "It's so hot I'm going to burn to a crisp before we get to the border."

Her fifth complaint of the morning was only half feigned. The journey might have been more bearable had she not whined and asked to stop every half hour, but the more she played the pampered princess, the lower her escort would drop their guard.

"Soon, Your Highness," Captain Silutar replied with a weary sigh. "Then we'll rest until the temperature cools enough to continue."

She exaggerated fanning herself. "I can't wait to get back to Tyrrath."

Eyes narrowed, Parker studied her. "Are we really going home?" she asked in an undertone.

Joss glanced at their escort, riding at a respectful distance in front and to their rear, before whispering back, "Not if I can help it."

"What about them?"

"Don't worry. I have a plan."

Parker groaned low in her throat and muttered, "Wonderful."

Chuckling, Joss returned her attention to the trail.

A few minutes later, a collection of blurry lumps appeared in the distant haze, coalescing as the group rode closer into a colossal statue half-buried in the sand. Part of one leg remained upright, and beside it, the toppled face stared up into the heavens, its features corroded beyond recognition by the desert. The torso lay sunken on its side behind them.

"What is that?" Parker asked.

"Leftover from the ancients," one of the guards ahead said. "It's a good spot to wait out the hottest part of the day."

Joss shifted in her saddle, and not just to dislodge more pesky grains. According to the map she had studied the previous evening, the statue was directly north of Vaan's retreat. The perfect place to make her move.

It took another twenty minutes to reach the broken statue, but despite the harsh conditions, their horses did not so much as sidestep before they dismounted. The Iskarian breed was certainly well-adapted to life in the desert.

Joss stroked Vale's nose and offered him another slice of dried apple.

"This way, Your Highness."

Captain Silutar led them around the head to a crude shelter formed from what appeared to be part of a hand resting on a couple of massive blocks. Whether it had been moved into position or had naturally fallen like that was hard to say, but the shade it provided from the blistering sun was a blessed relief.

Joss brushed as much sand as she could from her clothing and took a long drink from the waterskin the youngest guard handed to her. Her thirst slaked, she sat with her back resting against the cool stone and watched the guards go about various tasks as if they had done them a thousand times before, which they likely had.

None of them spoke while they worked. Whether they were too parched or exhausted by the morning's ride to converse or simply did not feel the need, she could not tell, but she savoured the peace the relative quiet brought.

One of the burly guards, the one without the scar, pulled an oiled cloth from the back of a supply horse and used it to line the space between a group of smaller rocks. Joss was about to ask what he was doing when the youngest poured water into it, creating a makeshift trough, and the horses dipped their heads to drink.

How clever. She mentally tucked the idea away for later use.

"Here. Take this." Parker held out a round of flatbread wrapped around some thick strips of meat and aromatic leaves with dark red sauce oozing from one end.

"Where'd you get it?"

Sinking down beside her, Parker jutted her chin at the guard with the eyebrow scar, who was slicing more meat off a bone at the other side of the stone hand.

They ate in companionable silence, and Joss got up for seconds. She considered a third helping but decided it would ruin the image she had adopted of a delicate lady too weak to possibly outsmart or escape her guards.

Instead, she wandered over to where the saddles had been left in the shadow of the statue's head, found Vale's, and retrieved the wine she had brought with her. She took it back to the guards, who were sitting in a circle on the cusp of the sheltered area, and held it up to them.

"Captain Silutar? I wanted to show my appreciation for your kindness in escorting us across the desert." She ducked her head. "And for putting up with me. Can I offer you some wine?"

She stepped closer to them, donning a wide-eyed, hopeful expression and pushing the wineskin towards the scarred-brow man. He took it awkwardly, then looked to his captain, who sighed, his brows furrowed, but nodded.

"Thank you, Your Highness," the burly guard said, the others chiming in behind him.

"Will you join us in a cup?" the captain asked.

"Oh, I couldn't possibly. It's my gift to you." She smiled as brightly as she could, turned, and headed for Parker, giving her friend a subtle shake of her head so she would not ask any questions.

The guards filled their cups with the wine and glugged it down, only the captain taking small sips. But even he accepted a refill, and the skin was soon empty.

Joss watched from the corner of her eye as first one, then the rest succumbed to sleep. Between the long ride, the draining heat, and the large meal, most people would probably opt for a nap, but the powder she had added to the drink ensured it.

When they were all lying flat on the sand with soft snores emanating from the non-scarred burly man, she crept over and peered down at each in turn. Not one of them so much as stirred at her movements. Good.

"What did you do to them?" Parker asked in a false whisper.

"Drugged them with the rest of the sleeping powder Noa gave you when we left the Free Isles."

Parker looked from Joss to the guards and back again. "You could have told me."

"I didn't want you to talk me out of it."

"Why am I not surprised?" Parker rolled her eyes. "How long will they be out?"

"Hopefully, until tomorrow morning."

Joss pulled out the map she had sketched the previous evening, spread it on top of a large rock, and turned it to match the angle of the sun's path. "We're here," she said, tapping the mark she had made between Dekarat and Jadhe. "And Vaan's retreat is directly south of us, here." She slid her finger down to the twin hills she had drawn according to Tammas's journal.

She looked up and scanned the horizon, then pointed to some distant dunes beyond the remains of the statue's feet. "So if we head in that direction, we should get there in a few hours."

"I'll fetch the horses," Parker said.

While she saddled their mounts, Joss loaded the lead supply horse with a day's worth of food and as much water as it could carry. If they could find the stone that evening and return the next morning, they would have plenty. And hopefully, their escort would not be too angry if they woke before then.

She was untying one of the other horses when Parker walked over and gripped her arm. "You're not setting them loose, are you?"

"Of course not. What kind of monster do you think I am?" Guilt ate at her, for she had considered it, though only for the briefest moment. But that would be cruel punishment for men who were only following orders and had treated them well.

She led the animal over to the water trough, tied it on a long line, and went back for the next. They would need to be able to drink while their riders slept. Parker filled the trough and fetched a bag of their feed from the pile of supplies at the back of the shelter.

By the time all the remaining horses were tied under the shade of the hand with easy access to both food and water, sweat prickled Joss's hairline. She took a long swig from her waterskin and wiped a handful of the precious liquid over her face and neck, feeling instant relief in the somewhat cooler temperature.

They were about to set out when Parker pulled her cloak from her pack, walked to the rear of the supply horse, and tied the cloak around its rump.

"What're you doing?" Joss asked, already in her saddle.

"Making sure we don't leave any tracks." Parker walked the horse a short distance, and the cloak's hem brushed the sand behind it, obscuring its hoofprints. She mounted, tied the lead rope to her saddle, and met Joss's gaze. "Just in case."

Chapter 28

Joss

The soft sand of the dunes slowed their progress, so the trip took longer than Joss had expected. Eventually, they spotted some hills in the distance that appeared to match Tammas's drawing. By the time they arrived, night had fallen, and moonlight painted the desert in silvery hues.

They dismounted and led the horses through the valley to the abandoned manor house, where they found a place to hide them among the ruins. While Parker made a water trough like the guards had earlier, Joss hung a couple of feed bags on the crumbling wall beside the animals and stretched her back.

Parker eyed her. "Should we wait till the morning to search for the stone?"

"No. I want to look now. I'll never be able to sleep otherwise."

"All right." The guard stoppered the waterskin she held and pushed to her feet. "Where first?"

Joss turned a slow circle. The hill to the east of the house rose in a gentle slope up to a rounded summit, but the one to the west climbed to an angular peak that resembled the outline on the map. Steeper and littered with outcroppings and crevices, it could easily hide several caves.

"There," she said, pointing to the pale traces of a path wending between the darker rocks.

They gathered a few supplies, lit two torches, and set out, inspecting every nook and cranny along the way. It took them some time to find the cave, and by the time Parker called Joss over to the entrance, night had long since cloaked the interior in pitch black.

The old fear placed a restraining hand on Joss's limbs. Closing her eyes, she told herself, "You can do this."

"Do you want me to go in and look around first?" Parker asked.

"No. We'll both go."

Joss lofted her torch higher, pressed her lips together, and walked inside.

The cave was the size of her bedchamber in Redcairn Palace and empty, save for a couple of faded and pocked murals and a bank of sand against one wall. The dark maw of a tunnel entrance gaped at the rear, and she thrust her torch inside for a closer look.

Cobwebs melted in the heat, more shimmering farther back.

"The ancient mages didn't destroy *all* life in the area, then." Parker's voice came from behind Joss, making her jump.

She spun on her friend and said, "Do you have to sneak up on me like that?"

Parker's brow rose. "It's not like you to be scared of a few spiders."

"I'm not scared." Joss nearly added 'of them', but that would have invited questions she had no desire to answer. "Come on."

She plunged into the tunnel, giving herself no time to fear the close confines. The webs petered out after a few lengths, and the floor sloped down as it snaked deeper into the rock. Another two caves opened off the passage, both as empty as the first, before it ended in a third.

Writing covered most of the left-hand wall, which was smoother than those of the other caves. Unfortunately, Joss could not decipher what any of it said, for it was written in the old tongue, some possibly in Dracestian, the language of the ancient mages.

If only Theo had been there, he could—

No. She cut the thought off before it led to dangerous places. Olivia. If only *her sister Olivia* had been there, she could have translated it for them. But they were alone.

Joss followed the wall around to the rear, where Parker studied a collection of symbols etched into the sandstone. A half sunrise caught her eye, and she traced it with a finger. The dragon stone she had found in Whistling Cove bore the same one.

But there was no dragon stone in the cave.

Aside from the wall carvings, there were no signs of life at all. Maybe it had been raided long ago and the stone already used. Though if that were the case, there surely would have been some evidence of it. She must have missed something.

She worked her way back up the passage and through the other caves, inspecting them more closely. The first might have once been used for storage. Several rows of evenly spaced holes in the wall suggested ancient shelving once hung there. The second provided no more clues than it had the first time she stepped inside.

Back in the outer cave, she studied the murals in detail. One depicted a verdant land with woods, meadows, rivers, and waterfalls. What remained of the sprawling city in the centre looked like the original had been carved from white stone and etched with patterns like fine lace. Could it have been Iskaria before the mage wars turned it into a desert?

The other mural was of a man and a dragon. The man leaned against the dragon's flank, wearing a rusty-coloured robe that could once have been either red or brown and the medallion of a fifth-rank mage. The dragon curled around him—protectively?—with its pale blue wing stretched above his head.

No hint of a stone in either painting.

Desolation swept through Joss, as complete as that which she found around her. After all they had been through—coming so far, fending off bandits and hunters, escaping capture, losing Theo—they had nothing to show for it, not even a new lead.

She slumped to the sand-strewn cave floor, too exhausted to walk back outside and down the hill to the ruins.

"I'll stand guard," Parker murmured.

"Sit with me," Joss blurted. "Please."

After only a brief hesitation, Parker planted her torch in the banked sand and lowered herself to the floor beside Joss.

They sat in silence as the air cooled and the torches burned low. Joss played with the sand by her thigh, doodling nonsense in it with her finger, then gathering it into a pile and flattening it again. A few stars twinkled in the night sky outside the cave entrance, oblivious to the sombre mood within.

"What will we do next, Milady?" Parker asked.

Joss flicked at the sand where she had absently written Theo's name. "I don't know anymore. Go home?"

"Whatever you decide." Parker rested her elbows on her knees and turned her face to Joss. "I go where you go."

The sincerity in her expression brought a lump to Joss's throat, and she ducked her head. "And you say we're not friends," she quipped.

She could feel the other woman roll her eyes without even looking. It freed a chuckle that grew into an uncontrollable bout of laughter.

Though there was nothing remotely funny about their situation and though Parker watched her as one would a madwoman, Joss laughed until her sides ached and tears dampened her cheeks. All the pain and frustration, the unbearable anger and utter futility of the previous months dissipated with the release, and when she finally got the giggles under control, it felt like a burden had lifted from her soul.

She wiped her eyes, sat straighter, and took one last steadying breath. “We’ll set out for home first thing in the morning. I need to help Maddie fend off those treacherous councillors and our despicable cousin.”

Yes. Focusing on the next thing was far better than thinking about the past. Lying back against the sandy slope, she clasped her hands across her middle and looked up at the roof of the cave, where shadows and torchlight danced together across the knobbled surface.

With the tension drained from her by the laughter and decision to leave, her eyelids drooped, her breathing evened, and she fell into the most peaceful sleep she had had in a long time.

Chapter 29

Theo

Theo tied his horse to a wizened skeleton of a tree outside the ruins of Vaan's manor in the early hours of the morning. Travelling at night had paid off. He had managed to avoid both the hunters camped outside Dekarat and the furnace-like heat of the desert during daylight hours.

Lighting a torch, he studied his surroundings, then headed for the steeper of the two hills flanking the ancient retreat. A faint path cut back and forth up the slope, allowing him to scour the scattered rocks and boulders for a cave entrance.

He found it two-thirds of the way up, hidden behind a large outcrop, and with a final glance around to ensure he was alone, slipped through the opening.

The first thing he noted inside was a large rock-painting of a mage and a dragon. The second was Kit asleep on a mound of sand beneath it. What was she doing here? He had watched from the opposite side of the gorge as she had left Dekarat for Jadhe the previous morning with an armed escort.

His feet took him a few steps towards her before he stopped himself.

She was not Kit. She was Princess Jocelyn.

An urge remained to move her to a more comfortable position or at least cover her with his cloak—the desert could get cold at night—but he could not. If he woke her, he would not be able to take the stone.

Part of him hated himself for what he did next. Turning his back on her and her guard, he crept past them on silent feet.

He found nothing of note in the rest of the cave, so he followed the tunnel to the next, and then the next, searching each as quickly as possible. The tunnel curved around and down to a final chamber that was covered in writing.

His heart kicked in his chest, and he hurried to the nearest wall, moving his torch across it to read the contents. When he found Yarin's half-risen sun emblem, he almost passed by it in his haste, doubling back to stare at it for a moment before inspecting the surrounding area more thoroughly.

Other than a circular indentation beneath the emblem, the rock was smooth and solid, cool to the touch. He took the keystone from his pouch and recited the riddle from his grandmother's letter again. "Iskaria's restoration lies beyond the sunrise."

Looking from the stone to the engraving and back again, he nodded to himself and clamped his teeth together. This had to be what it meant.

Slowly, he lifted the stone and held it over the emblem on the wall. It matched the indentation perfectly. He placed it in the hollow and pressed the emblem on the front, certain that nothing would happen.

What else could he try?

Red light spilled between his fingers, and he snatched his hand away. Then the rock around the keystone rippled and disappeared, exposing a small but deep alcove.

Cautiously, Theo leaned forwards and peered inside.

He patted the air where the cave wall had been only a moment earlier, then searched the edges of the alcove for some sort of mechanism. Nothing. A sound halfway between a laugh and a huff passed his lips. It would not be called magic if there were. He held the torch closer to the alcove and inspected the interior.

At the back, a large black stone sat on a raised base. Theo wiped the damp palm of his free hand down his trousers and slowly reached in to pick it up.

He did not know what he had expected, but thankfully, nothing sinister happened. No trapdoor opened up beneath his feet, no bolt of lightning struck him down. The dragon stone felt like any other, though when he pulled it out into the light, red veins swirled and glowed under the surface.

Kneeling, he set his torch on the cave floor, pulled the cloth from his neck, and wrapped the stone in it. The bundle was too precious to risk it falling from his pack, so he squeezed it into his waist pouch, stretching the fabric to near bursting.

Satisfied that it was secure, he picked up the torch and made his way back up the tunnel. The stone bounced against his hip with each step, so he dragged the pouch around his belt to the front.

His hand returned to it every few lengths, and he forced himself to relax. The stone was real. It was in his possession. And as soon as he could get it to Kasrkan, the magic that had destroyed Iskaria would be undone.

He turned the last bend into the outer cave and came to an abrupt halt.

Standing between him and the entrance, her hair awry and eyes blazing, Kit raised her bow and aimed an arrow directly at his chest.

Chapter 30
Joss

Joss stood in the middle of the cave, bow and arrow in hand, and listened for another bird call from outside. Parker had left to patrol the perimeter some time earlier and had yet to return, so Joss would have to deal with whomever had made the noise alone.

When the light on the cave walls flickered and shifted, her heart skipped a beat—their torches were both leaned against the entrance, blackened and dead. She spun towards the tunnel, and it felt like time stopped altogether.

Theo stood in the opening, a burning brand held high. Their eyes met, and his widened before sliding away, his hand going to his waist.

She tracked the movement and stared at the bulging pouch he failed to completely cover. "You found the dragon stone."

"Yes."

She swallowed, the taste bitter. "How?"

"The stone you found on the island." His gaze found hers for a split second. "It was the key to the alcove where Tammas hid it."

Her entire body sagged, the bow she held lowering. Had he known that all along? "You lied to me?"

"No. I found out after you left… Princess Jocelyn."

She winced. He knew who she was. "I didn't mean to hide that. It's just—"

"It was for your protection. Yes?" He glanced around the cave, presumably looking for Parker.

Joss nodded, mentally begging her friend to return quickly.

"I understand," he murmured.

She studied his earnest expression. He did?

Quieter, as if to himself, he added, "And it makes things easier."

Easier. To betray her? Now that she was a princess of another kingdom, it was easy for him to put Iskaria first, to ignore what he had made her feel? She raised her bow again, aiming at the centre of his chest.

"I never meant to hurt you." She had meant it to be an implied accusation. But she had stressed *never meant* instead of *I* and *you*, and it sounded to her ears more like a confession.

"And I don't want to hurt you either." He shot her a pained look that pierced her gut and twisted her insides into a knot. "I'm sorry, y sikani."

Not as sorry as he would be. She pulled the bowstring taut and steadied her breathing. "Give me the stone."

"I can't."

A tear rolled down her face.

"Theo…"

"You know I can't."

She kept her arrow trained on his heart as he skirted the wall towards the cave's entrance, but her fingers refused to release the string. "Don't," she warned. "Don't make me."

"I'm sorry," he repeated, and ducked outside.

Something metallic flashed beyond the opening.

She released the arrow and sprinted after it in time to see a black-clad hunter drop to the ground.

Farther down the trail, Theo glanced over his shoulder, and she met his eyes. He grimaced, turned, and ran.

Had he thought the arrow was meant for him?

She might have lost him, lost the stone, but she would not let the hunters kill him.

Notching another arrow, she searched the hillside below the cave for more threats.

A couple of bolts pinged against the rocks to her right as Parker dashed towards her from farther up the slope. Joss flinched but returned fire, hitting a second hunter in the shoulder.

Parker dived into the cave, pressed her back against the wall at the other side of the entrance from Joss, and peeked outside. "Thanks for the cover."

"Where've you been?"

"Scouting around the hill. I was on my way back when I saw them sneaking up on you. I dealt with two of them before I came inside."

“Did they follow us here?” Joss fired again, but her target lunged behind a large boulder and the arrow clattered harmlessly across the scree beside him.

“I think they’re a different group.” Parker threw a blade at the man Joss had injured, taking him down for good. “Probably stationed somewhere nearby and saw our light.”

Joss reached for another arrow but found only empty air. And her throwing knives were still in her pack, tied to her horse at the base of the hill. Cursing, she set her bow aside and pulled Maddie’s knife from its sheath.

When she spotted a hunter moving between the rocks just outside, she hesitated for only a second before throwing the precious gift. A direct hit. But it left her exposed.

Parker slammed into her as a bolt streaked past them. They thudded into the rock wall together, the air knocked from Joss’s lungs. Fire sliced across her upper arm, and she looked down to find blood blooming on her sleeve.

“Bind that, quickly,” Parker ordered, springing back up and drawing a knife from each boot.

She threw first one, then the other while Joss tore a strip from her cloak and tied it around her injured arm. Though it was only a flesh wound, the pain was enough to stop her from rejoining the fight. Not that she had any weapons left to use anyway, unless she could find the bolt that had cut her.

Before she could move, one way or the other, it was over. Parker looked around the hillside, then stood and stepped through the entrance. The knife she held disappeared into her clothing, and she signalled the all clear.

They watched the hunters scramble down the rocky slope, the tiny figures racing across the valley to their horses. Despite telling herself not to, Joss searched for Theo and spotted him in the distance, riding away from the ruins.

"Was that Theo I saw running away earlier?" Parker asked.

Joss worked her jaw and gritted, "Yes."

Her tone must have said what she could not voice—that he had the dragon stone—for Parker's eyes flicked to hers. The guard fisted her hands and looked outside then back at Joss's wound.

Joss put a hand on her friend's arm.

"There's no point. He's long gone, and…" And what? The explanation stuck in her throat. He had to save his kingdom, just as she meant to save hers.

But she had failed. Her father would die, and she would return to the prison of court life with no hope but to marry someone like Lord Ealley. And she would never see Theo again or know what happened to him if the mage hunters found him.

Her eyes burned, but she refused to let the tears fall. "Let's just go home."

Chapter 31

Theo

Forced to travel during the heat of the day to evade the hunters following his trail, Theo's vision wavered by the time he reached Kasrkan, despite having wrapped a head covering over his face. He gulped the last of his water and tossed the empty skin aside. If the dragon stone did not work, he truly would pay with his life.

He dismounted and left his horse at the edge of the sacred site with a couple of nuri fruits to ease his thirst. The stallion would not wander, whether tied or not. All of Theo's grandmother's horses had been trained to voice commands since they were foals.

Checking his waist pouch one last time, Theo strode past the petrified remains of a few ancient trees and on to the giant monolith that marked the source of Iskaria's magic-induced desolation.

It rose from the desert like an uneven thumb, the sandstone ridged and lumpy. According to the legends, it had forced its way up through the earth in response to the magical explosion and had stood on the spot ever since, unyielding to time or the desert's wrath.

If Theo was going to use the dragon stone to undo that catastrophe, the monolith was the best place to do so.

He tugged the stone from his pouch and carefully unwrapped it, then walked the monolith's circumference. The dragon stone did not seem to react to any particular position, the veins glowing dimly but steadily while he completed the circuit.

"All right, then." He faced the setting sun. "Here's as good a place as anywhere."

Hefting the stone in one hand, he filled his lungs and blew out through his mouth. There were no instructions for using the stone, but Master Garell had offered a few suggestions, and they were worth a try.

Theo gripped the stone tighter and said, "Undo the magic that was cast here."

He waited, breath held, but nothing happened.

A horse whinnied in the distance—the hunters were here. He did not have long.

Closing his eyes, he pictured what he wanted in his mind—Iskaria, healed, covered in green forests, lush grass, lazy rivers—focusing on that sole thought.

He cracked his eyelids open, and again, nothing appeared to have changed. But when he looked down, the stone glowed brighter. Crimson washed the surrounding rocks and sand, growing in intensity until he was forced to squeeze his eyes shut once more.

Blinding light flashed behind his lids, and rock rumbled as the ground shifted under his feet. The monolith slowly sank into the desert.

He dropped the dragon stone and staggered backwards, bringing up an arm to shield his face from flurries of displaced sand.

Grass sprouted around the stone, spreading out from the spot in a wide circle. A tree shot up in place of the monolith, and others formed nearby as the grass reclaimed more and more land.

His heart raced.

A gentle breeze stirred the air, caressing his face and bringing with it a different scent. No longer clogged with sand and foul magic, it carried fresh, earthy notes and the fragrance of long-forgotten plants.

A short distance away, chunks of stone thrust up through the sand, knitting together into an intricately carved fountain. The moment it was complete, water erupted from the top, cascading down the sides into a large bowl at the base.

Theo's mouth fell slack and his eyes widened. Water. In the middle of the desert. He dropped to his knees and watched in awe, the backs of his eyes prickling.

He had done it. He had restored Iskaria to life.

Farther out, buildings rose in a large square, the marble facades shining in the sun's fading rays. A city was reforming around him? It made sense, he supposed, if it had also been destroyed in the original explosion.

Someone cried out, and he spotted a figure lifted up into the air on a rooftop. Two more black-cloaked men rounded the corner of the nearest building on unsteady feet, ducking away from an emerging wall on their other side.

Theo scooted back against the tree, rested his forearms on his knees, and waited for them. There was no need to run now. The hunters could do with him what they would.

The men approached warily, their eyes darting around them, their weapons trained on him.

"What have you done?" the closest one demanded.

"He's doomed us all, that's what. That stone is destroying Iskaria."

"No." Theo gestured at the plants around them, though it was clear from the hunters' expressions that they were blind to the evidence. "It's restoring it."

"Lies! He's using magic to bewitch us."

To Theo's right, the ground ripped apart. Rocks flew through the air.

"If this is happening everywhere, it'll kill us all," the first hunter shouted.

"Stop it," the other demanded. "Now!"

Theo stood to face them. "I can't."

Another rumble shook the ground beneath them. The mage hunters both widened their stances, fear leaping into their eyes.

As soon as the tremor passed, the first man gestured at Theo and said, "Get him."

They closed in.

Theo pulled back his sleeve to reveal his clan tattoo. When he held his arm up for each of them to see, they hesitated, glancing between themselves. Good. At least they would not kill him straight away with the evidence of his powerful relations on full display.

"He's..."

"Is that real?" A short man with a hooked nose joined them as two more hunters emerged from behind the fountain.

"Of course it is," Theo replied. "To fake a tattoo is to court death."

"What do we do now?" the same man asked the one who had previously ordered the attack.

"Tie him up. We'll take him back to Jadhe to be tried as a mage. After what he's just done, not even the crown prince would defend him."

He allowed them to bind his hands, wincing slightly as the rope tugged at his skin, but a soft smile curved his lips as he took a deep breath of grass-scented air. He would have liked to have seen Princess Jocelyn one last time, but she probably did not feel the same.

Would the princess have fewer regrets if she could see this? He exhaled. Maybe not. But he could not have done anything differently.

Despite losing her, despite whatever judgement loomed in his future, peace washed through him.

He had done it. Life blossomed in Iskaria for the first time since the mage wars. He had fulfilled his vow and saved his kingdom.

Chapter 32

Joss

As the tension of fighting the hunters and losing the stone to Theo wore off and her heartbeat returned to its normal rhythm, Joss's mind and body seemed to shut down. She ate and slept at Parker's promptings, vaguely aware of rejoining their escort and Parker calming the furious but groggy captain. Of days passing as they travelled on to Jadhe and then north to cross the river into Tyrrath. But she could not formulate a single thought or muster any emotion.

By the time they arrived at a small town an hour north of the border, Parker's expression had set in a permanent frown. "We've reached Swallowdale, Milady."

Joss could only blink in response.

"Still not talking," the guard muttered. "I wish I knew what you were thinking."

Nothing. That was the problem.

Her thoughts led in so many different directions that her mind could not choose between them and had, instead, stranded her in this eerie blankness. And she had not the will to find her way out of it.

"Lavender!" a young voice called as they rode into the outskirts along a wide lane.

A girl of around five or six ran towards them, her arms swinging wildly as she pumped her little legs. Blonde hair flew loose around a square face and snub nose that were an exact match for Parker's.

"Lavender, you're home."

A flicker of interest flared in Joss's mind, and she lifted her head in time to see Parker wince. "Lavender?"

Parker spun to her, eyes wide, then grimaced. "Great. Now you pay attention."

"Your name's Lavender?" Joss's voice grated after days of not being used, and she cleared the gravel from her throat.

"Now you know why I go by Parker. Or Ven if I have no other choice." The guard handed her a waterskin, dismounted, and swept the little girl up in her arms. "Ahh, Daisy. You've grown so big."

"Lavender and Daisy," Joss mused.

Parker looked up at her over her sister's shoulder. "My mother loved flowers."

Joss merely nodded. She could not even summon the enthusiasm to tease her friend over the unfortunate name.

The little girl straightened and eyed Parker. "How long are you staying? Did you bring me a treat?" Before Parker could respond, she twisted around and studied Joss. "Is this your friend? She's very pretty, but she looks sad. Do you want a berry?"

She opened her hand, revealing a pulpy mess of yellow caeldon berries, and her face fell. "Oh. They're all smushed. But I can get you another one. Violet and me picked—"

"*I*," Parker interjected. "Violet and I."

"We picked a lot this morning."

Daisy wriggled out of Parker's grip and waved to someone farther along the lane.

Joss followed the direction of Daisy's gaze to another blonde girl who watched them with one hand shielding her eyes from the afternoon sun. Violet—another flower name. A thin shawl wrapped her shoulders, and a small basket sat by her feet, presumably filled with berries.

"Let's go then." Parker gathered her horse's reins and patted Daisy's shoulder, at which the little girl set off running back to her other sister. Parker turned to Joss. "I hope you don't mind, Milady, but I thought we could rest here for a few days. Just until you get your strength back."

As far as Joss was concerned, they could stay wherever the guard wanted. The longer she delayed having to face her family and admit her failure, the better. She dismounted and trudged towards the cottage where Parker's sister waited. "As you will."

Parker's family home was one of the larger on the lane, boasting a slate roof instead of thatch. A small wooden porch shielded the main entrance from the elements, and to one side, a fenced garden burst with flowers, the scent both inviting and soothing.

When they reached the front door, Parker turned to Joss and held up both hands. "Please. Wait here a moment?" She glanced around, chewing her lip. "There's a bench in the garden if you want to rest for a while.

"Violet, see to the horses, please." She handed the quiet young girl her reins and crouched in front of the youngest. "And Daisy, can you wash the berries in the stream?"

Daisy nodded vigorously, and the sisters dispersed, Parker casting an apologetic look at Joss before ducking inside.

Joss found the gate to the garden and wandered aimlessly around the flowery border and neat rows of vegetables. Bees hummed as they visited the various blooms, and a hen flapped out of her path, flinging up loose gravel and a couple of downy feathers. Otherwise, she was alone for the first time in what felt like forever.

When she sank onto the wooden bench tucked against the side of the cottage beneath a shuttered window, she heard voices filtering out from within.

"...a princess here. It's not appropriate," a male voice said.

"I didn't know what else to do," Parker replied. "I'm worried about her. She's not been herself for days—barely eating or sleeping and not saying a word—and if we keep going to Faerstolmere, I'm afraid she might collapse on the road."

The man blew out a long sigh. "We'll need to clean the house before you bring her in, and I don't know where she'll sleep..."

"She can have our room," a cheerful female voice said. "Iris can sleep in with the others, and I'll take the lounger."

"Thanks, Bee. I'll write to the palace tonight to let them know where…"

A young pig trotted over and snuffled around Joss's feet, distracting her from the rest of their conversation. Evidently finding nothing of interest, it twitched its tail and started digging up the nearest vegetables.

"How did you get out again?" Daisy ran from the rear of the house and shoved the runaway pig away from the plants.

It kept evading her and returning to its rooting, so Joss hauled herself from the bench to help. Between them, they herded it back to the pen where its siblings rested with their mother in the shade of an oak tree beyond the rear fence.

Daisy latched the gate and turned to Joss, her head cocked to one side. "What's your name?"

"Joss."

The little girl scrunched her lips as if deciding whether she approved or not. After a few moments, she asked, "Will you play with me? Everyone else is busy."

The thought of running around with a five-year-old made Joss want to disappear into a hole, but she could not bear to disappoint one more person. Mustering what energy she had left, she pasted a smile on her face and said, "Very well."

"Oh good. Can I do your hair?"

Before Joss could object that it was too gritty from travel, Daisy grabbed her hand and led her back to the bench. Then the little girl ran over to the flowerbed, plucked some lily of the valley, and returned to Joss's side. She sat down, carefully arranging the stems on the wooden seat beside her, and Joss dutifully turned her back to give the girl access to her plait.

To her surprise, Daisy produced a comb and proceeded to gently brush her tangled locks. One or two stubborn knots made her wince, but aside from that, the repetitive action soothed her more than she had expected, and she closed her eyes, enjoying the feel of the tines against her scalp.

"How many siblings do you have?" she asked, curiosity nipping at the edges of her mind.

"Six." Daisy set the comb aside and sectioned Joss's hair into three. "Lavender, Buttercup, Iris, Primrose, Lily, Violet, and me."

Seven girls. All named after flowers. "Your mother must love children."

"That's what Iris always tells me. Mama died when I was a baby so I never met her."

Oh. "I'm sorry."

"It's all right. I've got Papa and all my sisters here with me. Except Lavender because she lives in the capital. But she comes to visit twice a year, and she always brings me a treat." Her hands stilled. "Except this time."

The urge rose to apologise again, but before Joss could say anything, Daisy perked up and continued. "But she brought you instead, so that makes up for it. I like doing hair, but my sisters don't let me do theirs very often."

She tied Joss's braid and fell silent while she threaded the lily of the valleys into it, the sweet scent enveloping them.

"All done." She laid it over Joss's shoulder for her to see—a neat plait with clusters of tiny flowers tucked between the strands here and there.

Beaming, she ducked under Joss's elbow and nestled into her side, throwing a little arm across her middle. Her body was soft and warm, like Olivia's when she was still young enough to offer hugs freely. Failure's hold on Joss's mind loosened a little, and awareness of the world beyond her pain slid in with the memory.

Big blue eyes looked up into Joss's, brimming with hope, and Daisy asked, "Will you tell me a story?"

The request drew a rusty chuckle. How could she refuse? "Very well. Once upon a time, there was a…"

Daisy snuggled closer and shut her eyes. After a moment, Joss did the same, wrapping the young girl in her arms and seeing the story play out behind her closed lids as she spoke it to life.

The blacksmith was just about to trick the dark mage when real footsteps crunched on gravel, and Joss opened her eyes to find Parker in front of them. The guard glanced from her sister to Joss's hair, her lips twitching, but she said only, "Milady. If you'd like to come inside, we've prepared a meal for you."

The morning of their second full day in Swallowdale, Parker had Joss outside at dawn, practising her archery by the stream. She loosed her third arrow with the same result as the first two. It barely clung to the edge of the board the guard had propped against a large boulder several lengths away.

"You'll never hit your mark if you don't concentrate," Parker said.

Joss handed her the bow and sank onto a nearby stump. "I know."

Her friend's brow creased. "Never mind. We'll try again later."

A whoop from across the stream yanked Parker's attention around.

"Iskaria's turned green!"

Joss looked up.

A young boy with smudges of flour on his face and tunic ran along the far bank, shouting the news at the top of his lungs. He stopped opposite them and pointed in the direction he had come from. "Old Matthews just heard it from the tinker. The whole kingdom's come to life again."

He set off again, leaving Joss and Parker staring after him.

"The stone worked, then," Parker said softly.

Memories of Theo intruded. Joss's insides churned, love, guilt, and regret mixing together. "He must be happy."

Whatever response Parker might have made was cut off by the roar of a dragon. Joss searched the sky and soon found the beast's inky form in the clear blue to the north. It spread its wings, banked in a wide circle overhead, then dropped down behind the buildings closer to the middle of the town.

Less than five minutes later, a man who could only be the rider jogged along the lane, blond hair escaping his cap and fur-lined cloak askew. He slowed outside their cottage and walked over to the fence, lifting an arm to them.

"Is this the Parkers'? I'm looking for Princess Jocelyn."

Joss stood and walked over to him on leaden feet. "I'm here."

The man bowed and held out a folded paper sealed with Luc's wolf crest. "Your Highness. I've been sent by King Lucas to take you to Faerstolmere. How soon can you be ready to leave?"

After a moment of stunned silence, Joss tore open the missive and read the contents. Sure enough, Luc had asked the Brunnish messenger to collect them before returning home as it would be faster than her travelling by horse.

She turned to Parker and held up the paper. "Looks like we're going home by dragon."

Parker let out a strangled groan, to which the rider responded with an amused snort.

"What's your name?" Joss asked him.

He straightened to attention. "Henric, Your Highness."

"Very well, Henric. If we meet you on the green in an hour, will that be soon enough?"

"Yes, Your Highness." With a brief bow, he turned and jogged back the way he had come.

Joss and Parker headed inside. They packed their things and said goodbye to Parker's family.

When Joss turned to Daisy, the little girl hugged her as tightly as she had Parker and gave her a handful of berries. Then she hid her face in Buttercup's skirts, her shoulders hitching.

Parker waved for Joss to follow her outside while Buttercup stroked their youngest sister's hair and offered a silent farewell above her head. From the way the two eldest sisters' eyes met, it seemed this was a scene that had played out many times before.

Hefting her pack onto her shoulder, Joss cast one last look at Parker's family, a lump forming in her throat, and stepped through the front doorway.

"She'll be fine in a few hours," Parker said as they set off down the lane.

"Mm."

Joss followed behind, her mind turning from Daisy to her own sisters. What would she not give for one of Maddie's hugs, little though she deserved one? Squashing the painful thought, she focused instead on the houses, then shops they passed on their way through the town.

A small crowd had gathered by the time they arrived at the green. They clustered in doorways and around the edges of the grassy expanse, giving the dragon that sat in the middle a wide berth.

It appeared much larger up close, its body not black but the dark green of a pine forest. Wings the length of a carriage lay folded along its sides, and its head was the size of two large travel chests. It would have been a fearsome creature were it not for the fact that it had long since been dehorned, its claws filed to short stumps, and it was nuzzling its rider's waist pouch like an overlarge pup seeking treats.

"We're here," Joss called.

Henric looked up, then patted the beast's snout and walked over to where they stood beside a modest meeting hall. After bowing again, he said, "Your Highness, Lightfoot's still young, so I'll need to introduce you before you mount. May I take your packs first?"

He held out his hand, so Joss slid her bundle from her shoulder and gave it to him. Parker added hers with a distrustful glance at the dragon, and Henric made quick work of tying them to its back.

When he finished, he beckoned Joss forwards. "Just walk normally, Your Highness, but don't make any sudden movements. Good. Now hold out your arm, palm up, and let him take a sniff."

She did, and the dragon lowered its—his—massive head. Nostrils the size of apples twitched as they sucked in a rush of air that lifted her hand towards them slightly. Then he blew out a warm blast and made a low chuffing sound.

"That's it, Lightfoot. A friend." Henric patted the dragon's neck and led Joss around to his side, where the rider smoothed his palm down his mount's flank. "Now, give him a little stroke, like this."

When she reached out to touch it, the pebbled hide felt smoother than she had expected and cool beneath her hand. She stroked the dragon as she would her horse, cooing softly.

A rumble vibrated through Lightfoot's chest, and his tail swished back and forth over the grass.

"You can get on him now, Your Highness," Henric said. He showed her how to climb up Lightfoot's foreleg to the saddle and turned to Parker. "Your turn."

Parker hesitated but followed his instruction to walk forwards and let Lightfoot smell her. She squeezed her eyes shut and clamped her lips between her teeth while he snuffled her hand, and the sight would have made Joss laugh aloud had she not been trying to avoid spooking the beast.

That ritual complete, Henric guided Parker to Lightfoot's side, where she also stroked his hide.

"Are you sure this thing's safe?" she asked, pointing at the saddle, which was similar to that of a horse, though larger by at least twice.

Henric laughed. "Positive. The straps have been magically preserved, so they don't rot or wear away. This set's been used by three generations of my family and is still good as new."

Parker harrumphed but clambered into place behind Joss.

As soon as she was strapped in, Henric asked the townsfolk watching them to stand back and swung up onto Lightfoot's neck. The dragon unfurled his wings, which were a lighter green than his body, the pale shade of nightferns, and at Henric's whistle, they launched into the air.

Joss's stomach lurched at the sudden upwards movement, and she let out a little cry, clinging tighter to the handles on the dragon's harness. The roiling soon settled, and flight proved smoother than the initial jolt had indicated. She peered past the dragon's girth at the ground dropping away beneath them.

Each beat of Lightfoot's wings lifted them higher, until the town appeared no larger than a child's set of blocks and they headed north. Wind whipped Joss's cheeks and snatched away every word she uttered.

Unable to talk, she studied the passing landscape instead. A patchwork of pig farms and crops lay far below them with occasional villages and woods sprinkled across the land. The Arrol River meandered through it all, leading to Faerstolmere and home.

All excitement she felt at flying through the air on the back of a dragon disappeared with the reminder. When she arrived, she would have to tell her sisters she had failed. Her stomach roiled, and she swallowed hard. Would they blame her?

Like it or not, she would soon find out.

Chapter 33

Theo

Three days after Theo arrived in Jadhe and was thrown into the city's prison, a key scraped in the lock of his cell. He rolled over on the thin cot as a pair of guards entered.

"Time to find out your punishment," the older said.

Theo sat up and held out his hands to be chained, but the guard waved them down.

"No need for restraints."

Neither of them met Theo's gaze when he looked between them. The younger, barely old enough for the position, stepped aside and gestured for Theo to precede them out of the cell.

Unsure whether to laugh or sigh, Theo did as he was bid. He straightened his tunic and scraped a hand through his hair, then descended the stairs to the ground floor.

All the guards had treated him with deference since his cousin, Rai, had visited on his second evening there. Half an hour after they had said farewell, Theo was moved to an above-ground cell and served a meal of meat and vegetables instead of the thin gruel of the previous day. Such was the power of his extended family, despite the severity of his so-called crime.

Four mage hunters waited for them in the main entrance, shooting daggered looks his way. They fell in behind Theo and the guards flanking him, and the group walked out of the prison together. Would their reaction to him change when the expanding vegetation released by the dragon stone reached Jadhe, as Rai had said it soon would?

They emerged briefly into bright sunlight before turning onto a covered walkway that led to the Hall of Justice, where he would be judged for his crime. He started to turn left, towards the rear of the building, but the guards nudged him in the opposite direction. They ascended a flight of stone steps and stopped under a wide portico in front of the entrance to the high court. His case was being treated as significant, then.

While they waited to be admitted, Theo's roaming gaze caught on a puff of white above the opposite roofline. He stilled and watched it drift out into the clear blue sky. A cloud. The first over Iskaria since the mage wars? The tension in his body eased, and a smile crept across his face. Whatever he faced in the courtroom, it would be worth it.

"Summon the accused," someone intoned from within, and Theo's guards prodded him forwards.

At least a hundred pairs of eyes fell on him as he stepped through the oversized double doors into the grand chamber. Whispers rippled across the crowd filling the outer section. The weight of their scrutiny pressed down on him, and he struggled to keep his head up.

"I hope they strand him," an angry voice cried over the general murmurings. "It's his fault the kingdom's been thrown into chaos."

The bailiff banged his ceremonial staff on the ground, and the whispers cut off.

Theo walked down the central aisle, his footsteps on the marble floor echoing in the sudden stillness. The combined heat and scent of so many bodies grew stronger towards the front of the room, and he wiped his palms down his trousers.

His feet dragged up the steps to the accused's platform, but he forced himself to stand tall and look straight ahead. He had done the right thing, the best thing. For Iskaria and for those caught up in the conflict with Garellion.

The king himself sat in judgement, wearing his full regalia of a white, floor-length tunic with a wide sash belt and an open outer robe. Gold embroidery glittered at the neckline, waist, cuffs, and hem, and Iskaria's golden crown nestled in his salt-threaded hair.

Sharp brown eyes pinned Theo from a swarthy, bearded face, and Theo swallowed.

A double row of stern-faced judges sat to the right of the king's throne, and to the left, a collection of high-ranking officials and courtiers. Theo found Rai among them, and his cousin gave him a silent nod of support. Beside Rai sat his great-aunt, Theo's grandmother. Her face was a serene mask that could have been carved of the same stone as the chamber itself.

"Atheon Taskil," the king said, and Theo whipped his gaze back to the ruler in time to see him loft a brow at the document in front of him. "You are accused of using magic within our realm. How do you plead?"

"Guilty."

The word reverberated around the hushed chamber, flying back to him with lethal precision.

"But with mitigating circumstances," he added.

Lord Kavanasat, a high-ranking member of the Order, stepped forwards. He wore a red mourning band over the mage hunters' distinctive all-black clothing—for the man Theo had buried in Garellion?

"Your Majesty," the lord's deep voice rang out. "There can be no mitigating circumstances in this case. Magic is dangerous. We've seen this over and over throughout history, and now—"

The king held up a hand and studied Theo. "Mitigating circumstances, you say. Then tell me, what sand demon possessed you to use magic inside Iskaria's borders?"

"I did it to restore life to our kingdom."

"Restore life?" Lord Kavanasat released a disgusted snort. "Who knows what that stone's magic will do to us in the long run." He spun towards the king. "Your Majesty, we don't know if the plants spreading across Iskaria are safe. What if they're poisonous? Or attack us under the command of Garelli mages? The stone could well be a magical weapon planted by our enemies to finish what they started during the wars and wipe us out."

"That's ridiculous," Theo said. "The historical accounts I've read tell a different story, and the results so far prove it."

The lord's lip curled into a sneer. "Do they? We received warning of this, which is why we followed you and tried to stop you from using it. I can only regret that we failed."

Theo fisted his hands at his sides. "Magic is not evil, and we can't keep blaming mages for the state of our kingdom, not now the dragon stone's undone the damage. We need to stop persecuting them and end the conflict with Garellion before it turns to war."

"Well, the war effort has certainly stopped," one of the courtiers seated to the king's left said. "Between the desert disappearing and the number of commoners abandoning their posts to watch it happen, we're all too busy dealing with the chaos to prepare for any wider mage threat."

Lord Kavanasat pointed at the courtier who had spoken. "This is precisely the point. Magic is dangerous. It always comes with a heavy price. Using that stone has left us vulnerable to further attacks, even if it wasn't a weapon itself."

Lifting his eyes to the vaulted ceiling, Theo blew out a breath. How many times would he have to repeat himself before they listened to him? "The land being healed is good for Iskaria, and not all magic is a weapon. It's just a tool, like any other."

Lord Kavanasat opened his mouth to respond, but the king slapped his hand down onto the arm of his throne. The lord stepped back.

"I've heard enough." The king pinned his focus on Theo before continuing. "Magic may not be inherently evil, but it is outlawed here."

Theo bowed his head. "I acknowledge that and admit my guilt."

"Then I have no choice." The king looked to both sides of the court, and Theo could have sworn his grandmother gave a subtle nod. "I sentence you to stranding. You will be taken to the farthest point from the city and left with no food or water to return to us if you are able. May the desert purge you of your sins."

Stranding.

Iskaria's worst punishment, and in its most extreme form.

The air left his lungs in a whoosh, and he swallowed hard.

Then, an image of the cloud outside popped into his head, followed by the memory of the fountain at Kasrkan. Weight lifted, and a smile tugged at his lips. That was right—things were different now. A desert no longer held the kingdom in its fiery grip. Which meant that stranding was no longer the death sentence it once was.

Theo's head jerked up, and he met the king's steady gaze, reading knowledge and even approval in the warm brown orbs.

The room erupted as the spectators arrived at the same conclusion as Theo. Some called for a harsher penalty while others heartily agreed with the king's decision. One or two brave souls shouted their support, saying Theo should be released instead.

Lord Kavanasat's face clouded with thunder that was impotent in front of the king. His subordinates, the four who had accompanied Theo to the court, glared at Theo as one from behind their leader. If looks could inflict damage, he would have been flayed several times over.

Theo turned his back on them and sought out his grandmother and Rai among the officials whispering to each other and glancing his way. Though the elderly woman did not look directly at him, he felt the warmth of the smile playing at the corners of her lips.

Rai, on the other hand, openly laughed and sent Theo a knowing wink.

At a gesture from the king, the bailiff banged his staff on the floor again. The hard clang brought everyone's attention to the throne.

The king leaned forwards. "Does anyone wish to challenge my ruling?"

Silence followed his question.

He pinned the mage hunter with a glare, and the man bowed his head.

"Then the sentence may be carried out immediately."

Theo offered his liege a formal bow. "As you command, Sire."

He descended the steps from the accused's platform, his heart far lighter than when he had climbed them, and forced his legs to walk rather than run—or dance—back down the aisle to the main entrance where his guards waited. The sooner he got on with the stranding, the sooner he could return.

And then he would set out again, this time for Tyrrath.

Chapter 34
Joss

By the time Redcairn Palace came into view, Joss's thighs and rear ached, and cold nibbled at her fingers and nose, despite the sun shining in the clear sky above.

"Hold on for the landing," Henric shouted over his shoulder.

He brought them down in a wide spiral until they hovered just above the small field outside the palace wall, each beat of Lightfoot's wings kicking up clouds of dust and grass fragments. He landed with a soft thud that jolted Joss in her saddle and immediately tucked his wings into his sides and lowered his body to the ground.

Joss waved the dust away from her face as Henric leaped from the dragon's neck. He flashed her and Parker a grin before leaving them to dismount on their own and jogging along Lightfoot's flank to their packs.

The knots on the saddle straps yielded after a couple of attempts, and Joss swung herself around and slid down the beast's foreleg to the flattened grass. She stretched the kinks from her back and looked about the empty field while Parker dismounted, then turned to Henric.

He handed them their belongings and, with a hasty bow and brief word of farewell, climbed back up to his place.

"Thank you," Joss called out, but Lightfoot unfolded his wings, forcing her to retreat several paces.

He launched into the sky, throwing more dust and debris up around them, and banked towards Brunland, soon becoming no more than a black dot on the pale blue canvas to the west.

Joss turned to the palace. The red stone wall towered over her as if the building itself knew she had failed and sought to keep her out. A small door flew open at its base, and her sister Maddie strode out.

Her husband, Luc, hovered at her side, and Joss rolled her eyes at his vigilance. Until she studied her sister more closely. How had Maddie gained so much weight?

Joss stilled, her eyes fixed on her sister's abdomen. No. She could not be… But there was no denying the huge bulge beneath her gown. Joss ran forwards but stopped before hugging her sister. Would doing so unsettle the baby?

Maddie hugged her anyway, and after a moment, Joss returned her embrace. The familiar scent of sandalwood soothed her raw nerves and settled some of the churning in her gut.

"How—? When are you due?" she asked as they drew apart.

"Not until mid-autumn."

Joss tried to do the calculations in her head but failed. "I've only been gone a couple of months. Why didn't you tell me you were with child?"

Maddie tilted her head to the side. "It didn't seem the right time with everyone so worried about Papa. Besides, it was still early, then"—a gentle smile softened her words—"and you were too busy trying to leave."

The reminder hit Joss like an arrow to her heart. She lowered her head and swallowed back the sting of tears. "I'm sorry. I… I'm so sorry."

Despite her efforts, moisture blurred her vision and fell from her lashes, splashing onto the front of her tunic.

Maddie lifted her chin, and the salty droplets dribbled down her cheeks. "Come here," her sister said and pulled Joss into another hug.

Joss resisted at first, but Maddie squeezed her tighter, and she melted into her sister's arms.

"You've got nothing to be sorry about," Maddie whispered into her hair. "I only care that you're safe."

Before Joss could formulate a reply, something nudged her middle, and she started. Jerking back, she stared down at her sister's bulging abdomen. "Was that the baby?"

"Yes." Maddie stroked a hand over the spot. "She's saying hello to her aunt."

"Or he," Luc added, recalling Joss to his presence. He tucked his arm under Maddie's elbow. "We should go back inside."

Maddie gave him an exasperated look but allowed him to steer her towards the palace. Joss trailed after them with Parker a few steps behind.

When they had all passed through the door into the grounds, the guard on duty locked it behind them, and Parker drew to a halt. "I'll leave you here, Your Highness," she said to Joss. "I need to report to Captain Kaar."

Joss threw her arms around her, caught up in a whirl of emotion for the stoic guard-turned-friend, and after a moment, Parker patted her shoulder.

"I'm glad you're yourself again," she said, "but please, no hugging in public."

"Whatever you say, Lavender."

The guard groaned and stepped away, muttering something that sounded like "I should've known it was a mistake taking you home." She excused herself with a bow and jogged across the courtyard in the direction of the guard barracks.

Joss caught up with Luc and Maddie and followed them inside and up to their private solar, where Maddie had ordered tea and griddle cakes. Joss's favourite.

"Will you go and see Papa?" Maddie asked.

"Maybe later," Joss replied, not quite ready to face her father yet.

Luc plumped her sister's cushions and made her prop her feet up on the lounger before sitting beside her and turning to Joss. He jerked his chin at the griddle cakes. "You not having any?"

She shook her head.

"Eat something, Joss," her sister said, nudging the plate closer.

Joss glanced down at it. "I'm not really hungry."

Luc lifted a brow but, thankfully, said nothing.

Maddie, however, tried again. "For me?"

"Fine." Joss picked one up and nibbled the edge. The warm, buttery pastry crumbled in her mouth. She had forgotten how good they tasted. She took another small bite, then popped the whole thing in her mouth and reached for a second.

Maddie smiled.

When she had finished half the plate, washing the treats down with gulps of tea, Luc said, "All right, Joss. Tell us everything."

After wiping the crumbs from her fingers, she took a deep breath and did. She paced as she talked, her words racing to keep up with her feet, or the other way around. Every detail of her early journey poured out of her easily, but when she came to what happened with Theo after they reached the mage island, she glanced at Luc and faltered.

He sighed and pushed to his feet. "I need to speak to Tristan and Parker, so I'll leave you alone." He walked to the door but turned back as he opened it and smirked. "Maddie'll tell me what you said later anyway."

Joss threw a bolster at him, but he ducked out into the hallway, pulling the door closed behind him. The cushion thudded against it and slid harmlessly to the floor. She waited until his footsteps faded, then, fingers twisting together and cheeks flushing, she told her sister the rest.

"…and now I feel so stupid. Did he use me to get to the stone?" She knew that was not true even as she said it, but her thoughts tangled whenever they turned to him. She dropped onto the lounger beside Maddie. "And on top of everything else, I lost the dagger you gave me."

Tears streamed down her face again. All the tension of the previous weeks—the disappointment, grief, anger and self-recrimination—welled to the surface as if each droplet carried a piece of her pain with it. She jumped up and resumed pacing, needing the movement to counter the emotions overwhelming her.

"You mustn't blame yourself for giving up the stone," Maddie said, squeezing her arm. "It was the right thing to do, all things considered."

"But we're right back where we started. No, worse. Papa could deteriorate at any moment, and half the council are after his crown."

"That has nothing to do with the stone. Or you." Maddie grimaced. "It's me they're targeting."

Joss sat down and swiped at her face with the back of her hand. "What's the latest?"

Maddie lay a hand over her stomach. "News of the baby held them back for a while, but they've been stirring again recently, and Lord Elland's concerned."

It was no wonder the baby had made them pause. If it was a boy, he would be Tyrrath's next king, and anyone who opposed his mother would worry for their positions. But if Maddie's most senior advisor was concerned, the situation must be more serious than she had indicated.

"How bad is it?"

"There's more support for Lord Tuftridge than we thought. Lord Elland thinks nearly half the council are with him."

Half. Joss fisted her hands. How could they choose a distant relative over a direct descendent of the king? Or be so bold as to suggest ousting the current king for a usurper?

She picked up another griddle cake, but it had gone cold, the butter coalesced into claggy smears, so she dropped it back onto the plate.

"What do we do about it?" she asked.

"We've bought some time by arranging for a knowledgeable mage from the Aralan guildhall to examine Papa." Maddie pressed her lips into a thin line. "I've also agreed to remain in Tyrrath for as long as I'm ruling on his behalf."

Joss's eyes sprang wide. "What? But—"

"Luc agreed rather quickly to that condition." Her sister shrugged one shoulder. "He thinks it's better for the baby.

"And Lord Elland has sent someone to look into our cousin. If he can be proven unfit to rule, we can dismiss the notion outright when the council meets to discuss it. Until then, we're trying to sway as many of them as possible. We need all but the ringleaders on our side if we're truly going to beat them. Otherwise, we could face the same threat again in the future. I won't allow Papa to wake to a broken kingdom."

The words 'or for my child to inherit one' hung unspoken between them.

Resolve straightening her spine, Joss silently vowed to do everything in her power to help Maddie hold onto the kingdom. She had tried things her way and had failed. From now on, she would follow Maddie's lead, even if it meant being stuck in the palace or, creator forbid, in a political marriage. It was time to stop running away.

"Then tell me what I can do."

While Maddie talked, Joss stood and walked to the window, looking out at the rolling hills of Tyrrath. Guilt still gnawed at her, but its bite had less force than before. Despite everything, it was good to be home.

Chapter 35

Joss

Joss sat on the bank of the stream that ran through Mochynden Forest, dangling her feet in the water. Her bow and quiver lay propped against a rock beside her, and Parker stood at her shoulder, alert as always.

They had come to the forest to hunt, but after Joss's third arrow had thudded uselessly into a tree trunk instead of her prey, she had given up.

"Are you sure you won't sit down?" she asked Parker. "I'm perfectly safe here."

"Yes, because I'm standing guard."

"The water's nice and cool. Especially after we've been running around all morning." She kicked a leg and watched a handful of glistening droplets fly into the air before splashing back into the babbling flow.

Parker eyed her sideways, and Joss could almost hear her thinking that a bath back at the palace would be better. Her chest tightened at the image. A bath would lead to dressing in appropriate attire and then to being surrounded by courtiers and feeling trapped. She needed to escape that torture for a while longer.

It had been a couple of weeks since she returned to Faerstolmere. Weeks of meeting with various lords and impressing on them the importance of supporting her sister. Of wearing stylish, corseted gowns and maintaining perfect decorum. Of holding herself back behind the restrictive façade of a perfect princess.

Helping Maddie was worth her pains, but Joss felt like she was losing herself piece by piece. At least here in the woods, she could relax and be herself for a few hours.

"The time, Milady…"

Joss looked up at the sun, which peeked through the canopy from directly overhead, and slumped. "All right. Let's go back."

She shook the water from her feet, dragged her boots on, and picked up her bow and quiver. Drawing in a lungful of fresh air tinted with the scents of damp earth and tree sap, she turned her back on the quiet depths of the forest and strode along the trail that led to the palace.

The path took them up the rear of the hill on which the city stood, between ancient trees interspersed with ferns and shrubs. Joss trailed a hand over the soft fronds and rough bark, listening to several birds twittering and enjoying the pleasant warmth of the sun on her neck and shoulders.

How different from the burning heat of the southern kingdoms.

When the red stone of the palace's outer wall rose above the treetops, she pulled the gate key from her waist pouch and headed for the dense shrubs that hid the entrance. She found her discarded dress in the undergrowth and yanked it on over her hunting leathers, then unlocked the door and slipped inside.

A click sounded, and she glanced back.

Parker held out the key. "You left it in the lock again."

Joss glanced down at the dress covering her pouch.

Loosing a sigh, the guard tucked the key into her own pouch, and they padded along the passage between two outbuildings to the rear courtyard.

Though a hum of activity came from the front of the palace, the only people within view were a couple of kitchen hands peeling vegetables. Joss left Parker to report in and dashed across the cobbles, lifting her finger to her lips when they looked over at her.

She ducked through the archway into the gardens and wove through the kitchen plants towards a side door that would take her to her rooms.

As she rounded a large evergreen shrub, someone stepped out from the other side. Hands caught her arms in a firm grip, and she looked up into Lord Ealley's startled eyes.

He let go and all but jumped backwards, offering a short bow. "Princess Jocelyn."

His gaze remained lowered as he rose, his brows pulling together around a little vee. What was he staring at?

Joss looked down and grimaced. Her dress had caught on the handle of the dagger sticking out from the top of her right boot. She tugged the material loose and started to walk around the frustrating lord, but he held his arm out, stopping her.

"I'm glad I found you, Jocelyn. I need a word."

She bit back a growl at his use of her name, which would not have bothered her had it been anyone else. "What is it, Lord Ealley?"

"Some of the southern lords are worried." He glanced beyond the shoulder-high hedge bordering the kitchen garden from the roses, where a group of nobles—including Lords Brant and Lowden, both vocal opponents of Maddie's rule—stood, watching. "We need to make a good impression on the Iskarian emissary today. If they stop buying our goods now their kingdom's not a desert, it would devastate our income. A word of reassurance from you would go a long way…"

"I'm aware of the issue, and Princess Madeline and I will do our best."

"I know you will. I just…" He stepped closer, and she shuffled backwards to maintain the distance between them. "I'm here if you need me, Jocelyn. To lean on me for support. We have a special bond, after all."

She sighed. She did not have the fortitude to deal with him today. "I really have to go, Lord Ealley. I need to get ready."

Finally, he moved aside. "Yes, of course. I'll see you later. Look for me…"

Whatever else he said was lost on Joss as she rushed through the rest of the garden, inside the palace, and up to the royal family's private wing.

When she got to her room, her maid jumped up from a stool by the fireplace. "Your Highness. Your bathwater's gone cold. Should I—"

"Leave it. I can handle a lukewarm bath."

The young maid bit her lip and twisted her fingers together as though anything less than steaming hot water was unthinkable, and Joss rolled her eyes. "If you want to do something useful, you could fetch me something to eat from the kitchens. I'd rather avoid the lords downstairs for as long as possible, and I only had a handful of berries this morning."

"Yes, Your Highness." Her maid bobbed a curtsey and hurried out of the room, closing the door behind her with a soft clunk.

Joss headed for the wooden bathtub sitting in front of the hearth but paused by the bed, where a rust-red satin gown lay over the end of the mattress. She noted the narrow waist and tight-fitting sleeves, and pressure built in her chest as the walls closed in a little around her.

"It's fine," she said aloud. "I chose to do this."

She took a couple of steadying breaths and glared at the walls until they retreated to their proper place. Then she pulled off her clothes, leaving them in a pile on the floor, and climbed into the tub of cooling water to scrub her skin clean.

An hour or so later, her gown wrestled into place, Joss checked her hair in the looking glass. Hopefully, no one would notice that half of the knot pinned at her nape was still damp. She hurried out of her room, heading for the great hall, but winced when she looked along the upper hallway.

Maddie walked towards her, impeccably dressed in her finest emerald gown, not a hair out of place. "There you are. I was starting to worry you'd be late."

"Sorry." She grimaced and added in an undertone, "I bumped into Lord Ealley earlier."

"Oh?" Her sister guided her to one side of the hallway, away from a servant lighting the wall sconces.

"Yes. He said the southern lords are still worried about the changes in Iskaria affecting trade."

Maddie smoothed her skirts. "I've been told the same. At least it's distracted them from the issue of succession for a while. Maybe it's a blessing in disguise."

"Have you found out anything else about the emissary?" Joss asked as they descended the stairs.

"Just that he's a minor member of the royal family currently favoured by the king." Resting a hand on her enlarged stomach, Maddie gave her a meaningful look. "I'll be relying on you to entertain him during his visit."

Joss replied with a firm nod, "You can count on me."

They walked along a short passage to their private entrance to the great hall, where Tristan waited for them in his full captain of the guard uniform. With a smart bow, he held the curtain aside for them to walk through the archway. Then he escorted them up onto the raised dais where three thrones sat, one each for her, Maddie, and Olivia, who had returned from the local guildhall for the occasion.

Luc would wait upstairs during the welcoming ceremony, a deliberate choice made as much for the rebel lords as it was for the visiting dignitary.

The majority of Tyrrath's nobles milled about the rest of the room, gathered into their various factions and levels of perceived power. The nearest looked up as Joss and Maddie entered, their sudden silence drawing the attention of those behind in a ripple that spread to the very back.

Joss sank into her seat, feeling constrained by both their scrutiny and the tight ribbons of her gown. With all eyes on them, the hall seemed stuffy, despite being a spacious room with plenty of air and light pouring in through the row of bay windows along one side.

Olivia slipped through the curtained servants' entrance, clutching a book to her chest over her pale-yellow gown. She looked around the hall once, then ducked her head and mounted the dais.

As she passed Joss's throne, Joss asked under her breath, "How long have you been hiding back there?"

"Long enough to see you sneaking back from the woods." Hiding a shy smile, Olivia took her place on Maddie's other side. She slid her book behind her back, turned to their older sister, and whispered, "Just don't ask me to say anything, please?"

Maddie leaned over and patted her hand. "I won't. I promise."

The palace steward walked over and hovered at Maddie's shoulder. "Excuse me, Ma'am, but the emissary's waiting outside."

"Show him in," Maddie said.

Joss wiggled into a more comfortable position and considered how best to entertain the Iskarian emissary over the following days. Would he enjoy a cross-country ride? Or would she be stuck in the palace, pointing out various ancestors in the gallery? Hopefully, he would not have heard of her excursion through their kingdom.

The main doors opened and a column of people walked in wearing the opulent, flowing robes of Iskaria. They stopped a short distance from the dais and bowed as one, hands to their chests to display their clan tattoos.

A tiny part of Joss searched the group for Theo, though it was a futile effort. And not only because his presence there would be absurd. She could only see the tops of heads beyond those at the front, all of whom carried the ceremonial staffs of Iskaria's elite guards.

"Your Royal Highnesses," the nasally royal chamberlain intoned. "May I introduce His Grace, the Duke of Baankra, Atheon Sakanin."

The guards in the front row parted, and a familiar figure stepped forwards. It could not be… but it was. Tall, broad shouldered, his hair tied back in a neat queue and his full beard trimmed close to his jaw—Theo.

His name caught in her throat, and she clenched her hands around the wooden armrests of her throne so tightly her knuckles ached.

Theo was a duke. He was in Redcairn Palace. And his warm brown eyes were locked on hers.

Chapter 36

Joss

The pain in Theo's gaze mirrored Joss's own. It struck her like a physical blow, so intense it stole her breath and left a dull ache in her chest.

She turned her face away from him, hiding the moisture that sprang to her eyes. Why was he there? Tangling her thoughts and disturbing her hard-won calm? And how was he a duke? Had he been one all along, or was it his reward for undoing the magical curse on Iskaria?

Although, if he had been hiding it from her all along, that would explain how he had boarded the *Evening Star*, why Noa had called him by that name, and why he had accepted her identity as a princess so easily.

"Your Highnesses," he said, dipping his head again.

"Welcome to Faerstolmere, Duke," Maddie replied. "I hope your journey was uneventful. Is this your first time in Tyrrath?"

An image of him boarding the ferry at Dynnford in a hooded cloak rose in Joss's mind.

"I've visited the south, briefly," he said.

"Well, then. We'll have to arrange a tour during your stay." Maddie turned to Joss, her smile faltering as their eyes met. Concern clouded her features, but Joss gave a subtle shake of her head to reassure her sister that she was well.

Returning her attention to Theo, Maddie beckoned the steward forward and continued, "Hodges will see you to your rooms, where you can rest until the banquet this evening. Please let him know if you need anything."

"If I may be so bold, Your Highness, may I request a private audience with you and your sisters first?" He glanced at Joss. "There's an urgent matter we must discuss."

Whispers spread around the hall, and several lords shuffled uncomfortably. The same question etched frown lines in each of their faces—would he break off their trade so soon after arriving?

They would have their answer soon enough, for Maddie rose and gestured towards the entrance that led to the royal apartments and her study. "Certainly. This way, if you will."

Tristan stepped forwards from the rear of the dais, but she waved him off with a quiet, "The duke requested a private audience." Then she looked out at the rest of the gathering and said, "Please excuse us. We'll return in time for the banquet."

Joss trailed behind her sisters and Theo as they walked to Maddie's study. What could he have to discuss with them that he could not say in the great hall? She snorted. Part of her wanted to drag him into the nearest room, lock the door behind them, and demand answers to entirely different questions. The other part wanted to slip away and pretend he had never set foot in the palace.

When they reached the study, Maddie sat in one of the chairs by the fireplace opposite her desk, and Olivia took the one across from her. Theo turned the chair facing the desk around and dropped onto it, leaving the seat beside Maddie for Joss.

Maddie leaned towards her as soon as she was settled and said in an undertone, "I take it this is…"

"Theo," Joss replied. "Yes."

Her sister straightened and donned a neutral smile. "No wonder King Aber has favoured you of late. You brought Iskaria back to life. Is the title newly bestowed?"

Theo met her gaze without flinching. "No, Your Highness. It was always mine. My grandfather was the late king's brother, and I'm officially a Sakanin. But I'm rarely at court, and I've been using my mother's name, Taskil, for years." He turned to Joss and winced slightly. "I'm sorry I didn't tell you sooner. I'll explain everything when we have more time, but there's something important I need to share with you all first." He cleared his throat. "I brought someone with me who might be able to help your father."

"Help?" Joss whipped her eyes up to his. "How?"

"She's a mage." He held up a hand, forestalling their questions. "Before I tell you more, I have a condition."

"What is it?" Maddie asked.

He leaned closer, as though the painting of their grandfather above the mantelpiece or the books lining the other walls might be listening. "Her identity must remain a secret. No one outside this room can know she's here, or that she arrived with me. Even my escort doesn't know that she followed us here."

Joss could understand the secrecy. Even after healing Iskaria, associating with mages must still carry heavy penalties for Iskarians, even for a duke. She looked between her sisters and gave Maddie a single, firm nod.

"You have our word," Maddie said for all three of them.

A faint smile tilted his lips and was gone. "Thank you." Sitting back again, he spread his hands. "Her gift is hard to explain, but it's as if she can freeze someone, only without them being cold. They don't move or breathe, and their hearts don't beat, but they're perfectly fine when she releases them from the magic's hold.

"She used it once when someone was injured so they didn't bleed to death before they could be healed. I'm not sure how long she can make it last, but I thought it would be worth trying, to give you more time."

Joss stared at him. He had come to help them. He had taken the stone, but he had found a mage capable of helping her father.

So that he would not die.

"It's safe?" she asked. "There are no side effects?"

He shook his head. "None. I'll demonstrate it for you."

"Mouse could strengthen the mage's power," Maddie said almost to herself. "Couldn't you?" she asked Olivia.

"I think so. I might be able to keep it going afterwards as well, depending on how it works."

Theo gaped at Olivia. "You can do that?"

She ducked her head and nodded.

Joss jumped to her feet. "Where's the mage? Let's go and get her."

"We'll go," Maddie said, standing and tugging Olivia up beside her. "I need to speak to Lord Elland and Tristan anyway, and Mouse can show the mage to Papa's room. That way, they can discuss how to proceed without us hovering over them."

She turned to Theo, who said, "Her name's Chenne, and she's waiting outside the main gates."

"Thank you. You stay here, Joss. It'll raise questions if we all leave at once."

With that, Maddie crossed the room, all but shoved Olivia outside, and pulled the door closed behind them, leaving Joss and Theo alone.

Neither of them spoke. Joss sat back down and stared out of the window, drumming her fingers on her satin skirts and suppressing the urge to pace. Drat Maddie. She was not ready for this. Too many things stood unsaid between her and Theo, and she had no idea where to start.

He cleared his throat, and she looked up at him without thinking.

Eyeing her gown, he murmured, "You look beautiful."

She snorted. "I suppose you prefer this to the trousers I wore before."

"No." He met her gaze, a hint of sadness in his eyes. "You smiled more then. You look tense now."

Her mouth opened, but still, the words refused to form. How could he see her so clearly?

"I know what it's like to be born into the court but not feel like you belong," he added softly.

Joss jumped up and spun her back to him before he could read the truth of his statement in her face.

"Congratulations, Duke Sakanin," she said, deliberately using the two names he had kept from her. Her voice came out flat and tasted more bitter than she would have liked to admit. She forced herself not to wince. "You must be happy about becoming so popular in the Iskarian court."

Guilt bit deep as soon as the accusation left her mouth. Why was she lashing out at him?

"You know better than anyone that's not why I did it. I wanted to help my people and the mages being wrongly persecuted."

A question Joss had not thought to ask before popped into her mind. "Why is that? You're Iskarian. You must've been raised to hate mages, so why help them?" She glanced at the door. "Is it because you know one? The woman you brought with you?"

He scraped a hand through his hair, loosening his queue and leaving the shorter strands tousled. "Actually, I—"

Someone rapped on the door, and a moment later, it opened and a maid walked in. She bobbed a curtsey and said, "Her Highness said to tell you they're ready upstairs, Princess Jocelyn."

"Thank you, Bess. We'll be right there."

Joss stood to leave, but Theo blocked her way with his arm.

"Can we talk first?" he asked with an anxious look in his eyes. "There's something else I need to tell you."

Her gaze shifted to the door. "Can it wait? Please? We need to save Papa as soon as possible."

His shoulders drooped, but he nodded and stepped aside, allowing her to lead the way upstairs.

Joss's father lay in his canopied bed, the blankets pulled up to his chest, his cheeks sunken and pale. He had not moved from that spot, or even so much as flickered his eyelids, for over two years. Joss wished they were reviving him rather than merely preserving his life, but it was better than the alternative. If it worked.

"Freeze me first, Chenne." Theo pushed up his sleeve and walked over to one of the chairs by the fireplace.

The mage, an older woman with greying hair in a thick braid and bands of knotted embroidery edging her dress, joined him without a word of protest. She knelt beside him, looked up at Joss and her sisters, who stood by the end of their father's bed, and placed her hand on Theo's.

Nothing appeared to happen. No signs of magic being used or any discernible changes in him, but after a few moments, Chenne sat back, and said, "It's done, Your Highnesses. Come and see for yourselves."

Joss moved first. Bending close to Theo's face, she studied his closed eyes, his still chest, then reached forwards and tentatively touched his cheek. The skin under her fingers did not move or give at all. Pressing harder made no difference, nor did shaking his shoulder. It felt like trying to move a warm statue. She lowered her hand and checked for a heartbeat. Nothing.

Gasping, she pulled back and straightened. "Is he dead?"

Chenne chuckled. "Not at all. Just held still—that's what I call it."

"Can you bring him back, now?" Maddie asked.

"Certainly, Ma'am." The mage rested her hand on Theo's again, shut her eyes, and breathed in and out, a long, slow breath.

Theo's fingers twitched, then he sucked in air, opened his eyes, and looked up at them. "See?"

"What did it feel like?" Joss fisted her hands in her skirts to stop herself from embracing him.

"I didn't feel a thing. It's like falling asleep."

"This will work." Olivia stepped closer, her face lit from more than just the candles around the room. "And I can make it last much longer."

"You're sure?" Maddie asked her.

Olivia nodded. "Yes. I saw how Chenne's magic wrapped around him. I can increase her power and strengthen the bonds when it's in place. We can keep Papa alive for as long as it takes to break the curse."

Joss's entire body relaxed. She had not realised until that moment how tightly she had been holding herself since they had discovered the curse, but none of it mattered now. Their father would live.

"What are we waiting for, then?" she said. "Let's get started."

Chenne stood and walked to the bed, where she sat to the right of their father. Olivia took the chair beside her, and Maddie and Joss moved to his other side.

"I wish Luc were here," Maddie whispered.

"Where is he?" Joss whispered back.

"Keeping the lords occupied."

Ah. Joss gripped her sister's hand and shuffled closer to her chair. She glanced at Theo, who stood at the bottom of the bed watching the mage. How had he found her?

"Make sure you don't get too close to your father while we're working, Ma'am," Chenne said, drawing Joss's attention back to her.

The mage closed her eyes and drew in a deep breath, and Olivia rested a hand on her arm, doing the same.

As before, nothing appeared to happen, but a slight prickle raced over Joss's skin, like the energy that filled the air before a thunderstorm. Sweat beaded Chenne's temples, and Olivia clenched her jaw and free hand.

They stayed like that for what felt like long minutes but was probably only a few heartbeats. Then they fell back into their chairs, panting and spent.

"We've done it," Olivia said.

"Papa's safe?" Maddie asked at the same time as Joss asked, "It worked?"

"Yes… He should stay like that… for quite some time." Chenne turned to Olivia, her eyes wide. "You have so much power… I felt like I was flooded with it."

Olivia ducked her head, covering a shy smile.

"You should both rest." Maddie scooted forwards and slid her hand over their father's. "Thank you, Chenne. And you, Duke."

Joss stilled. She had almost forgotten he was there. "Yes, thank you for arranging this, Your Grace."

"Please, call me Theo. And it was the least I could do."

The warmth in his tone made her look up. His eyes locked on hers for the second time that afternoon, and something inside her shifted. She dragged her gaze from his and jumped up, almost knocking her chair over in her haste to escape. "I should tell Lord Elland it worked."

She needed time to think. If she was not careful, she would fall even more in love with Theo than before. But she could not afford for that to happen. Too much stood between them now, their choices an impenetrable barrier she could not break.

And even if he did still care for her, he was a duke now. He would need power and influence to maintain his position as Iskaria's emissary, which meant he would want a demure wife who followed the rules of the court, like all the other nobles. And the thought of being trapped in that life, acting as a perfect princess all the time, made Joss break out in a cold sweat.

Chapter 37

Theo

By the end of the next day, it was clear to Theo that Jocelyn was avoiding him. What he could not figure out was why. Did she blame him for not telling her earlier that he was a duke? Or did she just hate him for taking the dragon stone? Maybe she still believed he had deliberately kept the keystone from her.

Regardless of the cause, he could not change her mind unless he could talk to her alone, so he did the only thing he could think of. He requested she accompany him on a ride along the river the following morning. Maybe if he could get her outside, where she felt comfortable and free, she would open up to him.

But when he arrived in the palace courtyard after a hasty breakfast, ten guards in full uniform waited beside her.

Parker stood among them, appearing so different in the tabard and helmet that he almost did not recognise her. He caught her eye, and she gave him a one-sided shrug, though whether to acknowledge her status as guard rather than cousin or in sympathy with his plight was hard to tell.

He studied Jocelyn as he approached. She stood with her back to him, her hair caught up at her nape, a thin, rust-red cloak over her ample skirts. So different from the tunic and trousers she had favoured in the southern realms.

"Good morning, Princess Jocelyn," he said with a dip of his head.

"Good morning, Duke."

He looked up at the clear sky. "It's a beautiful day for a ride. We should've packed some lunch so we could stay out longer."

Her eyes lit. "We could always—" She pressed her lips together, appearing torn, but the light in her eyes faded. "I have a meeting later. We'd better get going."

So, she did not hate him completely. He hid a smile. It was a start.

They mounted and rode through the gates in silence, the guards too close for him to speak to her in private. The cobbled street wound through the city, past guildhalls and inns, workshops and grand houses, down the hill towards the lake.

When they emerged from the last of the cottages nestled outside the city wall, Jocelyn broke free of their escort and pulled ahead on a wide, packed-dirt path that followed the lakeshore. Theo watched her for a few moments. Her skirts flew behind her to reveal the trousers she wore underneath, and her thick braid bounced against her back. This was the woman he knew and loved.

He tapped his heels into his horse's sides and chased after her, determined not to waste the opportunity presented.

They galloped south, neck and neck, moving in perfect harmony with the horses under them. Theo's heart pounded in time with the hoofbeats, his breath snatched away as they sped along the path towards the mouth of the river.

Lake Arrol sparkled on their right, and the forest blurred into a dark green mass on their left. Ahead, a riverboat laden with barrels and crates sailed into view from around a bend, likely heading for Faerstolmere to trade.

The boat reminded him of sailing downriver with Captain Butts on the way to Eindal. His chest ached. If only they could return to when they were simply Kit and Theo not Princess Jocelyn and Duke Atheon. Before they knew the stone could only be used once, before so many secrets and opposing loyalties had come between them.

She slowed her pace as they drew level with the boat, and he eased his mount closer to Shadow so they could talk.

"Do you ride here often, Kit?" He winced at the name that slipped out. Eyeing her, he asked, "Is that a pet name?"

"No, my sisters call me Joss." She snapped her mouth shut as though she had also spoken without thinking.

He repeated the nickname in a soft voice. "Joss… May I call you that?"

She jerked her head around, meeting his eyes for the first time that morning.

Theo gave her a hopeful smile. “We’ve been through too much together to be so formal with each other.”

“What do you want, Your Grace?”

A sigh escaped. Winning her back was going to be an uphill battle. But he was prepared for that, starting with telling her the whole truth. “I want us to get to know each other again, with no secrets this time. I’m the same man you met in Garellion. I just—”

“Have a title?” she finished, looking away from him.

“Yes. So do you. But there’s something else you need to know. I’ve never used it because…”

Hoofbeats approached from behind, and he looked over his shoulder. The guards had caught up. Strand it. He could not afford for them to overhear his deepest secret.

He steered his horse farther from hers as the guards surrounded them once more. Maybe they would drop behind again on the way back to the palace.

Unfortunately, Jocelyn stayed close to them for the rest of their ride. He gritted his teeth and tried to enjoy the scenery. He would bide his time for now, but later… Later, he would find an opportunity to have a real conversation with her, and he would not leave Tyrrath until he had told her exactly what she meant to him.

Chapter 38

Joss

Joss had not been able to avoid Theo entirely during the days following his arrival, but she had found ways to keep from being alone with him. She had invited several lords on their stroll through the gardens, taken extra guards on their ride along the lakeshore, and spent as much time as she could talking to the locals on their tour of Faerstolmere and the surrounding farms.

Fortunately, much of his time was taken up in meetings with Maddie and various members of the council. Unfortunately, he sat between her and Joss at the banquet held in his honour, and thanks to her sister being heavily pregnant, and married, he turned to Joss when the time came for the first dance.

"Shall we, Princess Jocelyn?" he asked once the tables had been cleared.

She looked from the hand he held out to her up into his warm eyes and pressed her palms into her thighs. "You can do this. It's just a dance," she murmured, then reached out and slid her hand into his.

He held it loosely—unlike some of the local lords, who always seemed to want to either impress or possess her—and led her to the middle of the great hall, where space had been made for them. His hand was warm, the callouses on his fingers the only rough thing about his grip.

More couples joined them, forming two lines opposite each other. When they were ready, she nodded for the musicians sitting in the upper gallery to begin.

They struck up a lively tune, and Theo led her in a promenade between the rest of the dancers. At the end of the line, they parted to circle back to their places, the next couple already following behind.

Theo's arm was ready for her when they transitioned into a turn, supporting her back when they spun faster. They moved well together, their steps perfectly in sync, and she lost herself in the rhythm of the dance.

The freeing sensation reminded her of dancing with him on the *Evening Star*, the great hall momentarily replaced in her mind by the ship's deck, raucous sailors, and a beautiful sunset.

And their first kiss.

Her feet stumbled at the memory, and the hall came sharply back into focus. Heart racing, face surely aflame, she tensed as Theo caught her around the waist to stop her from falling.

He had told her on the ship that he wanted to spend more time with her, and she had planned to accept him until...

She shook her head to clear it. What was she thinking? None of that mattered anymore.

The dance ended, and Theo asked, "Are you all right? You nearly fell during that last—"

"I'm fine. Thank you."

He offered his hand to lead her off the floor. "There's something I've been trying to tell you."

"Can we talk later? I need to… get some fresh air." The hall *was* considerably stuffier than it had been earlier, not even the vaulted ceiling enough to dissipate the combined heat of so many bodies. Her excuses made, she dipped her head and hurried away from him, heading for the nearest entrance to the gardens.

She had just set foot outside when a voice called out, "Princess Jocelyn."

Lord Ealley.

Under normal circumstances, he would have been the last person she wanted to speak to, but the sight of Theo in her periphery made her turn towards the lord.

"Jocelyn. I'm glad I found you. Come, let's go somewhere quieter to talk." He snatched her by the hand, his grip so tight it pinched, and towed her through an archway to the rose garden, where night blooms released a sweet scent into the air.

As soon as he stopped, she shook him off and rubbed her squashed fingers.

They were still close enough to the palace that sounds of merriment reached through the hedges and trees to them, and lanterns hanging from a nearby arbour cast a soft glow over the formal borders. They highlighted the square planes of his face and lit his eyes with a sheen of excitement.

"I've just been talking to Lords Lowden and Deuring," he said, "and they might be willing to support your sister at the council meeting. If you come with me now, I think we can secure their votes."

"Really?" Joss took a step towards him, her usual caution forgotten in the face of such good news. "That would be wonderful."

"Of course. I know Lowden's been giving you trouble, so I've been spending more time with him recently. We make a good couple, you and I. We just need to show him that."

The back of her neck prickled, and she stilled. What had he told Lowden to change the old man's mind?

"Maybe we could announce our engagement soon too. Give the lords even more to celebrate. I've been courting you for some time now, and we're certainly compatible."

Every muscle in her body tightened.

Until that moment, she had considered him to be merely an annoyance. A lord who loved the idea of her, the public face she was forced to wear, without stopping to notice who she really was underneath. But maybe he was more calculating than she had imagined. Otherwise, how could he blackmail her into marrying him like this? And with a smile on his face as he did so?

Political alliances were common within the nobility—even Maddie had initially married Luc for the sake of their kingdom—but every part of Joss balked at the idea of acquiescing to Lord Ealley's proposition.

Her future with him rolled across the night sky, bound to his every decision, forced to submit to his will.

Her freedom stripped from her while he enjoyed the benefits of marrying into the royal family. But she needed his support, his and the rest of the southern lords he called friends.

Joss wiped damp palms on her skirts and swallowed past a knot in her throat. Her heart beat loudly in her ears. Her greatest duty stood on one hand; on the other, her greatest fear.

She tried to clear her mind, but Lorad Ealley was still speaking, and his voice grated across her skin.

"…so I think it would be best to avoid any more of your excursions into the woods until we secure the votes of the other lords. We need to show them the Dalbots can be trusted with the kingdom, and it's hardly dignified for a princess to run around in trousers."

Anger flickered in her gut, and she fisted her hands, the nails digging into her palms. Through gritted teeth, she said, "What I choose to wear in private should have no bearing on my sister's rule."

"But you must—"

Footsteps crunched on gravel behind her, and Theo stepped through an archway covered in trailing vines. The low light made him look like a pirate come to claim her as his own, his dark eyes glittering in the shadows. "Ah, Princess Jocelyn. And…?"

"Lord Ealley." The lord dipped into a low bow, an ingratiating smile plastered over his face when he rose. "It's a pleasure, Your Grace."

Theo kept his focus entirely on her and asked, "Would you care to go hunting with me in the morning? After such a fine evening, I could use a ride, and I've heard your private forest has plenty of game." He flicked a glance at Lord Ealley before frowning at her skirts. "Be sure to wear trousers, though. Dresses get caught in everything and scare off the prey."

Joss suppressed a smirk. Had he overheard them?

Lord Ealley answered before she could. "I quite agree, Your Grace. Skirts must be a terrible nuisance on a hunt. And we wouldn't want anything to spoil your enjoyment of our capital."

"Thank you, Lord Ellin. Would you mind giving us a moment?" Theo asked.

She swallowed a bubble of laughter at his butchering of Lord Ealley's name. Had it been deliberate?

The lord's brows pulled together as he looked between them, but he quickly smoothed his expression and bowed to Theo. "Of course, Your Grace." Turning to Joss, he grasped her upper arm, said, "I'll see you later," and scurried back to his friends.

"What was that about?" Theo asked when they were alone. "You looked like you wanted to run away."

"He offered to help us with the lords asking for Papa to abdicate," she said before she could think better of it. Why had she told him that?

"Mm. I heard about that. Is there anything I can do?"

Turning towards the palace, she snapped, "I wouldn't want to inconvenience you, Duke."

He stopped her from leaving, his hand on her arm as gentle as always, such a contrast to Lord Ealley's determined grip. "Jocelyn, wait. You know me. I'm the same person you met in Garellion."

She spun on him. "But you're not the same. You're Atheon Sakanin, not Theo Taskil. You lied to me."

"Not about anything important." He stepped closer. "Besides, you lied about your identity too."

"Yes, but I didn't claim to be interested in you." Her traitorous cheeks heated.

He growled low in his throat. "It wasn't a claim. I meant every word. I love you. And I think you love me too."

"I do not."

"Really?"

He closed the remaining gap between them, and her breath hitched, her gaze moving unbidden to his lips. When he touched them to hers in a slow, deliberate kiss, she did not pull away.

"Liar," he whispered as he lifted his head from hers. "Whatever's holding you back, it's not that you don't have feelings for me."

His low voice rumbled over her objections and straight into her heart, leaving his presence indelibly stamped there.

She blinked, and the world around her came back into focus. What was she doing? Only a few minutes earlier, another man had forced a proposal on her, which she still might have to accept.

She could not love Theo. She could not. But despite everything that stood between them—the lies and betrayals, their opposing roles and duties, and possibly one calculating lord—the voice in her heart told her that she did. She loved him very much.

Backing out of Theo's reach, she turned and ran, heedless of the direction her feet took her.

"I'm not going anywhere," he called after her, and she was not certain whether it sounded like a threat or a promise.

Chapter 39

Theo

Theo needed help. He walked towards the library, his feet sinking into the thick runner, his troubled thoughts at odds with the bright morning sunshine streaming through the windows that lined one wall of the corridor.

He knew Jocelyn loved him as much as he loved her, but something was keeping her from acting on it. And he had no idea what it was.

She had looked so pale when he found her and the lord in the gardens the previous evening, the mask of calm she wore failing to hide the tightness of her mouth and eyes. Her hands had clenched her skirts with such force that he would not have been surprised had she been unable to let go.

But she would not talk to him. Had run away, even. How could he make amends if she kept avoiding him?

He paused outside the library door and straightened the hem of his tunic. It was time for a change of tactics.

That morning, he needed to find one of her sisters instead. Surely, they would know what she was thinking.

As he reached for the handle, Princess Madeline called out from behind him, “Your Grace. May I have a word?”

Did she want to discuss something to do with their kingdoms’ trade? He glanced at the door. He had hoped to seek out the younger princess for advice, more comfortable with minor royalty, but he could not refuse his host’s request. With a mental shrug, he turned and offered a polite bow. “Of course, Your Highness.”

She led him to her study, where she sat by the fireplace and gestured for him to join her. “Please.”

A pot of steaming dakka and a plate of griddle cakes lay on the side table between their chairs, and she poured him a cup before speaking again. “Would you mind telling me about your time searching for the dragon stone with my sister?”

He met her eyes over the rim of his cup, then set the drink down. This was the very subject he wished to broach, but the princess’s perceptive gaze unnerved him. His palms turned clammy, and he wiped them surreptitiously on his thighs. “If you’ll offer me some advice in return.”

One side of her mouth twitched as though she were suppressing a grin. She took a small sip of her dakka and said, “Gladly.”

And so, he did, starting with his first impression of the woman who called herself Kit, how they had grown close as they researched the stone, made silly bets over it, and evaded mage hunters during their journey to the

Free Isles. He skipped over the pain he had felt when he woke to find her gone but told her honestly about his regret at having to take the stone for himself. "…and even then, she helped me escape with it." He scraped a hand through his hair and shook his head. "It's been an incredible adventure from beginning to end."

The princess studied him for a long moment. "Do you have feelings for her?"

Were all the Dalbot sisters so blunt? He leaned forwards and rested his elbows on his knees to give himself time to think. "She already knows this, so I can tell you I've loved her since the third time we met, when she put herself between me and an inn full of angry Garellis. She's bold, brave, loyal, and just. I love how talented she is at archery and how she always needs to be active. She'd do anything for the people she loves, and the only thing she fears is tight spaces. She's nothing like any woman I've ever met before, and I'd spend the rest of my life with her if she'd let me."

"It's not just tight spaces she fears." Princess Madeline frowned. "Joss is afraid of anything that makes her feel trapped or controlled. Tight spaces, corsets, but also court rules, marriage…"

"Marriage?" His eyes jumped to hers. "That's why she's running away from me?"

The princess sighed and set her cup down. "Yes. It all stems back to an incident that happened when we were young. Joss has always been energetic and lively. She was the first one into the water when we visited the coast, the first to climb a tree or explore new places… Always running everywhere, always laughing.

"Then, after our mother passed, Papa hired a governess to teach us court etiquette. Mistress Lytchett was incredibly strict. She insisted that we should be still and silent to maintain our royal dignity, which was so difficult for Joss."

Theo's teeth clenched.

"She did something one morning while I was with Lord Elland—I can't remember what it was—and Mistress Lytchett locked her in a chest as punishment. She was in there for almost a whole day before we found her."

"What?"

"Papa dealt with Mistress Lytchett—we never found out how, but I suspect she was banished—but Joss changed after that. She had a hard time with anything tight or enclosed, and she associated being a princess with having to hide her natural inclinations. Laughter turned to little grins, running turned to tapping her fingers. Everything she did in front of others became… smaller, quieter."

Theo fisted his hands, recalling how Joss had trembled inside the wardrobe in Firstport and the look of terror on her face in Dekarat's prison. He closed his eyes and swallowed the bile that rose in his throat. What he would not give to find that governess and shove her in a chest for a day. Or longer. "That explains a lot of things."

"I imagine it does, from what she's told me of your journey." Princess Madeline let out a soft sigh. "For Joss, getting married is just another form of being controlled. It doesn't help that most of the lords in Tyrrath want quiet, respectable wives."

"And that's why she's so determined to refuse me."

"I'm afraid so."

He stood and looked out of the window, barely taking in the courtyard or the tree standing over it. Pushing the air from his lungs, he turned back to Princess Madeline and asked, "Why are you telling me all this?"

"You calmed her fears in Firstport. Not many people can do that. And I see the way she looks at you. I think you can make her happy."

Theo read her approval in her expression, and in that moment, they came to an understanding. Nevertheless, he said, "I promise you, I'll never try to take away her freedom or crush her spirit. That's the reason I fell in love with her."

"Then I'll help you as much as I can."

"Thank you, Your Highness."

She smiled warmly. "Call me Maddie."

"And I'm Theo," he replied in kind.

Chapter 40

Joss

Joss sat beside Maddie in the council chamber, feeling the eyes of her ancestors boring holes into her from the paintings hanging along the west wall. Would she and her sisters be the last of their line to sit at the head of the council?

Only Lord Brant and two of his closest allies had voted to depose their father in favour of his second cousin, Lord Tuftridge, but the rest of Maddie's detractors could have another plan in motion.

She caught her lips between her teeth as Maddie asked, "And those against?"

One by one, the lords arrayed around the long table lifted their arms into the air. Lord Ealley stuck his straight up, high above his head, and his friends did the same, for which she was grateful.

She turned towards Lord Lowden, who stared down at the table, his mouth set in a grim line. Both hands rested on the polished wooden surface, the left crabbed with rheumatism, and she willed him to move one.

Slowly, as if in answer to her prayer, he lifted his right hand up until it was level with his cap of white hair.

The lords to his right and left immediately followed his lead, until all but the three who had brought the motion to the council indicated their support for Maddie's rule.

Joss released the air in her lungs and squeezed Maddie's hand. They had done it. The majority of the council had chosen to remain loyal.

"Then this meeting is adjourned." Maddie stood, signalling the lords' dismissal. She spoke briefly to Tristan in a voice too low for Joss to hear and strode from the room, no doubt headed straight for her husband with the good news.

Slumping back in her chair, Joss returned her attention to Lord Lowden. The elderly man had been almost as vocal in his disdain for a female ruler over the previous weeks as Lord Brant. Why had he changed his mind?

It could not be because of Lord Ealley's influence. She had told her unwanted suitor in no uncertain terms the previous evening that she could not marry him. For the sake of her kingdom, she had considered a marriage alliance with him, but the prospect of being bound to his will sent a spike of panic through her. If she had to give up her precious freedom, it needed to at least be with someone she loved, and she did not love Lord Ealley.

She pushed to her feet and rounded the table to catch Lord Lowden before he left the council chamber. "May I have a word, Lord Lowden?"

"Certainly, Your Highness." He dipped his head briefly and shuffled closer to the wall to allow the lords behind him to pass.

When they were alone, Joss gestured for him to take one of the chairs beside them, but he stomped his cane and straightened as much as he was able. Mentally, Joss sighed. If he insisted on standing to talk, so be it.

"Thank you for siding with my family today," she said. "I know you don't approve of my sister ruling in Papa's place. If you don't mind me asking, why did you vote to keep him as king? Did Lord Ealley convince you to?"

"That young fop?" The elderly lord snorted. "No. It was the Iskarian emissary."

Joss started. "Theo… How? What did he say?"

Lord Lowden pursed his lips like he had just swallowed a sour berry. "He agreed to buy pigs and grain from the southern lords every year for the next five and trade fifty thoroughbred horses, already broken, in return for teaching his men how to work the land." He peered at her, leaning more heavily on his cane. "On condition that King Johnathan remains on the throne. Apparently, Iskaria would never trade with a kingdom that ousted its ruler for fear of inciting rebellion in their own land."

"I see. Thank you, Lord Lowden."

Theo had used his position as emissary to save her father. Again. Had he hurt Iskaria's interests to do so? No, he would never do that. He loved his kingdom too much to betray them. But he had still found a way to help her family.

She only half noticed the lord take his leave, mumbling something as he walked past her. The sharp tap of his cane on the wooden floor pierced her musings, however, and she rushed to follow him out. She needed to find Theo and confirm a few things.

Unfortunately, he was not in the antechamber, or the entrance hall.

But Lord Ealley was.

He broke away from a group of the other lords when she rounded the corner from the west corridor and walked towards her.

Glancing around, she ushered him to one side of the central staircase and said, "Thank you for voting for Papa today. After I… Well, you could have sided with Brant, but you didn't. I appreciate it."

"You think I only planned to support the king if you married me?" The hurt in his voice was like a punch to her gut. "I've always been loyal."

"I'm sorry. I know that," she hurried to say. "I should never have said otherwise." What a mess she was making. She drew in a steadying breath and started again. "I apologise. I shouldn't have implied that. And I'm sorry I can't marry you, too. You'll find someone else soon. Someone better. A lady with the same interests as you who won't embarrass you with her wild behaviour."

He studied his feet. "I thought we were well-matched, and that I'd be a good support for you."

She glanced around, wishing Maddie were there. Her sister knew how to soothe the nobles far better than Joss could.

“Maybe I could introduce you to some of the other court ladies?” she offered.

He flinched, and his shoulders drooped even lower. “Thank you, but no,” he said with a shake of his head. “I’m going to return to my estate for a while. I need to speak to my steward about the next shipment to Iskaria.” His voice dropped to a whisper. “And I need some time…”

The rest of his unfinished thought hung in the air between them, and another stab of regret nearly pushed a third apology from her. But that would only make things more awkward, so she clamped her lips on the urge and tapped her fingers on her thigh.

Forcing herself to smile, she wished him the best and quickly excused herself.

She crossed the entrance hall and continued her search for Theo. He was not in the great hall, or the library, his rooms, the kitchen, or the gardens. A trip to the training yard and around to the stables yielded no results either. He must have gone into the city. Though why he would blithely wander the capital while her father’s rule was being debated was beyond her.

With a huff of air directed at the curl falling over her forehead, she headed back inside. She would have to find him later. In the meantime, she climbed the stairs two at a time and turned towards the royal family’s private wing.

Maddie would be celebrating their victory with Luc, and Joss had no desire to witness that, so she bypassed their rooms and let herself into her father’s chamber. Between what Lord Lowden had told her and Lord

Ealley's decision to leave the capital, she had plenty of news to relate.

Theo's face popped into her mind, his ultimatum to the southern lords still muddling her thoughts. She let out a long sigh. If only her father could offer advice in return.

Chapter 41

Joss

The next morning, after a measly three hours of sleep, Joss woke much later than usual. Her eyes were full of grit, her limbs had turned to lead, and her left arm tingled where she had twisted into an awkward position during the night. She fought her way out of the tangle of blankets and sat up.

Light spilled through a crack in the curtains, far brighter than it should have been. Stretching her arms and back with a deep yawn, she searched for water to wet her dry mouth. A spare waterskin sat on the nightstand, but when she leaned across for it, her fingertips landed a few inches short. She groaned. She would have to move to reach it.

A knock brought her head up. The door eased open, and Maddie peered around the edge. "You're up late this morning. May I come in?"

"I didn't sleep well." That was an apt enough description for the fitful hours Joss had spent tossing and turning, her mind a whirlpool of contrasting emotions.

Sitting on the edge of the bed, Maddie asked, "What are your plans for the day?"

"I want to find the duke this morning, and then—"

"Theo? He already left."

Joss jerked her gaze to her sister, her lethargy forgotten. "What?"

Maddie pointed towards the window. "He set off with his full escort before sunup."

"What?" Throwing the blankets aside, Joss scrambled out of bed and searched for her boots. She needed to stop him before he got too far.

Her sister cleared her throat, and when Joss glanced at her, she held the boots up and gave them a little shake. Joss hurried to retrieve them, but instead of letting go, Maddie held on and said, "What will you do if you catch up with him?"

"I'll tell him…" The ramifications of chasing after him swirled through her mind, clarifying into one inescapable truth. She would have to admit how she felt about him, and then there would be no turning back.

She sank onto the mattress beside her sister, nausea roiling in her stomach. "Forget it. Maybe it's better if he does leave."

Maddie studied her. "Are you really going to let him go? You might never see him again."

"Mm." Joss did not trust her voice in that moment. She clenched her hands so tightly her fingernails dug into her palms and focused on the pain in an attempt to block the deeper ache in her chest. It did not work.

In a whip-sharp voice, Maddie said, "I've never known you to be a coward before, Joss."

Joss flinched as if struck. “I’m not a coward.”

“Forget everything else for a minute. Just look me in the eye and tell me you don’t love him.”

“I…” She turned away.

“Exactly. And he loves you too. Why else do you think he came all the way here? He could have demanded a marriage as part of the trade agreement, but he didn’t. He helped us defeat Brant and Tuftridge’s plot, and he even found a mage to save Papa.”

“But the stone—”

“Was used exactly as it always should have been.” Maddie picked up her hand. “And it brought you together. Don’t let misguided guilt and childhood fears steal your chance at true happiness, or I’ll never forgive you.”

When Joss met her eyes, they twinkled with humour but also challenge. “Fine. I’m going,” she said, jumping up to resume dressing. “Happy?”

“Exceedingly.”

Joss pushed Shadow as fast as she dared through Faerstolmere, shouting for people ahead of her to move aside. One elderly man leaped from her path at the last moment, and she winced as she passed him, throwing an apology over her shoulder.

Normally, she would have stopped—or not raced along the streets so recklessly in the first place—but Theo’s ship could set sail at any moment.

She arrived at the lake in record time, only to find the dock utterly empty. Where was the boat? She scanned the water farther out, but it was as flat as a mirror, reflecting the cloudless sky without a single interruption in either direction.

Her shoulders slumped. She was too late. She had missed him.

Turning for home, she spotted horses in the distance. Iskaria's banner fluttered above them, and she blew out a breath. Thank the creator, Theo had chosen to ride rather than sail downriver. She would never have caught him otherwise.

Digging her heels into Shadow's flanks, she chased after him along the lakeside path. As soon as she was within earshot, she called, "Theo. Theo, wait."

After the third try, one of his rear guards glanced over their shoulder, and a moment later, the group slowed to a stop. Theo turned his horse, rode back a little way from the others, and dismounted.

She reined in a couple of lengths short of him, slid from her saddle, and ran over to where he stood waiting. "You're leaving?" she asked between panted breaths.

His brows collided in a confused frown. "Just out for a morning ride."

She blinked, then surveyed his escort, none of whom carried supplies on their mounts. Her jaw clenched, and she thumped her leg—Maddie had tricked her.

"Why are you here?" Theo asked, drawing her attention back to him.

"You saved Papa's throne," she blurted. "I wanted to thank you."

His lips quirked into a brief smile. “I just did what I could. I’d do anything for you.”

“Please don’t go,” she whispered, her eyes fixed on the grass at her feet. “I…” She swallowed and looked up, directly into his eyes. “I love you. I should have admitted it earlier, but I was too afraid.”

He stilled, then asked in a hoarse voice, “Of what?”

“Of being trapped in a golden cage. I love my family, and I take my responsibilities seriously, but I’m not built to be still and look perfect all the time.”

Sadness shadowed his eyes, and he shook his head. “Ah, sikani. I never wanted that.”

“But you’re a duke, and you came here as the emissary—”

“Only to find you.” He lifted his hands to her shoulders. “I’ve been trying to tell you that since I got here. I don’t want power or influence. I don’t even use my title normally, and I’ve always avoided the court. I’m happier helping the people through my talents.”

Letting go of her, he groaned and shoved a hand into his hair, gripping it in his fist. “I’m going about this all wrong,” he muttered. Then he dropped his hand, looked around, and led her to a fallen tree trunk between the path and the lakeshore.

When she was seated, he took a deep breath and faced her again. “I don’t want there to be any more secrets between us, so I need to tell you something important. You know Chenne, the mage who helped your father? The truth is, she’s my aunt.”

Joss felt her eyes widen. “What?” The question came out in a squeak, and she coughed before trying again.

"You're Iskarian royalty. How can your aunt be a mage?"

He winced. "My mother was one too. That's why I've always stayed away from the palace. My ba found her outside Akkia, beaten half to death and hiding from mage hunters. He married her to keep her safe, and they eventually fell in love." His face softened, presumably from reliving memories of his parents. A moment later, his smile fell, and his eyes turned serious again. "Apart from my ama, no one outside my immediate family knows the truth, not even my cousin."

Neither of them spoke for some time, the only sounds the gentle lap of water against the rocky bank and some birds chattering in the nearby trees.

"Are you gifted as well?" Joss asked.

He shrugged one shoulder, his eyes wary. "I don't know. I never dared find out in case I was caught."

She jumped up and tugged his hand for him to follow her. "We should ask Mouse. She'll be able to tell us—"

"Wait. That's it? You're not…"

Her forehead puckered. "Not what?"

"You're not afraid of me."

"Why would I be?" Pain lanced her at the confused doubt in his expression. She lifted her hand and rested it on his chest, feeling the rapid beat of his heart beneath her palm. "I'm not Iskarian. You being a mage makes no difference to how I feel about you."

He loosed a sigh, and his shoulders relaxed. Then, pulling her closer, he wrapped his arms around her and whispered into her hair, "I love you, sikani. Please say you'll marry me?"

“I—” She froze, her mouth drying and skin prickling. “I still need my freedom.”

“You’ll have it. I promise. Whenever being Princess Jocelyn gets too much for you, we’ll be Kit Parker and Theo Taskill for as long as you need.”

Only half joking, she asked, “What if I run away from you as well as everything else?”

“Then I’ll just have to follow you, to the ends of the earth if need be.”

“All right, then.”

He started and, gripping her shoulders, stepped back to look her in the eye. “Is that a yes? You’ll marry me?”

She nodded. “Yes.”

His lips were on hers before she could take a breath. Then kissing her cheeks, her nose, her eyes, her forehead.

“Stop kissing me,” she said with a giggle. “Your guards can see us.”

“They’re not looking.” He picked her up and spun her around. “Besides, you kissed me in public first.”

She gaped at him. “I did not.”

Lowering her to her feet, he kissed the tip of her nose again and said, “Let’s make a new bet. If I can prove you did, you have to marry me within the next month.”

Joss grinned. She would not mind even if she lost. “Deal.”

He straightened and held up a finger like a tutor about to deliver a lecture. “You kissed me on our last night in Ilderdell, right here.” He touched his cheek. “You were just so drunk that you don’t remember it.”

Her face burst into flame. She had? "That doesn't count. Our first kiss was on the *Evening Star*, and you were the one who started that."

He shook his head. "Uh-uh. Ilderdell, and Parker can confirm it. You even complained that my beard was scratchy."

Vague images of clinging to him as he helped her to her room drifted across Joss's mind, and a smile tugged at the corners of her mouth. It looked like she would soon be wed.

He peered at her. "You concede?"

She nodded.

A beaming smile lit his face. "You won't regret it, sikani. I promise."

Chapter 42

Joss

The morning of Joss's wedding dawned bright and clear. It was not, however, within a month of Theo's proposal.

Much to her frustration, the council insisted on following all the protocols of a grand royal marriage. She had tried arguing that they had ignored them for Luc and Maddie, only to be told that her sister's hasty wedding made it even more important for hers to be done properly.

So, it was late in the following spring when they finally stood in the palace's chapel—Joss had outright refused to wed in Faerstolmere's cathedral, which seated an overwhelming number of people—and performed the marriage rites.

As soon as the wedding banquet had been cleared and they had greeted and received gifts from the requisite dignitaries in attendance, they sneaked out of the great hall and up to her rooms.

Theo helped her remove the numerous jewelled pins from her hair, dropping them into a box on her dressing table and combing his fingers through each loosened lock. Then he rubbed her shoulders, relieving the tension from her tight muscles, but his hands disappeared far too soon.

When she turned to stand, he stopped her, saying, "Stay right there. I've got a surprise for you."

He crossed to the chest of his belongings a servant had brought to her chambers that morning and rummaged through it. Picking something up, he straightened and returned to her side, where he cleared a space on the table between her throwing knives, the box of pins, and a bag of dried fruit.

"Here." He spread a notebook in the gap with a drawing of a leafy plant on the open page.

She looked from the notes scribbled around it to him. This was her surprise?

"It's called a taefern," he said, leaning over her shoulder and pointing at the writing at the top of the page. "It only grows in the far north, and it has magical properties."

Her brows shot up. "I've never heard of magical plants before."

"They were made by the ancient mages. It's like what happened in Iskaria but in reverse. There, the magic they cast stripped all life from the surrounding area, but in this case, the magic seeped into the ground and the nearby plants. I found a story about a man who drank broth made from taefern roots after he'd been hit with a bolt of magic, and he was completely restored. I think we might be able to use it to break the curse on your father."

"Really?" She stared at the drawing again, taking in the details, then jumped to her feet and spun to the door. "Let's go and find it."

He caught her by the hand. "Steady your ropes, sikani. We've got all the time in the world."

"Sikani." She huffed at the nickname he had given her. "You might think I'm impatient, but you're still as slow as a tortoise."

Chuckling, he tugged her closer. "It means precious one."

Precious…? She stared at him, open mouthed, her mind replaying all the times he had called her that.

He nodded slowly, his eyes not leaving hers, then planted a soft kiss on her forehead. "Balaya, w sikani. I love you."

"I love you too." She melted into his embrace, until his discovery popped back into her mind. "But the plant is out there, just waiting to be found."

Groaning, he backed up to the bed, where he sat down, pulled her onto his lap, and looked her straight in the eyes. "Let me make something completely clear, Jocelyn Sakanin. I've waited nearly a year to make you mine. Neither of us is going anywhere tonight."

"But why sleep here when we could be—"

"I never said we'd be sleeping." He leaned forwards and kissed her collar bone, her neck, her jaw. "In fact, I don't plan on either of us getting a wink before dawn."

Heat followed the path of his lips across her skin. "Oh."

He was grinning when he pulled away, a twinkle dancing in his eyes. “Exactly. And I plan to be as slow and thorough as a tortoise, my beautiful Kit.”

Acknowledgements

Of all my books to date, this has been the hardest by far to write. Between burnout, health issues, and scheduling conflicts, there've been times I thought I'd never finish it. Which is why I truly mean it when I say it wouldn't be in your hands right now without the following people. Each and every one of them has been a godsend on The Dragon Stone's perilous journey to publication.

First and foremost, I have to thank my husband, Dave, who not only offered his usual encouragement and support this time but also rolled up his sleeves and dived into edits with me, noting everything from plot holes to typos. I love you, and I value your input more than you think.

Then there's my writing sister, Cathy, and my mum, Marion, who read the ugly early drafts, listened to me ramble through difficult sections, and picked me up whenever I cried because my brain wouldn't cooperate. You are both absolute gems without whom I wouldn't be where I am today.

Sabine and Michele, thank you for your ideas and enthusiasm, and the mini deadlines that forced me to write when I needed it. I've never been so happy about someone demanding regular word counts before.

To my beta readers, Kate, Karen, Nina, and Sophia, your excitement and enjoyment of the story provided inspiration for marketing and the will to face another round of edits. I owe each of you a hug.

I should probably also acknowledge Aesop (and my nieces). Without the challenge of adapting fables for modern fantasy romance readers, this story would never have crossed my mind, let alone made it onto the page. I'm so glad it did because, despite everything, it's one of my favourites.

For offering the name of what should have been a throwaway character, I have to thank Miranda Eley. Whether due to you or his own tenaciousness, Lord Ealley wormed his way into the plot and refused to leave. Bless him.

And for inspiring another of the characters Joss meets on her journey, I can only hope that Bruno reads this someday. Mum and I will never forget your roadside assistance when our tyre burst in Senlis, France. Your kind spirit and refusal to accept any form of payment were both a blessing and an inspiration. As requested, I've already paid it forward.

Thanks to Bianca at Moonpress Designs for another stunning cover, to Andreas for a second beautiful map, and to Jenelle for a piece of artwork so good it made me rewrite a scene to match it.

And last, but not least, I must praise my awesome God. You've brought me on a journey I never expected to take in this lifetime, and I thank you every day for the blessings I've discovered along the way.

Coming Next

THE LION BOND

Tales of Tyrrath 3

She's been kidnapped… but can she change his heart before hers is crushed?

Olivia Dalbot has spent the last three years mastering her magical powers and avoiding the intrigues of the royal court. When she refuses yet another marriage proposal from the neighbouring kingdom of Brunland, she is taken from her home by force.

Granted increased strength and endurance by a magical bracer, her captor is impossible to escape, but when they barely survive an ambush by more enhanced warriors, she convinces him to help her. Unfortunately, the only way out is to flee north, where the mountains are plagued by wild dragons.

With winter closing in, enemies at every quarter, and an unwanted bond growing between them, will Livi and Felix succumb to the forces aiming to control them or fight for a different destiny, together?

Find out more about me and my books here:

laurenhsalisbury.com

www.ingramcontent.com/pod-product-compliance
Lightning Source LLC
LaVergne TN
LVHW041102080826
845145LV00007B/1656

* 9 7 8 1 9 1 5 4 3 8 0 7 2 *